THE SHADOW GIRLS

Also by Henning Mankell

Kurt Wallander Series

Faceless Killers

The Dogs of Riga

The White Lioness

The Man Who Smiled

Sidetracked

The Fifth Woman

One Step Behind

Firewall

Before the Frost

The Pyramid

The Troubled Man

Fiction

The Return of the Dancing Master

Chronicler of the Winds

Depths

Kennedy's Brain

The Eye of the Leopard

Italian Shoes

The Man from Beijing

Daniel

Non-fiction

I Die, but the Memory Lives on

Young Adult Fiction

A Bridge to the Stars

Shadows in the Twilight

When the Snow Fell

The Journey to the End of the World

Children's Fiction

The Cat Who Liked Rain

Henning Mankell

The Shadow Girls

Translated from the Swedish by
Ebba Segerberg

Harvill Secker
LONDON

Published by Harvill Secker 2012

2 4 6 8 10 9 7 5 3

First published with the title *Tea-Bag* in 2001
by Leopard Förlag, Stockholm in arrangement with
Leonhardt & Høier Literary Agency, Copenhagen

First published in Great Britain in 2012 by
HARVILL SECKER
Random House
20 Vauxhall Bridge Road
London SW1V 2SA

www.rbooks.co.uk

Addresses for companies within The Random House Group Limited can be found at:
www.randomhouse.co.uk/offices.htm

The Random House Group Limited Reg. No. 954009

A CIP catalogue record for this book is available from the British Library

ISBN 9781843430599 (hardback)
ISBN 9781846556722 (trade paperback)

Typeset in Minion by Palimpsest Book Production Ltd.

Printed and bound in Great Britain by Clays Ltd, St Ives plc

THE SHADOW GIRLS

1

It was one of the last days of the twentieth century.

The girl with the big smile was awakened by the sound of raindrops hitting the tent cover above her head. As long as she kept her eyes closed she could imagine that she was still back in the village by the cold, clear river that spilled down the side of the mountain. But as soon as she opened her eyes she was thrown out into an empty and unfathomable world, one in which nothing of her past remained except disjointed images of her escape. She lay still and slowly let herself float up into consciousness, trying not to leave her dreams without preparing herself. These first few minutes of the morning often determined the way her day would turn out.

During the three months in the refugee camp she had developed a morning ritual that helped her avoid being overcome with sudden panic. The most important thing was not to rush up from her uncomfortable cot with the misguided notion that something momentous was about to occur. By now she knew that nothing ever happened here. This was the first lesson she learned after she had dragged herself onto the rocky European beach and been greeted by guard dogs and armed Spanish border guards.

Being a refugee meant being lonely. This was something that was true for them all, regardless of what country they had come from or what circumstances had forced them to flee. She didn't expect her loneliness to leave her soon, in fact she had prepared herself to live with it for a long time.

As she lay with her eyes closed she searched for a foothold in the confusion of all that had happened since her arrival. She was being held in a refugee camp in southern Spain, lucky to be one of the few survivors from that mouldering ship from Africa. She could still remember the air of expectation aboard. Freedom has a scent, she thought, which only grew more overpowering as land approached. Freedom, security, these were what they wanted. A life where fear, hunger, and hopelessness were not the only reality.

It had been a cargo-hold of hope, she thought; although it was perhaps more correct to call it a cargo-hold of illusions. Everyone who had been waiting on the Moroccan beach that night and who had placed their lives in the hands of the ruthless human smugglers had been ferried over to the waiting ship. Sailors who were little more than shadows had forced them down into the cargo area, as if they were modern-day slaves.

But there had been no iron chains around their ankles. What had ensnared them were their dreams, their desperation, all the fear that had driven them to break up from various hells-on-earth in order to make their way to freedom. They had been so close to their goal when the ship hit a reef and the Greek sailors had left in lifeboats, leaving the people in the cargo hold to save themselves.

Europe let us down before we even arrived, she thought. I will never forget that, whatever happens to me in the future. She didn't know how many people had drowned, nor would she ever find out. The cries for help still pulsated like a pain in her head. At first she had been surrounded by these cries, then one by one they had fallen silent. When she hit land she had praised her luck. She had survived; she had arrived. But for what? She had quickly tried to forget her dreams. Nothing had turned out as she had imagined.

A harsh spotlight had picked her out as she lay on the cold and wet Spanish beach. The dogs had run up to her and then the soldiers surrounded her with their shiny weapons. She had survived. But that was all. Afterwards she had been placed in the refugee camp with its barracks and tents, leaky showers and dirty toilets. On the other side of the wire fence she could see the ocean that had released her, but nothing else, none of the future she had imagined.

The people in the refugee camp, so varied in their language, dress and terrible experiences – imparted through a look or sometimes words – had only this in common: nothing to look forward to. Some had been there for many years. No country was willing to admit them and all of their energies were devoted to avoiding being sent back. One day, as she had been waiting in line for her daily rations, she spoke with a young man from Iran – or was it Iraq? It was often hard to know where people came from since they invariably lied about it in the hope that it would make their applications for asylum more attractive. He said that the camp was simply a large death chamber, a holding place where the clock ticked on relentlessly towards death. She had immediately understood what he meant but tried to ignore the thought.

His eyes had been full of sorrow. They surprised her. Since she had grown to be a woman all she had seen in men's eyes was a kind of hunger. But this thin man seemed not to have noticed her beauty nor her smile. This had frightened her. She could not stand the thought that men did not immediately desire her, nor that the long and desperate flight had been for nothing. She, like all the others who had been caught, lived in the hope that her ordeal would one day be over. Through some miracle someone would one day appear before her with a paper in his hand and a smile on his lips and say: Welcome.

In order not to drive herself insane she had to be very patient. She understood that. And patience could only arise if she did not allow herself any expectations. Sometimes people in the camp committed suicide, or at least made serious attempts. They were the ones who were not strong enough to stifle their own expectations and the burden of thinking that their dreams would one day be realised finally overcame them.

Therefore, every morning when she woke up, she told herself that the best she could do was to rid herself of hope. That and never mentioning her true country of origin. The camp was always a hotbed of rumours about which countries offered the best chances for asylum applicants. It was as if the camp were a marketplace of countries where the possibilities for entry were recorded on a kind of stock market. No investments were ever long-lasting or secure.

A short while after she arrived, Bangladesh had been highest on the list. For some reason that they never understood, Germany was granting immediate asylum to all people who could prove that they came from Bangladesh. During an intense few days people of all complexions and appearances waited in line in front of the exhausted Spanish bureaucrats and argued with great fervour that they had suddenly realised they were from Bangladesh. In this way at least fourteen Chinese refugees from the Hunan province made their way to Germany. A few days later Germany 'closed' Bangladesh, as they said in the camp. After three days of uncertainty a rumour was started that France was prepared to take a certain quota of Kurds.

She had been unsuccessful in her attempts to research where the Kurds actually came from or what they looked like. Nonetheless she stood in line with the others and when she at last stood in front of a red-eyed clerk with the name tag 'Fernando' she smiled her sweetest smile. Fernando simply shook his head.

'Tell me what colour you are,' he said.

She immediately sensed danger, but she had to say something. The Spanish didn't like people who didn't answer their questions. A lie was better than silence.

'You are black,' Fernando said in reply to his own question. 'There are no black Kurds. Kurds look like me, not you.'

'There are always exceptions. My father was not a Kurd, but my mother was.'

Fernando's eyes seemed only to redden. She continued to smile. It was her strongest weapon, it always had been.

'And what was your father doing in Kurdistan?'

'Working.'

Fernando threw his pen down in triumph.

'Ha! There is no Kurdistan. At least not in any official capacity. That is exactly the reason that Kurds are fleeing their country.'

'How can they leave a country that doesn't exist?'

But Fernando lost patience with her. He waved her away.

'I should report the fact that you have been lying,' he said.

'I'm not lying.'

She thought she could suddenly see a spark of interest in his eyes.

'You are speaking the truth?'

'Kurds don't lie.'

The spark in Fernando's eyes died away.

'Go,' he said. 'It is the best thing you can do. What is your name?'

She decided in that moment to give herself an entirely new name. She looked quickly around the room and her gaze fell on the teacup on Fernando's table.

'Tea-Bag,' she replied.

'Tea-Bag?'

'Tea-Bag.'

'Is that a Kurdish name?'

'My mother liked English names.'

'Is Tea-Bag even a name?'

'It must be since that is what she called me.'

Fernando sighed and dismissed her with a tired wave. She left the room and did not let the smile leave her face until she was out in the yard and had found a place by the fence where she could be alone.

*

The rain continued to fall on the roof of the tent. She pushed away all thoughts of Fernando and her failure to impersonate a Kurd. Instead she tried to recall the uneasy and wild dreams that had rushed through her head all night. But the only impressions still left were like the ruins of a burned house, the blurry shadows that had surrounded her as she slept, shadows that seemed to creep out of her head, put on strange plays and then disappear again into the depths of her brain. She had seen her father curled up on the rooftop in their village. He had been cursing his imaginary enemies, threatening to kill the living and raise the dead, and he had stayed up there until he fainted from exhaustion and rolled off, landing in the dry sand where Tea-Bag's distressed mother had tearily pleaded with him to return to his senses.

But little of this remained when Tea-Bag awoke. There was only the fading impression of her father on the roof. There was nothing left of her other dreams, only the fleeting faces of people she wasn't sure she recognised.

Tea-Bag pulled the dirty blanket up to her face. Was the dream trying to tell her that perhaps she was the one who was now on that rooftop, sharing the pain that her father had suffered? She didn't know, didn't find any answers. The rain fell steadily against the sailcloth of the tent and the thin light that came in through her eyelids told her it was seven or seven-thirty in the morning. She fumbled for the watch that she had stolen from that Italian engineer. But it had disappeared after the shipwreck. She still had very few memories from that night. There were no precise details, she could remember only their desperate attempts to survive, not to be pulled down and die a few metres from the land that meant freedom.

*

Tea-Bag opened her eyes and looked up at the tent. Outside she could hear people cough, sometimes saying words in a language she didn't understand. They moved around slowly, just as she would do when she got up, the movements of a person without hope. A heavy, reluctant gait, since they had no goal. In the beginning she had kept track of the days with small white stones that she gathered down by the fence. But then they had lost meaning for her. During that time she had been sharing her tent with two other women, one from Iran and the other from Ghana.

They had not got along well, had chafed in the limited space inside the tent. Refugees were loners; their fear meant they couldn't stand to have people come too close to them, as if the sorrows and despair of others were a contagious disease.

The woman from Iran was pregnant when she first arrived. She had cried all night long because her husband had disappeared somewhere along the way during their long journey. When her contractions started the Spanish guards put her on a stretcher and Tea-Bag never saw her again after that. The girl from Ghana was an impatient type, someone who couldn't see a fence without immediately plotting to climb over it. One night she and a couple of boys from Togo, who had sailed to Europe on a raft made of empty oil barrels that they had stolen from a Shell depot, had tried to climb the fence. But the dogs and the spotlights caught her and she never returned to the tent. Tea-Bag assumed she was now in the part of the camp where those labelled 'difficult' were held under stricter supervision.

Tea-Bag sat up in bed. Loneliness, she whispered, is my greatest source of suffering. I can walk out of this tent and immediately be surrounded by people. I eat with them, I walk along the fence and look at the sea with them, I speak with them, but still I am alone. All refugees are alone, all are surrounded by invisible walls. I have to get rid of all hope if I am to survive.

She put her feet on the ground and shivered from the cold. At the same moment she was again reminded of her father. He would always plant his feet firmly on the ground when confronted with an unexpected difficulty or anything he was not prepared for. This gesture was among her earliest memories, and connected with her understanding of the potential for mysterious action that even the people closest to her were capable of. Later, when she was six or seven, her father had explained to her that a person needed to have a secure foothold when facing unexpected troubles. If she remembered this rule she would also be able to remain in control.

She pressed her feet firmly into the ground and told herself that nothing special was going to happen this day. If something did occur, it would be a surprise, nothing she had been waiting for.

Tea-Bag sat up and waited for her strength to return, the strength to carry on another day in this camp in which people were forced to renounce their identities and were constantly searching for signs of where they might be welcome.

When she felt strong enough she got up, pulled the old nightgown over her head and put on a T-shirt that the girl from Ghana had given her. It had a Nescafé logo on the front. The logo obscured her identity in the same way that the camouflage uniforms had hidden the soldiers who took her father away.

She shook her head to rid herself of these thoughts. She could allow herself to dream about him sitting on the roof until he fell to the ground of exhaustion. She could think about the way in which he used to press his feet into the ground. But she could not allow herself to think about his disappearance, except sometimes in the evening. She felt strongest right before sunset, filled with supernatural powers for a few short minutes. Then it was as if she slowly started to sink, her pulse grew slower and her heart tried to mask its stubborn beat deep inside the hidden recesses of her body.

Tea-Bag folded back the flap of the tent door. It had stopped raining. A damp mist clung to the camp, over the long row of barracks and the tents that looked like dirty fettered animals.

People were slowly wandering around as if towards a goal that only existed inside of them. Guards were patrolling the fence with gleaming weapons and dogs that seemed relentlessly intent on picking out danger from the sea. Danger in the form of leaky ships with cargo holds filled to the brim with desperate people, or curiously crafted rafts and rowboats, even doors that some people used as floatation devices.

I am here, Tea-Bag thought. I am in the centre of things here, in the centre of my life. There is nothing behind me: there may not be anything ahead. I am here, that is all. I am here and I am not waiting for anything.

*

Another day had begun. Tea-Bag walked over to one of the barracks where the women's showers were located. As usual there was a long line. She had to wait for about an hour until it was her turn. She closed the door behind her, took off her clothes and stepped into the spray of water. She was reminded of the night she almost drowned. The difference, she thought to herself as she soaped her body, the difference is something I'll never understand. I survived without knowing why, but I also don't know what it is like to be dead. Once she had dried herself off and put her clothes back on she stepped outside to let the next woman in line take her place, a fat girl with a black scarf wrapped over her head so that only two eyes looked out like dark holes. Tea-Bag wondered absently if the girl took off the scarf when she washed herself.

She walked on between the rows of barracks and tents. Whenever she met someone's eye she smiled. In an open area under a hastily erected iron roof she received some food, doled out by two heavyset and sweaty Spanish women who maintained a ceaseless conversation with each other. Tea-Bag sat down at a plastic table, wiped away a few breadcrumbs and started to eat. Every morning she was afraid that she would lose the will to eat. Sometimes it seemed as if the ability to feel hunger was what kept her alive.

She ate slowly as a way to make the time go by. She thought about the watch that lay on the bottom of the sea. She wondered if it still worked or if it had stopped at that moment when she herself ought rightfully to have died alongside the others. She searched for the name of the Italian engineer whom she stole the watch from that lonely night when she had sold her body in order to get the money together for the trip. Cartini? Cavanini? She didn't know if it was his first or last name. Not that it mattered.

She got up from the table and walked over to the women who were still doling out portions from their huge pots while they continued their endless conversation. Tea-Bag put her dish with the other dirty dishes on a trolley and walked down to the fence to look out at the sea. There was a ship far out towards the horizon.

'Tea-Bag,' she heard someone say.

She turned around. Fernando was looking at her with his red eyes.

'There's someone who wants to speak to you,' he said.

She was immediately on guard.

'Who?'

Fernando shrugged.

'Someone who wants to talk to someone. Anyone. It might as well be you.'

'No one wants to talk to me.'

She was even more suspicious now, using her big smile as a way to keep Fernando at bay.

'If you don't want to talk to him I'll find someone else.'

'Why would he want to speak to me?'

Tea-Bag sensed danger; she hoped an opening in the fence would suddenly appear so she could jump through. To ward off the threat she made her smile even wider.

'A reporter. Someone who has taken it into his head to write a story on refugees.'

'What kind of a story?'

'I'm assuming he's writing an article for the paper.'

'And he's going to write about me?'

Fernando made a face.

'I'll ask someone else if you don't want to do it.'

He turned and started to walk away. Tea-Bag had the feeling she was about to make one of the most important decisions of her life.

'I'll talk to him, if he wants to talk to me.'

'Just remember that it won't be to your advantage if you criticise the camp.'

Tea-Bag tried to understand what he was getting at. The Spanish guards always spoke a language where the most important message lay beneath the surface.

'What would be to my advantage?'

Fernando stopped and took out a piece of paper from his pocket.

'I am pleased to say that the Spanish authorities treat us with the utmost compassion and humanity,' he read aloud.

'What is that, exactly?'

'That's what you should say. Everyone who works here has a

copy of it. Someone in the Ministry of the Interior wrote it. That's what you should say to the journalist. It could be to your advantage.'

'My advantage? How?'

'So you will continue to be treated with compassion.'

'What exactly do you mean by "compassion"?'

'To help you reach your goal.'

'What goal?'

'The goal you have set for yourself.'

Tea-Bag had the feeling she was walking around in a circle.

'Does that mean I can leave the camp?'

'Actually it will mean the reverse. You can stay on.'

'But that's what would happen anyway.'

'Don't be too sure. You could be deported to your homeland. Wherever that really is.'

'I don't have a homeland.'

'You will be deported to the country of last domicile.'

'They won't accept me.'

'Of course not. You will be sent back whereupon we deport you again. You will find yourself in what we call the circular route.'

'And what is that?'

'A route in which you circulate.'

'Around what?'

'Around yourself.'

Tea-Bag shook her head. She didn't understand. There was nothing that could make her as frustrated as when she didn't understand.

'I've heard of a man who claimed to be from a central African republic,' Fernando continued. 'He has now lived in an Italian airport for twelve years. No one wants him. Since no one will pay his airfare it has turned out to be cheapest simply to let him remain at the airport.'

Tea-Bag pointed to the note Fernando held in his hand.

'That's what you want me to say?'

'Just this. Nothing else.'

Fernando gave her the note.

'He's waiting in my office. He also has a photographer with him.'

'Why?'

Fernando sighed.

'They always do.'

*

Two men were waiting outside Fernando's office. One was short with red hair and a raincoat that flapped in the wind. He was carrying a camera. Next to him was a tall and thin man. Tea-Bag thought he looked like a palm tree. His back was slightly bent and he had bushy hair that stood out like palm fronds. Fernando pointed to Tea-Bag then left them alone. Tea-Bag smiled and the man who looked like a palm tree smiled back at her. He had bad teeth. The other man picked up his camera. His raincoat rustled.

'My name is Per,' said the palm-tree man. 'We're doing a series on refugees. We're calling it "People without a face". We want to tell your story.'

Something about the way he spoke rubbed her up the wrong way. She sent him a blinding smile. She was furious.

'But I have a face.'

Per looked puzzled.

'We mean it in a symbolic way. "People without a face". People like you who are trying to come to Europe without being welcome.'

For the first time since she had been here, Tea-Bag suddenly felt an urge to defend the camp, the red-eyed guards, their dogs, the fat women who doled out the meals, the men who emptied the latrines. All this she wanted to defend, just as she wanted to defend the other refugees in the camp and those who never made it that far, who drowned or committed suicide in their despair.

'I won't speak to you,' she said, 'until you have apologised for saying that I have no face.'

Then she turned to the man in the raincoat who was constantly moving about and snapping pictures of her.

'I don't want you to take any more pictures of me.'

The photographer flinched as if she had slapped him and put his camera down. Tea-Bag wondered if she had made a mistake. Both of the men in front of her seemed friendly and their eyes were not red from exhaustion. Tea-Bag quickly decided to retreat.

'You may speak to me,' she said. 'And you may take your pictures.'

The photographer immediately started working again. Some children who were drifting around the camp stopped and looked at them. I'm speaking for them, Tea-Bag thought. Not only for me but for them.

'So how are things here?' the reporter asked.

'What do you mean by that?'

'What it sounds like. Life here in the camp.'

'I am treated with compassion and humanity, I am happy to say.'

'It must be terrible to be in the camp. How long have you been here?'

'A few months. A thousand years.'

'What is your name?'

'Tea-Bag.'

The man asking the questions had still not said anything that could provide a door for her, a door through which she could escape.

'Excuse me?'

'My name is Tea-Bag. Just as yours is Paul.'

'Per. Where do you come from?'

Careful now, she thought. I don't know what he wants from me. He may have a door somewhere but he could also be someone who wants to send me back, someone who wants to reveal my secrets.

'I almost drowned. Something hit me in the head. I have lost my memory.'

'Have you been examined by a doctor?'

Tea-Bag shook her head. Why was he asking all these questions? What did he want? She became suspicious again and tried to retreat.

'I am treated with compassion and humanity by the Spanish authorities.'

'How can you say that? You're a prisoner here!'

He has a door, Tea-Bag decided. He is simply trying to determine if I am worthy of it. She had to restrain herself so she would not throw herself into his arms and embrace him.

'Where do you come from?' Now she was the one asking the questions.

'Sweden,' he said.

What kind of place was that? A town, a country, the sign on a door? She didn't know. The names of so many cities and countries were constantly circulating around the camp like swarms of bees. But had she heard the name 'Sweden' before? Maybe, she couldn't be sure.

'Sweden?'

'That's in Scandinavia, in northern Europe. That's where we come from. We are writing a series on people without faces, refugees who are desperately trying to enter Europe. We want to tell your story. We want to give you back your face.'

'I already have a face. What is he taking pictures of if I have no face? Can you smile without teeth, without a mouth? I don't need a face, I need a door.'

'A door? You mean somewhere to go where you will be welcome? But that's just why we came down here. We want you to find somewhere to go.'

Tea-Bag strained to understand the words that reached her ears. Someone was trying to help her? This tall man who was still gently swaying must have access to a secret door that he was not showing her.

'We want to tell your story,' he said. 'Your whole story. As much as you remember.'

'Why?'

'Because we will print it in our newspaper.'

'I want a door. I want to get out of here.'

'That's exactly what this is about.'

*

Afterwards Tea-Bag never understood what had made her trust him. But somehow she sensed that door was actually opening for her. Perhaps she had been able to follow her intuition because her feet were firmly planted on the ground, just as her father had taught her, the only thing he had been able to give her. Or perhaps it was because the man asking the questions had seemed genuinely interested in her answers. Or perhaps it was because he didn't look tired. In any case she needed to make a decision and she decided to say yes.

They went into Fernando's office where the dirty teacup that had given her her name still sat on the desk. But she said nothing of that. She started by telling them about her village, somewhere in a land whose name she had forgotten, about her father whom she had not forgotten and who was one morning led away by soldiers, never to return. Her mother had been harassed, they belonged to the wrong kind of people, the kind of people who were not in power. Her mother had urged her to escape, which she had done. She skipped parts of her story and said nothing of the Italian engineer and how she had sold her body to him in order to get the money for passage on the ship. She kept as many secrets as she told. But she was still swept up by the emotion of her story and she saw that the man in front of her who had turned on his tape recorder was also moved by it. When she came to the part about the terrible night in the cargo-hold when the ship began to sink she started to cry.

She had been speaking for four hours when she reached the end. Fernando had appeared in the doorway from time to time and she always weaved in words about 'compassion and humanity' when he appeared. The reporter seemed to accept this as a kind of secret code.

Then it was over.

The reporter who packed away his tape recorder had not in fact provided her with a way out of the camp. But she had still found her door. She had the name of a country far away where people actually wanted to see her face and were interested in hearing her story: Sweden. She decided that that was where she was headed, nowhere else. Sweden. There were people there who had sent out someone to watch out for her.

She walked them to the front gates of the camp.

'Is your name just Tea-Bag?' he asked. 'Nothing else? What about a surname?'

'I don't have one yet.'

He looked at her curiously but smiled. The photographer asked one of the guards to take a picture of the three of them.

*

It was one of the last days of the twentieth century.

It started raining again in the afternoon. That evening Tea-Bag sat on her bed and pressed her feet against the cold floor for a long time. Sweden, she thought. That's where I'm going. That's where I have to go. That's my goal.

2

Jesper Humlin, one of the most successful writers of his generation, was worried about losing his tan. This fear easily surpassed his other anxieties, such as the fate of the impenetrable collections of poetry he published every year on the sixth of October, which happened to coincide with his mother's birthday. This morning, a few months after his latest book had come out, he was looking at his face in the mirror and noted to his satisfaction that his tan had an unparalleled evenness of tone. A few days earlier he had returned to a chilly Sweden from a month-long sojourn on the South Seas, first in the Solomon Islands and then on Rarotonga.

Since he liked to travel in comfort and stay in the most expensive hotels he would not have been able to undertake this trip if he had not received the Nylander grant of 80,000 kronor. It was a newly established grant, the donor a shirt manufacturer from Borås who had long nourished the dream of becoming a poet. He had been bitterly disappointed to see his dreams of poetry disappear in a lifelong battle with arrogant shirt designers, suspicious labour unions and unhelpful tax authorities. His time had been spent on button-down collars, colours and fabric swatches. In an attempt to come to terms with his own disappointment he had established the fund that would go to 'Swedish writers in need of peace and quiet for completion of their work'. The first grant had gone to Jesper Humlin.

*

The phone rang.

'I want a child.'

'Right now?'

'I'm thirty-one years old. We either have a child or it's over.'

It was Andrea. She was a nurse anaesthetist and never knocked on doors. Humlin had met her at a poetry reading he had done a couple of years earlier when he had just sworn off the bachelor lifestyle and decided to settle down with one woman. With her slim face and dark hair he had immediately been attracted to Andrea. He had also fallen for her enthusiastic response to his poems. When she was angry at him, which was a fairly common occurrence, she liked to accuse him of having picked her in order to have constant access to someone in the medical profession, since due to his hypochondria he was always convinced that he was suffering from a fatal illness.

This time she was furious. Humlin wanted children, many children. But not right away and possibly not with Andrea. Naturally this was not something he was prepared to discuss with her, at least not by phone.

'Of course we'll have children,' he said. 'Many children.'

'I don't believe you.'

'Why not?'

'You're always changing your mind about everything. Except, apparently, about waiting to have children. But I'm thirty-one.'

'That's no age at all.'

'For me it is.'

'Maybe we could talk about this a little later? I have an important meeting coming up.'

'What kind of meeting?'

'With my publisher.'

'If you think your meeting is more important than this conversation then I want to break up with you right now. There are other men.'

Humlin felt a pang of jealousy arise in him and escalate to painful proportions.

'What other men?'

'Men. Any men.'

'You mean you are prepared to leave me for some man, any man out there?'

'I don't want to wait any longer.'

Humlin sensed that the conversation was spiralling out of his control.

'You know, it's not good for me to have these kinds of discussions so early in the morning.'

'And you know I can't talk about these things at night. I need my sleep because I have a job that starts early in the morning.'

The silence travelled back and forth between them.

'What did you do in the South Pacific anyway?'

'I rested.'

'You don't seem to do anything else. Were you unfaithful again?'

'I haven't been unfaithful. Why would you think that?'

'Why not? You've done it before.'

'You *think* I have. That's not the same thing. I went to rest.'

'To rest from what exactly?'

'I happen to write books, as you well know.'

'One book a year. With about forty poems. What's that – less than one poem a week?'

'I also write a wine-tasting column.'

'Once a month, yes. In a trade paper for tailors that no one else reads. Now, *I* could have really used a trip to the South Pacific to rest.'

'I invited you to come with me.'

'Since you knew I couldn't get away. But I'm about to take some time off. There's something I want to get started on.'

'And what's that?'

'I'm going to write my book.'

'About what exactly?'

'About us.'

Humlin felt an unpleasant pain in his stomach. Of all the things he had to worry about, the thought that Andrea might prove the more talented writer seemed to him to be the worst. Every time she brought this up he felt as if his very existence was threatened. He sometimes lay awake at night and imagined the sensational reviews of her new book, how the critics embraced her as a new talent and wrote him off as a has-been. For this reason he always devoted an extraordinary amount of time to her whenever her authorial ambitions kicked in. He cooked her dinners, talked about the inordinate amount of suffering and hard work it took to complete a book and had, up until now, always been able to talk her out of her plans.

'I don't want you to write a book about us.'

'Why not?'

'I want my private life to remain private.'

'Who said anything about your private life?'

'If this book is about us, it involves my private life.'

'I can call you Anders.'

'What difference would that possibly make?'

Humlin tried to take the conversation in a different direction.

'I've thought about what you said.'

'About being unfaithful?'

'I haven't been unfaithful. How many times do I have to tell you that?'

'Until I believe you.'

'And when are you going to believe me?'

'Never.'

Humlin decided to retreat from this topic.

'I've been thinking.'

'What about?'

'That you're right. We should have a child.'

'Are you sick?' Her voice was sceptical.

'Why would I be sick?'

'I don't believe you.'

'I'm not sick. I meant it. I'm a very serious person.'

'You're childish and vain. Are you serious?'

'I'm neither childish nor particularly vain.'

'Are you serious? You don't think we should wait?'

'I'm at least prepared to take it into serious consideration.'

'Now you sound like a politician.'

'I'm a poet, not a politician.'

'If we're going to have a baby, we can't talk about it over the phone. I'm coming over.'

'What do you mean?'

'What do you think? If we're going to have a baby we have to go to bed first.'

'I can't. I have a meeting with my publisher.'

Andrea hung up. Humlin returned to the bathroom and looked at his face, looking past his suntan to the warm long nights on the Solomon Islands and Rarotonga. I don't want to have any children, he thought. At least not with Andrea.

He sighed, left the bathroom and poured himself a cup of coffee in the kitchen. In his study he leafed through the latest reviews of his book that the PR department had forwarded. Humlin had given them careful instructions as to what kind of reviews he wanted to read. He only wanted to see the good ones and had an old-fashioned ledger where he noted which papers and critics continued to praise his work as 'the primary representative of mature poetry at the end of the twentieth century'.

Humlin read the latest reviews, made some notes in his ledger, and noted that the *Eskilstuna Courier* had once again given his work too little notice. Then he walked over to the window and looked out. Andrea's latest outburst worried him. There was a chance he would soon face the prospect of either making her pregnant or accepting the fact that she might finally write her book.

At seven he called a taxi service, giving the receptionist plenty of time to recognise his name. He got in the taxi and gave the driver the address. The driver was African and spoke poor Swedish. Humlin wondered grumpily if he would actually be able to find his way to the little restaurant in the Old Town where he was going. It was not, as he had told Andrea, his publisher he was going to meet. That meeting was tomorrow. But this was something equally important.

Once a month he met fellow writer Viktor Leander. They had met when they were still young and unpublished and had taken to meeting regularly to compare notes and pick each other's brains. They had never liked each other very much. They were competing for the same market and were always afraid that the other was going to have a brilliant idea and leave his rival in the dust.

The driver had no trouble finding his way among the narrow

alleys of the Old Town. Humlin took a few deep breaths before getting out. Viktor Leander was waiting for him at their usual table in the corner. He was wearing a new suit and had let his hair grow somewhat longer than normal. Viktor Leander was also tanned. A few years earlier he had managed to purchase his own solarium bed with a couple of well-paid articles about 'new horizons' in a magazine for data consultants.

Humlin sat down.

'Welcome back.'

'Thanks.'

'I got your postcard. Nice stamps.'

'It was a good trip.'

'I look forward to hearing about it.'

He knew the man on the other side of the table had no interest in hearing about either the Solomon Islands or Rarotonga, just as Humlin had no real interest in hearing about Leander's experiences.

They ordered their food. Now came the delicate task of interrogating the other.

'I had a whole bunch of debut novels and poetry with me on the trip. That was hardly relaxing.'

'But educational. I know exactly what you mean.'

It was part of their ritual to speak badly of the latest batch of new writers, especially if any of the debuting authors had been particularly praised.

Humlin lifted his glass and toasted his colleague.

'What are you working on these days?'

'A crime novel.'

Humlin almost choked on his wine.

'A crime novel?'

'I want to show up all these upstart bestseller types who can't write. I'm going to give this genre a literary treatment. I've been reading Dostoevsky for inspiration.'

'What is the book about?'

'Oh, I haven't come that far yet.'

Humlin sensed a door being shut. Of course Leander knew what he was planning to write. But he didn't want to give Humlin a chance to steal his ideas.

'Sounds like a great idea.'

Humlin was irritated. He should have thought of this himself. A crime novel from one of the country's greatest poetic talents would gain a great deal of attention. It could be a bestseller, as opposed to the small editions of his poetry books. His trip to the South Pacific had been a mistake. If he had stayed here he would no doubt have had the same thoughts as Leander. He hastily tried to find a counter-blow.

'I've been thinking of writing for TV myself.'

Now it was Leander's turn to choke on his wine. When they last met, a few days before Humlin was leaving on his trip, they had spent most of the dinner talking disdainfully about the quality of programming on TV. Humlin had not had any thoughts then of writing plays or series. When he was younger he had tried, of course. But after two rejections, one from the City Theatre and one from the Royal Dramatic Theatre, he had decided not to keep writing dramas. But television was the only thing he could think of to counter Leander's idea of a crime novel.

'And what are you writing about?'

'Reality.'

'How interesting. Which reality is this?'

'The unbearable *tristesse* of everyday life.'

Humlin sat up. He sensed that Leander had taken a blow.

'There will also be an element of crime.'

'You're going to write a crime series for television?'

'Not at all. The crime will remain in the background. I think viewers are tired of the conventional police drama. I'm envisioning something completely different.'

'Such as?'

'I haven't decided yet. There are various possibilities.'

Humlin raised his glass. A certain equilibrium had been restored.

'Reality and the *tristesse* of everyday life, he said. 'An under-examined subject in our time.'

'What in the world is there to say on the matter except that it is boring?'

'Quite a lot, actually.'

'I can't wait to hear it.'

'It's too early for me to tell you any of this in greater detail. If I say too much now I might lose all inspiration.'

They ordered dessert and dove into a neutral topic as if by silent agreement. Both of them enjoyed this part of the evening – gossip.

'What's happened since I left?'

'Not much.'

'Something always happens.'

'An editor at one of the major publishing houses hanged himself.'

'Who?'

'Carlman.'

Jesper Humlin nodded thoughtfully. Carlman had once almost refused to publish one of his earliest books of poetry.

'Anything else?'

'The stock market is wavering.'

Humlin poured them both more wine.

'I hope you haven't been silly enough to put any money in the new tech companies.'

'I have always had a soft spot for the two pillars of the Swedish economy: timber and iron. But everything is tumbling.'

'I know. That's why I switched to bonds some time ago. Boring, but safe.'

The economic competition between them was also ongoing. Both of them had checked the other's figures in the public tax records and confirmed that the other was not expecting a significant inheritance.

*

After precisely three hours, when all gossip had been divulged and discussed, they split the bill and left the restaurant. They walked as far as the Munkbro bridge.

'Good luck with your thriller.'

'Crime novel, not thriller. It's not the same thing.'

Viktor Leander's voice took on a stern note. Jesper Humlin was left with the feeling that he still had the upper hand.

'It's been a pleasure, as always. See you next month.'

'Until then.'

They hailed taxis and left in different directions. Humlin gave the driver an address in Östermalm, the upper-class part of town, then leaned back and closed his eyes. He was happy with the evening since he felt that he had succeeded in giving Leander a real jab. This infused him with energy, despite the task that awaited him.

Three evenings a week Humlin visited his elderly mother. At eighty-seven, she was still full of vitality but was also stubborn and suspicious. He could never predict what turn their conversations would take, although he always planned out a couple of harmless topics beforehand. Whenever they had an argument he always left hoping she would die soon. But when they occasionally spent a pleasant time together he would get sentimental and wonder if he should write a book of poetry for her.

It was a quarter to eleven when he rang the doorbell. His mother Märta was a night owl. She rarely got up before noon and didn't go to bed until dawn. Her best time was right around midnight. While Humlin was waiting for her to open the door he thought about all the evenings he had spent fighting exhaustion while she grew more and more animated.

When she opened the door it was with the expectant yet suspicious energy that was typical of her. This evening Märta Humlin was wearing a trouser suit that resembled a uniform and which reminded him vaguely of the kind of clothes people wore in films from the thirties.

'I thought you said you were coming at eleven?'

'It is eleven.'

'No, it's a quarter to eleven.'

Humlin started to get angry.

'If you like I can wait in the hall.'

'If you don't keep better track of the time you will never get anywhere in this life.'

'I already have got somewhere. I'm forty-two years old and I'm a successful writer.'

'Your last book of poetry is worse than anything else you've written.'

Humlin decided to leave.

'I'll come back another time.'

'Why would that make any difference?'

'Do you want me to come in or not?'

'Why would I want us to keep talking out in the hall?'

He followed her into the apartment and almost tripped on a large cardboard box.

'Watch your step.'

'Why is this box here? Are you moving?'

'Where would I move?'

'What is in this box?'

'That's none of your business.'

'Does it have to be right here so people trip over it when they come to visit?'

'If you're going to be like this all evening perhaps it would be better for you to come back another time.'

Humlin sighed, took off his coat and followed her into the rest of the apartment, which reminded him of an overstocked antique store. Here his mother had squirrelled away everything that she had ever come across. Humlin could still remember fights his parents had had about things Märta had refused to get rid of. His father had been a quiet man, an accountant who had treated his children with a mixture of surprise and general goodwill. For the most part he had been a silent partner to his energetic wife, apart from those times when he found his desk or his side of the bed covered with newspapers that his wife refused to throw away. Then he would have a violent outburst of temper that could last for days. But it always ended the same way, the newspapers or the knick-knacks remained in the apartment and he fled back into silence. In contrast, Humlin could not remember a single occasion when his mother had been silent. She was possessed by a deep-seated need to always make herself heard. If she was in the kitchen she banged her pots, if she was on the balcony cleaning the rugs she beat them so the blows echoed in the courtyard.

Humlin had often thought that the unwritten book closest to his heart was the one about his parents. His father, Justus Humlin, had devoted his youth to the hammer throw. He had grown up in Blekinge, in a village close to Ronneby. He had trained with his homemade hammer behind the family farmhouse. Once he had thrown it so far that it would have set a Nordic record under controlled circumstances. Unfortunately, he was only accompanied by his two younger sisters. They measured his throw with an old tape measure. The Nordic record at that time was held by Ossian Skiöld and measured 53.77. Justus Humlin measured his throw four times and came up with 56.44, 56.40, 56.42 and 56.41. He beat the Nordic record by over two metres. Later, when he started competing regionally, he never managed to throw the hammer past fifty metres. But he insisted until he died that he had once thrown it further than anyone else in Scandinavia.

Märta Humlin had never been interested in sport. Her world had been that of culture. She had grown up in Stockholm, the only child of a successful and well-to-do surgeon. Her dream had been to become an artist, but she had not been talented enough. Furious, she had turned to the dramatic arts and started a theatre with the financial help of her father. There she created some scandalous performances which involved her dragging herself across the stage in an almost completely transparent nightdress. Later she had owned a gallery, then she turned to music. Lastly she had been involved in the film business.

She was seventy and newly widowed when she realised she had never seriously thought of dancing, at which point, with her usual verve, she founded a dance company. There was no dancer younger than sixty-five in her troupe. Märta Humlin had reached for almost everything in life but almost nothing stayed in her restless grip.

Jesper had been the youngest of four and had seen his siblings leave home as quickly as they had been able. At twenty he informed his mother that his turn had come. When Jesper woke the following morning he couldn't move. His mother had tied him to the bed. It took him a whole day to talk her into letting him go. First she had forced him to promise to come and see her three times a week for the rest of her life.

Humlin lifted a box of skating laces from his chair and sat down. Märta Humlin went into the kitchen and returned with a bottle of wine and two glasses.

'I don't want any, thanks.'

'And why not?'

'I've already had a bottle this evening.'

'And with whom, might I ask?'

'Viktor Leander.'

'I have no idea who that is.'

Humlin was shocked. He stared at his mother who was in the process of filling his glass to the brim. He was bound to spill some when he lifted it, which would give her yet another reason to chastise him.

'But you've been to a number of his readings.'

'Well, I certainly don't remember him. I'm almost ninety years old. My memory is not what it once was.'

As long as she doesn't start to cry, Humlin thought. I don't have it in me to go through her emotional blackmail tonight.

'Why do you pour me wine when I say I don't want any?'

'Isn't it good enough for you?'

'It's not about the wine. What I'm saying is that I've already had all the wine I could want tonight.'

'You don't have to come over and see me if you don't want to.'

Here it comes, Humlin thought. *I'm used to being alone.*

'I'm used to being alone.'

The satisfaction he had felt at giving Viktor Leander a good jab had already dissipated. His mother already had him pinned him to the ground. He picked up his glass, spilling wine on the tablecloth as he did so. It was going to be a long night.

3

When Humlin walked in through the doors of his publishing company the following day he was very tired. The conversation with his mother had lasted long into the night.

He knocked on his publisher's door at a quarter to one. The name on the sign was Olof Lundin. Humlin always entered Lundin's office with a certain trepidation. Although they had worked together for many years now – and Humlin had never had another publisher – their conversations often led to hopeless circular discussions of what kind of books the market wanted. Lundin was one of the most unclear thinkers Humlin had ever met in the book business. He had often wondered with irritation how such an intellectually confused man as Olof Lundin had actually been able to climb to the heights of the publishing world.

'Didn't we say a quarter past one?'

'No, it was a quarter to one.'

Olof Lundin was overweight and a rowing machine sat among the manuscript piles that littered the floor. He also had a blood-pressure cuff beside the overfilled ashtray. When the company in its negotiations with the unions decided to institute a complete non-smoking policy it had led to war. Olof Lundin had simply refused to play along. He threatened to leave effective immediately if he were not allowed to keep smoking in his own office. Since a graphic designer had taken a similar position and been summarily denied, the matter had been taken up at the highest executive level. The publishing company which had been family owned for over a hundred years had suddenly been sold to a French oil company. The oil company had been interested in investing in media with the huge profits they had made from their Angolan oil fields. It was the directors of the oil company who finally debated the matter of Lundin's refusal to obey the non-smoking policy on their table. At last a compromise had been reached and the company had a powerful ventilation system installed in Lundin's office – at his expense.

Humlin lifted a few manuscript piles from a chair and sat down. It was always chilly in the room since the ventilation system drew in air directly from the outside. Olof Lundin was wearing a woollen cap and mittens.

'How is the book doing?' Humlin asked.

'Which one?'

Humlin sighed.

'The last one.'

'As expected.'

'What does that mean?'

'Not as well as we had hoped.'

'Is it possible for you to clarify the matter for me?'

'We don't expect any book of poetry to sell more than about one thousand copies. To date your book has sold one thousand, one hundred copies.'

'So it actually sold more than you expected?'

'No, not really.'

'How is that possible?'

'What don't you understand?'

'If a book sells more than you expected, how can it then possibly not have done as well as you had hoped?'

'Naturally we always hope that our expectations have been set too low.'

Humlin shook his head and pulled his coat tight. He was cold. Olof Lundin pushed some piles of paper out of the way in order to have a clear view of him.

'How is the new book coming along?'

'I just came out with a new book. I'm not a factory.'

'Well; how is the book that you are going to write?'

'I don't know,' Humlin said.

'I hope it will go well.'

'I hope so too.'

'I just have some advice for you,' Lundin said.

'And what's that?'

'Don't write it.'

Humlin stared at him.

'That's your advice?'

'Yes.'

'You don't want me to write the book that you nonetheless hope will go fine.'

Lundin pointed to the ceiling.

'They're a bit nervous upstairs.'

'Perhaps I should write a book of poetry about oil?'

'It's easy for you to laugh. I have them to answer to. They are pressuring me to show better profit margins.'

'And what does that mean, practically speaking?'

'That we shouldn't publish any book that we don't expect to sell at least fifty thousand copies.'

Humlin was taken aback.

'How many of the books that you presently publish sell fifty thousand copies?'

'None,' Lundin answered cheerily.

'Is the company about to go out of business?'

'No, far from it. But we are going to start publishing books that sell fifty thousand copies.'

'I don't think there's ever been a book in the history of Swedish literature that has sold so many copies, at least in a first edition.'

'That's why I advise you not to write the book that you are planning to write. The one that I naturally hope would go well.'

Humlin was starting to get a stomach ache. Had he just been black listed? Was he one of the authors the company was planning to ditch?

'Do you plan to drop me?'

'Not at all. Why would I do that? Haven't I always told you that you are one of our cornerstones?'

'I don't particularly appreciate being likened to cement. But you know as well as I do that the kind of books I write will never sell fifty thousand copies.'

'That's why I don't want you to write books like that any more. I want you to write something else.'

'What?'

'A crime thriller.'

Humlin suddenly thought he saw an unpleasant resemblance between Lundin's and Leander's faces.

'I am a poet. I don't write crime fiction, and don't particularly want to try. I have my artistic integrity to thank for what little respect I still get. I wouldn't even know how to begin writing something like that.'

Lundin got up, pushed some papers aside with his foot and got onto his rowing machine.

'I'm not so sure you wouldn't know how to do it.'

Humlin always had trouble concentrating on the conversation when Lundin started rowing.

'I don't like crime fiction. I think whodunnits are boring. I couldn't care less about reading a book where the only point is to guess who the murderer is before the book is over.'

'That's fine. That's just what I had expected.'

'Do you have to do that right now?'

'I have to take responsibility for my high blood pressure. My doctor tells me I'll be dead in four and a half years if I don't exercise regularly.'

'How can he be so exact?'

'He retires in four and a half years. He's planning to move to the Azores Islands.'

'Why?'

'Supposedly they have the healthiest population on the planet.'

'I'm not writing a crime novel.'

Lundin paused the machine.

'That's the spirit.'

'What do you mean, that's the spirit? I thought you wanted me to write one?'

'I believe I've made it as far as Möja.'

'What do you mean?'

'I row back and forth to Finland about once a month.'

Humlin felt exhausted.

'I just want to make myself understood. I don't write crime fiction. What do oil executives know about good literature?'

Lundin resumed his rowing.

'Nothing.'

'I'll be turning in my usual book of poetry.'

'A crime novel, you mean?'

'No, no crime novel. How many times do I have to say it?'

'It will be a sensation. A renowned poet who neither cares to nor knows how to write one does so anyway. It will be completely different from what others are writing. But excellent. Perhaps it will be a very philosophical crime novel?'

'If you no longer want my poem there are other publishing companies. Ones that are not owned by oilmen.'

Lundin dropped the oars and stood up. He lit a cigarette then placed the blood-pressure cuff around his arm.

'Aren't you supposed to rest before doing that?'

'I'm just checking my pulse. Of course I want your poems.'

'They don't sell fifty thousand copies.'

'But your crime novel will.'

'I don't write whodunits. I am a poet.'

'You will continue to write poetry. Just as you always have. The crime novel comes in between.'

'What do you mean?'

'My pulse is at ninety-eight.'

'I don't care about your pulse right now. I want to know what you mean.'

'It's very simple. You write a crime novel where the poem at the start of each chapter gives the reader some clues.'

'What kind of clues?'

'Most likely the kind that it will take some literary knowledge to decipher. I am convinced it will be a sensation. A philosophical thriller. Jesper Humlin is treading a new path. It will be wonderful. I think it will go to sixty-two thousand copies.'

'Why not sixty-one?'

'My instinct tells me this one will go to sixty-two thousand.'

Humlin looked at the time and got up. He felt a need to escape from this room that was starting to look more and more like a battlefield.

'I have a reading in Gothenburg tonight. I have to go.'

'When can I expect the manuscript?'

'I'm not writing a thriller. That's it.'

'If I get it in April we can have it out by September. The title should be something along the lines of "Deathly Rhyme".'

Humlin left the building and took a few deep breaths when he got out onto the street. The conversation had both unsettled and angered him. Usually these conversations only left him exhausted. As he collected himself he realised that Lundin was serious about this. Viktor Leander was not the only one who was convinced that crime novels were the way of the future.

While he walked to the Central station he thought about the cover design of the last book. He had protested against it until the last, right until he left for the South Pacific. He had made a number of angry phone calls to Olof Lundin. The cover had nothing whatsoever to do with the content, and to top it off it was extremely ugly, hastily sketched in the sloppy style that was in fashion. Lundin had insisted it would help sales. Humlin could still recall their conversation. He had been at the airport on the morning of his trip and decided to make a last attempt to change Lundin's mind.

'I hate the cover and I will never forgive you if you give it the green light.'

'Just because your poems are unreadable doesn't mean the cover has to be.'

'And what do you mean by that?'

'Just what you think it means.'

'You're insulting me.'

'I don't mean the poems are bad, I mean they're difficult. They require a great deal of their reader.'

'If that's what you really mean you should say so.'

'I'm saying it now.'

'I hate the cover.'

'It's a good cover.'

He had to end the conversation because his name was called on the intercom system. Recently, it had become a habit of his to wait until the last minute to board, just to get his name read aloud and thereby enjoy the small buzz of attention it garnered him.

*

The train pulled out of the station. Humlin decided to mull over the conversation with Lundin until he reached Södertälje, at which point he had to start thinking about tonight's reading. He had been planning to do this first thing, but the visit to his mother's last night had made that impossible.

His phone rang. It was Andrea.

'Where are you?' she demanded.

'On my way to Gothenburg. Have you forgotten about my reading?'

'I haven't forgotten about it since you never told me about it in the first place.'

Humlin sensed that she might be right. He decided against having an argument he was bound to lose.

'We'll talk when I get back.'

'When I see you I want to talk about reality, not your poetry.'

Andrea ended the conversation abruptly, as she often did. Humlin kept thinking about what Lundin had said. He grew more and more agitated.

When the train left Södertälje, however, he forced all thoughts of crime novels out of his head and thought about the evening ahead. He liked jetting about the country and speaking about his work. Leander had once – after an especially inebriated dinner – accused him of being nothing more than a vain impresario. Humlin especially enjoyed speaking at libraries and adult education settings. He was more sceptical of high schools and plain fearful of any school at a lower level. This evening in Gothenburg promised to be to his liking. A civilised evening at the library with a focused audience of upper-middle-aged women who clapped heartily and never asked difficult questions.

He decided which poems he would read and which version of his journey to authorship he would present. He had tried a variety of different stories over the years and had finally settled on three accounts that he could choose between at will. The first of these was the closest to the truth. He talked about his sheltered upbringing and the frightening fact that he had never felt the need to rebel in adolescence. He had done well in school, never joined any radical factions nor travelled too adventurously. It usually took him about twenty minutes to talk about this abnormal normality.

The second version of his life was mostly lies. It consisted of a far more colourful youth and since his old classmates sometimes turned up in the audience, he had made sure to only claim such experiences as would be impossible to verify.

The third story was about a long and uncertain path to becoming a writer. In this account he claimed to have written his first novel at the age of eight but that he had burned it when he published his first real book. This version came the closest to describing the man he wished he had been. But he would never have admitted that any of these things he said about himself were not true.

*

The train arrived on time. He took a taxi to the Mölndal library and was greeted by a young librarian.

'So is anyone coming to see me tonight?'

'All of our tickets are gone. We're expecting one hundred and fifty people.'

'Whoever said the Swedish Folk Movement was dead?' Humlin said with fitting humility. 'One hundred and fifty people are coming to listen to a simple poet on a dark and cold night in February.'

'There are some groups coming.'

'What kind of groups?'

'I don't know. The other librarian should know.'

Later Humlin would regret the fact that he never took the time to seek out the other librarian and ask her about these groups. He assumed they were a book club or perhaps a retired persons' association. But when he stepped up to the lectern at seven o'clock he saw a group of people that reminded him neither of retirees nor of book lovers. In the usual audience of beaming older women he noticed some people he couldn't quite place.

In the front row there were a group of middle-aged men who did not look like the kind of audience members he usually saw, neither in their clothing nor their looks. Many had long hair and pierced ears and wore leather jackets and jeans, often torn over the knees. Humlin immediately grew more guarded. He also noticed a group of dark-skinned women sitting together. Immigrants, or so-called New Swedes, were not a usual part of his following, apart from a Chinese man who lived in Haparanda and who often sent him long letters with complicated and altogether incomprehensible analyses of his poems. Nonetheless there was an immigrant group here in this library in Mölndal listening to him.

Jesper Humlin drew a deep breath and launched into his lecture, the one that was closest to the truth and took twenty-one minutes. Afterwards he read a few poems from his latest collection that he thought would go over best. The whole time he was speaking he kept a surreptitious eye on the men in the front row. They listened attentively and he began to think with increasing satisfaction that he seemed in fact to have reached a new reading public. But the atmosphere in the room changed when he started reading his poems. One of the men in the front row shifted restlessly and started rocking back and forth in his chair as he sighed audibly. Humlin started to sweat. He skipped a whole stanza in the poem he was reading out of sheer nervousness, making the already challenging poem completely incomprehensible.

When he finished the poem, he looked up to find the men in the front row staring at him. None of them clapped. Humlin leafed through his book and hastily decided to change his approach and only read a few more of the shortest poems. At the same time his mind was ever more desperately trying to figure out who these men with their leather jackets and torn jeans could possibly be. The other unusual group, the immigrants, were staring at him impassively. They clapped dutifully but without enthusiasm. Humlin had the distinct impression that it was all going to hell, but without really being able to say why. He had never experienced a reading quite like this one.

He finished the final poem and wiped the sweat from his brow. He looked up at the people he considered his *normal* public and received their enthusiastic applause. The men in the front row were staring at him with what he now saw were glazed eyes. He lay aside his book and smiled, trying to hide his fear.

'I am happy to take any questions that you may have. After that there will be a short time for book signing.'

A woman put up her hand and asked him to define his usage of the word *charity*. She felt it was a concept that underpinned the whole collection. Humlin thought he heard a low growl from the front row. He started to sweat again.

'Charity, in my opinion, is simply a more beautiful word for kindness.'

The man who had shifted restlessly during Humlin's poetry reading stood up so violently that his chair was knocked to the floor.

'What the fuck kind of question is that?' he shrieked. 'What I would like to ask you, Mr Poet, is what you think you're doing when you force us to listen to this stuff. If you like I can tell you what I think.'

'Please do.'

'I don't understand how all this shit fits between the covers of such a little book, one that costs three hundred kronor, by the way. I have only one question I would really like to get an answer to.'

Humlin tried to control his voice as he replied.

'What's your question?'

'What do you get paid by, the word?'

A shocked mumble arose among those members of the public who had enjoyed the reading. Humlin turned to one of the librarians who was sitting behind and slightly to one side of him.

'Who are these people?' he hissed.

'They're clients from a halfway house outside Gothenburg.'

'What the hell are they doing here?'

The librarian gave him a stern look.

'One of my most important duties is exposing people who have never previously had the opportunity, to the world of literature. You have no idea what I had to go through in order to get them here.'

'I think actually I have some idea. But you see the kind of questions this man is asking.'

'And I think he deserves an answer.'

Humlin collected himself and looked at the man who had still not seated himself. He was tensed like an angry wrestler.

'I don't get paid by the word. As a general rule poets get paid very little for their work.'

'I'm glad to hear it.'

The woman who had asked about charity got up and thumped her cane into the floor.

'I think it is indefensible and rude to ask Mr Humlin about these sorts of financial matters. We are here in order to discuss his poetry in a calm and civilised manner.'

Another one of the men in the front row got up. Humlin had noticed him earlier since he had been nodding off most of the time. Once he got to his feet he swayed and had to take another step to balance himself. He was clearly intoxicated.

'I don't know what that old bitch is talking about.'

'How do you mean?' Humlin said helplessly.

'Isn't this a free country? Why can't we ask what we want? It's all the same to me anyway. I'm with my pal Åkesson here. I've never heard worse shit in my whole life.'

A flash went off. Humlin hadn't seen them, but at some point during the reading a local reporter and a photographer had sneaked into the auditorium. This is going to be a scandal, Humlin thought desperately, picturing the headlines in the national papers. As with other writers, there was a place inside himself where he doubted his own talents, a place where he was nothing more than a literary charlatan. Humlin was about to plead with the photographer not to take any more pictures when Åkesson unexpectedly came to his aid.

'Who gave you permission to take my picture?' he screamed. 'Just because I've done time doesn't mean I don't have human rights.'

The photographer tried to ward him off but now all the men from the front row gathered around him. The librarian tried to calm everyone down as most of the audience started filing out of the auditorium before a fight broke out. Humlin was dumbstruck. He had never in his life imagined that his poetry would lead to the kind of tumult he now saw playing out before his eyes.

But the chaos dissolved as quickly as it had begun. Suddenly Humlin was alone in the big room. He could still hear agitated voices in the corridor outside. Then he realised someone else had stayed behind in the room as well. It was a young dark-skinned woman from the immigrant group. She was alone in the sea of chairs and she had raised one arm. The most striking thing about her was her smile. Humlin had never seen a smile like it before. It was as if she gave off light.

'Did you want to ask me something?' he asked.

'Have you ever written about anyone like me?'

Are there no straightforward questions any more? Humlin thought.

'I don't think I know exactly what you're getting at.'

The girl spoke with an accent but her Swedish was clear.

'I mean people who have come here. We who were not born here.'

'It has always been my view that poetry is about crossing borders,' Humlin said, but he heard how hollow it sounded.

The young woman got to her feet.

'Thank you for answering my question.'

'I am happy to answer more.'

'I have no other questions for you.'

'May I ask you something?' Humlin asked.

'I have not written any poems.'

'What's your name?'

'Tea-Bag.'

'Tea-Bag?'

'Tea-Bag.'

'Where do you come from?'

She continued to smile but did not answer this last question. Humlin watched her as she slipped out into the corridor where angry voices could still be heard.

*

Humlin left the auditorium by a back door and left Mölndal in the taxi that had been waiting for him. He had not signed a single book and had not said goodbye to the librarians. He leaned back in his seat and looked out the window. They drove past a frozen lake that glinted in the headlights. Humlin shivered. Then his thoughts returned to the young woman in the auditorium with the beautiful smile. Her I think I would be able to write a poem about, he thought. But nothing is very certain any more.

4

When Jesper Humlin woke up the following morning in his hotel in central Gothenburg he suddenly came to think of his old friend Pelle Törnblom who lived in a suburb called Stensgården. Pelle Törnblom was a one-time sailor who had finally returned to land and started a community boxing club. They had seen a lot of each other when they were young. Pelle Törnblom had also nourished literary ambitions for a short while. Over the years they had kept in sporadic contact with phone calls and postcards. Humlin tried to recall when they had last seen each other. The only thing he was sure of was that Törnblom had been working on a barge at the time, directing timber transports along the coast of northern Sweden.

Humlin decided to look for Törnblom's telephone number after breakfast. First he nervously checked the morning paper but found nothing about last night's events. That calmed him for the moment, though he feared the scandal was simply being held over for a day. He thought about having a word with the librarian whose brilliant idea it had been to invite a bunch of ex-cons to his poetry reading, but knew there was nothing to say. She had genuinely worked to draw in a group of people who were not usually exposed to the world of books.

The cell phone rang. It was Olof Lundin. Humlin did not want to talk to him.

'Olof here. Where are you?'

Once upon a time people asked you how you were, Humlin thought. Now they ask you where you are.

'This connection is bad. I can't hear you.'

'Where are you?'

'This connection is bad. I'm in Gothenburg. I don't want to talk to you.'

'What are you doing in Gothenburg?'

'You arranged two readings for me here.'

'I'd forgotten about that. The library?'

'Yesterday I was in Mölndal and tonight I'm going out to a place called Stensgården.'

'Where is that?'

'You should know since you set it up. I can't keep talking. And anyway, I can hardly hear you.'

'Why can't you talk now? Did I wake you up?'

'I'm awake, I just can't hear you very well.'

'You can hear me fine. Kudos for your performance in Mölndal, by the way.'

Humlin drew his breath in sharply.

'How do you know about that? You didn't even know where I was.'

'Now you seem to hear fine.'

'The connection got better.'

'The librarian called me. She was very pleased.'

'How can she be pleased? There was almost a fight.'

'It's not very common for a poetry reading to lead to such violent reactions. I've been calling the evening papers trying to get them to include it in tonight's issue.'

Humlin almost dropped the phone.

'What have you done?'

'I talked to the evening papers.'

'I don't want anything in the evening papers!' Humlin yelled. 'There were just a bunch of drunk men who spewed forth about my poetry. They wanted to know what I make per word.'

'An interesting question.'

'You think so, do you?'

'I can work it out for you, if you like.'

'Why would I want to know that? Should I start writing longer poems? I don't want you to speak to any papers, in fact, I forbid you to.'

'Sorry, it's getting harder to hear you.'

'I said, I don't want to see anything about this in the papers!'

'Call me back and try to get a better connection. I must get back to the evening papers.'

He hung up. Humlin stared furiously at the phone. When he tried calling back he was told that Lundin was in a meeting and would not be reachable until the afternoon. Humlin lay down on the bed and decided he would change publishers. He didn't want anything more to do with Lundin. As a kind of revenge he spent an hour thinking out the basic plot of a crime novel, although he promised himself he would never actually write it.

*

In the late afternoon as the rain had begun to drizzle down over Gothenburg, Humlin took a taxi to Stensgården. It was a depressingly generic city suburb with rows of concrete apartment buildings laid out like blocks. He got out on the windy main square of Stensgården where the library lay wedged in between McDonald's and the government-owned wine store. Once again his taxi driver had been an African man, and once again he had found the address without any problems. The sign for the library was broken and the front door was covered in graffiti. Humlin went in search of the librarian in charge who turned out to be almost identical to the woman at Mölndal library. He asked with obvious trepidation if she had invited any special groups to the reading.

'What kind of groups?'

'I don't know. Perhaps you've been doing a community outreach of some kind to bring in a new clientele to the library.'

'And what kind of people are we talking about?'

'I don't know. I was just asking.'

'I don't know what you're talking about, but I should warn you that we are not expecting very many people tonight. At best I think we'll have ten.'

Humlin looked at her with horror.

'Ten people?'

'We normally only get that many for poets. If we have a writer of crime fiction we naturally draw a larger crowd.'

'How many more?'

'Last time we had a hundred and fifty-seven people.'

Humlin had no more questions. He placed his overnight bag in the librarian's office and left. Once he was back out in the deserted main square he tried to call Lundin again. This time he was there.

'I hope you didn't talk to any media people.'

'Of course I did, but unfortunately they didn't seem very interested.'

Humlin felt a huge weight lift from his chest.

'So there will be no story?'

'Probably not. But I'm not going to give up just yet.'

'I want you to give up.'

'Have you given any more thought to your crime novel?'

'No.'

'You should. Let me know when you have a title.'

'I'm a poet. I don't write detective fiction.'

'Let me know when you think of a title.'

Humlin put the phone back in his pocket, pulled his coat more tightly around his body and started wandering across the square. After a few steps he realised that there was something different about this place. At first he didn't know what it was, then he understood that it was the people. It was as if he had suddenly crossed over an invisible line into a foreign country. The people he saw on the street were different in colouring, dress and posture.

It struck him that he had never spent any time in this other new Sweden that was emerging, the ghetto-like city suburbs where every immigrant or refugee ended up. It also struck him again with fearful clarity that only ten people were coming to his reading tonight. What did his poetry possibly have to say to these people?

He walked around the square until he got too cold. He went into a cafe with Arabic music playing over the loudspeakers and looked for Pelle Törnblom's phone number. He found it under 'Törnblom's Boxing Club'. Then he turned to the dark-skinned girl behind the counter and asked her if she knew where the boxing club was located.

'On the other side of the church.'

Humlin did not recall having seen a church. The girl walked over to the fogged-up window and pointed it out to him, then returned to her magazine.

Humlin finished his coffee and walked over to the church and the ramshackle industrial building where a small sign on the door read 'Pelle Törnblom's Boxing Club'. Humlin hesitated before ringing the bell. Why was he looking him up after all these years? What would they have to say to each other? He decided to go back to the library, but at that moment the door opened. It was Törnblom. Humlin saw at once that he had gained weight. Earlier he had kept himself fit. Now he had a large belly and a red face. The shirt under his leather jacket strained across the middle. Törnblom nodded in recognition.

'We're coming to see you tonight,' he said with a smile.

'Who's we?'

'Amanda and I.'

'Who is Amanda?'

'My wife. My fourth and last wife.'

'Then that brings us to twelve people. The librarian is expecting ten.'

Törnblom invited him in. They walked up a narrow staircase and entered a room that smelled of old sweat. There was a boxing ring in the middle of the room. Weights and other tools for strength training were lined up along the walls. Humlin instinctively looked around for something that resembled Lundin's rowing machine.

'Thursdays are my day off,' Törnblom said. 'Otherwise this place would be full of kids.'

Törnblom escorted him to a small office in the back where they sat down. Törnblom seemed to take the measure of him.

'Why are you so tanned?' he asked.

'I've been travelling.'

'It doesn't look natural.'

'What do you mean?'

'It's too even. It looks like you keep it up in a solarium.'

Humlin was now convinced he had made a mistake in looking up his old friend.

'I've been out travelling in tropical places. It makes you tan.'

Törnblom shrugged.

'You look like you've gained weight,' Humlin said as a counter-attack.

'I'm married for the fourth and last time now. I can let myself go.'

'What about your health?'

'I'm only this heavy in the winter. I lose weight in the summer.'

'Tell me more about this Amanda.'

'She's from Turkey, although to be precise it is more like Iran. But her father was born in Pakistan. He lives in Canada now.'

'So she's an immigrant?'

'She was born in Sweden. Whatever that makes her.'

'I saw a lot of immigrants around here as I was wandering around the square.'

'It's probably only me and the alcoholics that hang out in front of the liquor store who are what you would call ethnic Swedes. Everyone in my boxing club has another nationality. I've counted nineteen different ones so far.'

'I can't imagine I'll see many of them at the reading tonight,' Humlin said, and noticed to his surprise that the thought disappointed him.

'You'll meet them later,' Törnblom said cheerfully, and reached for a coffee maker that had been sitting high up on a shelf.

'After the reading?'

'I couldn't convince anyone to come to the library, but they're all coming to the party afterward.'

'What party is this?'

'The party we're throwing for you. It'll be here.'

Humlin felt a new wave of anxiety wash over him.

'No one said anything to me about a party.'

'Of course not. It was going to be a surprise.'

'Unfortunately I'm not going to be able to attend. I just have enough time after the reading to catch the last flight out for Stockholm.'

'Then why don't you leave tomorrow?'

Humlin saw Andrea's face in his mind's eye.

'I can't. Andrea will go crazy.'

'Who is Andrea?'

'She's the woman I guess I share my life with.'

'Are you married?'

'No. We don't even live together.'

'Call her and tell her you need to stay overnight. She'll understand.'

'No, she won't. You don't know Andrea.'

'Not even one night?'

'I can't do it,' Humlin said.

'Everyone will be very disappointed if we cancel the party. All the kids were looking forward to it. They've never met a famous bestselling author before.'

'I'm not a bestselling author. And I'm not even particularly famous.'

Pelle Törnblom had managed to get the coffee maker to work. He offered Humlin a cup, but the poet turned him down.

'I didn't think someone like you would have it in you to

disappoint a group of young immigrant kids. Some of their parents are coming too.'

Humlin gave up. He tried to imagine how he would explain staying overnight to Andrea, but realised there was no way in which it would not be turned against him.

'Some gypsies are coming to play music,' Törnblom said encouragingly.

Humlin didn't answer. Instead his gaze fastened on an old poster advertising a match between Eddie Machen and Ingemar Johansson.

*

Thirteen people came to the reading, since one of the janitors working in the building came in at the end of his shift. They could have been as many as seventeen, since a group of drunk men who had been hanging around outside the liquor store wanted to come in and warm up. Humlin, who still had not worked up the nerve to call Andrea, stared glumly out over his audience. But when the drunks from outside tumbled into the room he collected himself and said he refused to read his poetry to people who were clearly intoxicated and only interested in getting warm.

Right before he was about to start, Törnblom and his wife entered the room. Humlin immediately fell in love with her. She had a beautiful face, with deep-set eyes. During his reading he directed his inner attentions towards her, reading his poems for her and no one else. The rest of the audience consisted mainly of the retired, among them a man whose breath rattled worryingly in his chest. In Humlin's mind the breathing came to sound like stormy waves smashing up against a rocky shore. After the reading there were no questions. Törnblom smiled and Humlin grew suspicious. He looks down on me, he thought. When we were younger the literature we had in mind was of a completely different sort. We were going to write deadly critiques of oppressive regimes. I ended up in the world of poetry, he in a barge and then a boxing club.

While the librarian was presenting Humlin with a small bouquet of flowers for his troubles – among the smallest he had ever received – he decided he would leave through a back door and take a taxi straight to the airport. He realised this would likely make any future contact with Törnblom impossible. But he was genuinely afraid of Andrea's reaction. When the room was almost empty Pelle Törnblom and his wife approached him.

'I did not understand your poems,' Amanda said simply. 'But they were very beautiful.'

'I understood them,' Törnblom said. 'But I didn't think they were very beautiful.'

'Let me just get my coat,' Humlin said. 'Then I'll meet you down at the boxing club.'

Törnblom looked closely at him.

'I thought we could walk over there together.'

'After a reading I always like to have a little time to myself to clear my head.'

'I think we should walk over together. But we don't have to talk.'

He senses I'd like to get out of this, Humlin thought. When he came back into the room with his coat he still wasn't sure what he was going to do. The thought of calling Andrea and telling her of the change in his plans seemed too much. He got out his mobile phone to call a taxi when his phone rang. He didn't recognise the number that appeared on his display. He answered. It was his mother.

'Where are you?'

'Why don't you ask me how I am?'

'We live in a new age now. With mobile phones one never knows where people might be. Why don't you ask me where I am?'

'I don't recognise the number. Where are you?'

'I've been invited out to a restaurant.'

'By whom?'

'A secret admirer.'

'Who?'

'I'm not going to tell you.'

'Is that why you called? So you can tell me you're not going to tell me who has invited you out to dinner?'

'I'd like you to drop by later this evening. We have something important to talk about.'

'I can't come by this evening. I'm out of town.'

'I spoke to Andrea earlier. She said very definitely that you were coming home tonight.'

Humlin felt trapped.

'I could be dead by tomorrow night. I'm almost ninety years old.'

'You're not going to die tonight. I'll be over tomorrow evening.'

'That's not possible. Andrea is coming over then.'

'Andrea?'

'I'd like to see you tonight and her tomorrow.'

'Why can't we come over together?'

'I have some important things to tell you. But I would like to speak to you separately.'

Humlin tried to understand what could be going on with his mother.

'I'll be by if I make my flight.'

'Where are you?'

'Andrea didn't tell you?'

'She couldn't remember if it was Luleå or Malmö.'

'I'm in Gothenburg.'

'I don't have any more time to talk now. I'll be home after midnight. We'll have a glass of wine.'

'I don't want to have any wine.'

The connection was already broken. Humlin called the taxi company but the number was busy. He found a phone book on a shelf in the hallway where he quickly looked up other companies. Everyone's number was busy. Humlin was starting to sweat. I don't want to go to a party, he thought. Maybe I would like to be alone with Amanda and explain the meaning of my poetry to her.

He called the first company again and got through this time.

'We can send a taxi out to you in twenty minutes.'

'That's too late. I'm trying to catch a flight.'

'There's a medical conference on in town. That's why we're so busy tonight.'

'I need a cab out here immediately.'

'I'm sorry, sir. It doesn't look like we can help you.'

Humlin decided he would try to wave one down on the street. He found the back exit and thought to himself that he was leaving by the door of the Failed Poets. Bestselling crime novelists probably always left through the front door.

But when he got outside Törnblom was there waiting for him.

'Amanda went the other way,' Törnblom said. 'We were afraid we might lose you.'

Humlin felt humiliated.

'I saw it in your face that you were going to try to stand us up,' Törnblom said accusingly. 'I have to look out for my kids, for everyone who's going to be disappointed if you don't show.'

'You don't know Andrea.'

Törnblom held out his hand impatiently.

'Give me your phone. I'll call her.'

'What are you going to say?'

'That you're indisposed.'

'She knows I never get ill. She's a nurse. She knows me.'

'I'll say you had a fainting spell.'

'I've never had one before.'

'Diarrhoea. That can happen any time.'

'You don't understand. Even if I actually had a heart attack she would accuse me of not keeping my promise.'

Törnblom seemed to see the seriousness of the situation. He thought for a moment.

'What time does the plane leave?'

'In exactly seventy-seven minutes.'

'Then let's wait one hour and call and say that the car broke down while I was taking you to the airport.'

'She won't believe me.'

'She doesn't need to believe you, just as long as she believes me.'

Törnblom's voice was firm. Humlin realised there was no longer any point in trying to resist going to the party that had been organised for him. He handed Törnblom the phone.

'Call Andrea whenever you feel is the best time. But remember that I'll have to suffer an unimaginable nightmare if you aren't convincing.'

'Don't worry.'

Humlin's anxiety increased.

They walked across the barren square that was now empty of people. Humlin thought he should ask more about the event they were headed to but Törnblom beat him to it.

'You're lucky none of the kids heard your poetry.'

'I already know you didn't like it.'

Törnblom shrugged.

'It's like most poetry.'

'And how is that?'

'Generally uninteresting.'

They kept walking in silence. Humlin's sense of discomfort and low self-worth increased with each step.

When they arrived at the boxing club they saw some candles flickering outside the front door, which was slightly ajar. Humlin stopped Törnblom right before they went in.

'What exactly do they expect of me?'

'You're the guest of honour.'

'So what's expected of me?'

'That you behave like a guest of honour.'

'And how is that?'

'You answer questions. Sign autographs. Show them you're grateful for the attention.'

'Who am I to them?'

Törnblom seemed surprised by the question and had to think for a while before answering.

'Someone from a world foreign to them. You're from Stockholm but you might as well be from outer space.'

*

Just as Humlin had feared Andrea blew up when Törnblom delivered the message about his car breaking down. Even in the din from the gypsy orchestra Humlin could hear her voice on the other end. It came out of the phone and whirled around Törnblom's head like a torch blower's flame. He flinched and held the phone away from his head.

'What happened?'

'She didn't believe me.'

'What did she say?'

'You told me she wouldn't believe either one of us, and you were right.'

Törnblom acknowledged defeat.

'We should have stepped out before making the call.'

'You mean you should have stepped out. You were the one making the call.'

'I guess it didn't sound much like I was calling from a broken-down car with the gypsy music in the background.'

'What did she say?'

'She started talking about some book that she's going to start working on tonight.'

'Don't say anything else. I don't want to know.'

Humlin had decided he was not going to drink at this party. But now he decided to throw caution to the wind. One has to have one's last meal somewhere, he thought. It can even be at a party in a boxing club. He started to drink; having some drinks, at first slowly and methodically, then becoming more manic. He and Törnblom were the only ones drinking wine. All the rest were drinking sodas. Törnblom introduced him to many people, all immigrants, and many of them spoke such poor Swedish that he couldn't understand what they were saying. But people were constantly coming over wanting to talk to him, most of them young. His patience was stretched trying to understand and then answer the questions they put to him.

Then someone pulled him up into the boxing ring to dance. Humlin hated dancing. He had never been good at it and had always envied those who could make their bodies move smoothly to the music. As he tried to climb out of the boxing ring he tripped and fell head over heels. Luckily, since he was extremely drunk by this time, he fell gently and did not hurt himself. Amanda helped him into the back office where he and Törnblom had spoken earlier. He wanted Amanda to stay with him but she only blushed very attractively when he groped after her and told her how beautiful she was. She hurried out of the room and closed the door behind her.

Suddenly Humlin was alone. The sound of music and excited voices filtered softly into the room. Without knowing why, he began to think of the young woman he had met in Mölndal, the one who said her name was Tea-Bag. He closed his eyes. No more poems, he thought. But I'm also never going to write that crime novel that Lundin wants me to. What I'm going to write next, and if I will be up to it, I have no idea.

The door opened and a girl with a Middle Eastern appearance looked in.

'Am I disturbing you?' she asked.

The whole world is disturbing to me right now, Humlin thought.

'Not at all,' he said.

The girl spoke broken Swedish but Humlin had no trouble understanding her.

'I want to be a writer,' she said.

Humlin flinched as if he had been jumped from behind. Although he was drunk he couldn't help feeling the same worry and suspicion he always felt when a person stood in front of him and declared their intentions to become a writer. He always feared that the other person would prove to be the greater talent.

'What on earth for?'

'I want to tell my story,' she said.

'And what story is that?'

'My story.'

Humlin looked at the girl who was maybe eighteen or nineteen. He was so drunk that the room was rocking but he managed to keep his eyes fixed on her. She was very fat. She was wearing a shawl that concealed much of her body but he could still tell that she was more than just a little chubby. Her face was covered in acne and was shiny with sweat.

'Where do you come from?'

'Iran.'

'What's your name?'

'Leyla.'

'Are you a boxer?'

'I'm here because my brother asked me to come. He does boxing here.'

'And you want to be a writer?'

'I just need to know how it's done.'

Humlin stared at her. He didn't know where his next thought came from but it was fully formulated and clear, the way he very occasionally saw a whole poem appear before his eyes and never had to change a single word. *I just need to know how it's done.* Humlin straightened his back. Viktor Leander can write his crime novel, he thought. What I'm going to do is help this girl write her story. And in turn she'll help me write about the people who live in Stensgården. Humlin pulled over the wine bottle that Amanda had left behind and finished off its contents. Leyla looked disapprovingly at him.

'I can help you,' he said when he put the bottle down. 'If you give me your phone number, I'll call you.'

Leyla jumped.

'I can't do that.'

'What do you mean?'

'I can't give out my phone number,' she said.

'Why not?'

'My parents won't like it if I start getting calls from a man.'

'Just tell them who I am.'

She shook her head.

'It won't work. It's not proper. Call Pelle Törnblom or Amanda.'

Then she smiled.

'Are you sure you want to help me?' she asked.

'I am. If I can remains to be seen.'

Leyla left. Humlin stayed put and stared at the tattered posters on the wall. The outlines were still unclear but he finally had a sense of what he was going to write. Not the book Leander was working on, not the one Lundin wanted him to do. Something completely different.

*

Törnblom took him to the airport the following day. Humlin had a bad hangover and was not completely sure of what had happened towards the very end of the party. He had woken up to find himself lying on a training mat next to the ring. He had a pounding headache.

'It was a great party, wasn't it? I'm glad you decided to stay. Andrea will have cooled down by the time you get home.'

Humlin shuddered at the thought of what awaited him when he got home. He thought longingly of the beer he was hoping to get at the airport.

'She won't have cooled down one bit.'

'Your visit meant a lot to the kids back there.'

Humlin didn't reply. He thought of that fat girl, Leyla, and the idea that had come to him last night. In the grey light of the morning after he could no longer tell if he thought it was a good idea or not. And this suddenly frightened him more than the thought of what Andrea would say when he returned.

5

Everyone was against it, but for different reasons. Andrea, who had been waiting furiously for him to return, didn't even want to hear a word of his new plan.

'I can't take my eyes off you for a second, can I? The only thing you ever put any thought into is how you're going to sneak around without getting caught.'

'I'm not unfaithful to you, Andrea.'

'Then who is Amanda?'

Jesper Humlin stared back at her with surprise. They were sitting across from each other at her dinner table in the apartment in Hagersten some days after his return from Gothenburg.

'Amanda is married to a good friend of mine, Pelle Törnblom. He runs a boxing club.'

'When did you ever let that stop you? You called out her name in your sleep.'

'So what? What matters is I've been inspired to write a book about – and *with* – immigrants.'

'And what makes you qualified to do this?'

'You can't deny that I am a writer.'

'Soon you'll be telling me you're going to write a bestseller.'

Humlin looked at her with horror.

'What makes you say that?'

'It just sounds like you think you can write whatever you please without effort. I think you should leave this poor girl alone.'

Humlin stopped trying to convince Andrea of his new idea. The rest of the evening was spent discussing his inadequate commitment to having children. Then she left for her night shift at the hospital. Before she left he promised her he would spend the night in the apartment and be there when she came back.

As soon as she left he went into the bedroom and started looking through her papers and diaries. He found a draft of something that described one of their early encounters. He sat down in the living room and read it through thoroughly. His anxiety returned. It was good, unnervingly good, actually. He put the piece of paper down with a grimace. His first thought was to end the relationship immediately, or at least threaten to. But he wasn't sure where that would lead.

According to his usual habit he then proceeded to read her diary. She had an old-fashioned model, the kind that teenage girls used, with a small heart-shaped lock. He knew how to pick the lock with a hairpin and he eyed the entries she had made since last time. He was indifferent to most of it since it was mainly about work-related matters. But he studied the few passages about marriage and children very carefully, poring over her jerky handwriting. A couple of the sentences caught his eye. *I must keep asking myself what I want. If you don't keep stoking the fire of your will, it dies.* He decided to write them down in his own notebook immediately. He hadn't written a poem on the topic of will yet. Her formulation here could perhaps be developed and used in his next poetry collection.

After the assault on her diary he started to feel better. He poured himself a glass of grappa in the kitchen, then lay down on the sofa with one of her fashion magazines that he read in secret.

Humlin, exhausted after his evening with Andrea, had just gone to bed when his mother called.

'I thought you were coming over,' she said.

'I've just gone to bed. I was tired. If you like, I can come over tomorrow.'

'Is Andrea there?'

'She's working.'

'So should you be. It's only half past eleven. I've set out a little supper for us. I went to a delicatessen just for your sake.'

Humlin put his clothes back on, ordered a taxi and noticed, as he looked in the hall mirror, that his South Pacific suntan was already fading. His taxi driver was a woman who couldn't find her way at all in the inner city.

'I'm a third-generation Stockholmer,' she announced cheerfully after she had made a large detour to get to the one-way street his mother lived on. 'I'm born and bred in this city but bless my soul if I can't find my way to save my life.'

She also had no change, as it turned out, nor could she accept credit cards. In the end she took down his bank information and promised to send him the change.

*

Märta Humlin had bought oysters for supper. Humlin hated oysters.

'Why did you buy oysters?'

'I like to give my son the best. Isn't this good enough for you?'

'You know I've never liked oysters.'

'I've never heard any such thing.'

He realised the futility of continuing the conversation. Instead he told her about the idea he had had in Gothenburg. At times his mother had been able to give him valuable feedback.

'That sounds like a marvellous idea,' she said when he finished.

His surprise was genuine.

'Do you really think so?'

'You know I always say what I think.'

'I see. Then how come everyone else I've talked to has been against it?'

'It doesn't matter. You should listen to me, and I'm telling you to go ahead and write about this girl from India. It will be very romantic, very moving. Is it a love story?'

'She's from Iran, not India. I was thinking more of something along the lines of a socio-realist novel.'

'A love story is better. I think you should write something thrilling about a Swedish author and a beautiful woman from a foreign land.'

'She's fat and ugly, mother. And anyway, I can't write love stories.'

Märta Humlin fixed her eyes on him intently.

'I thought the whole idea was to break away and try something new.'

'I want to write about something real. The way things are,' he said.

'Tell me how they are. And why aren't you eating your oysters?'

'I'm full. I want to write about how hard it is to come to a new land and try to set down new roots.'

'And who in God's name would want to read about a fat girl with a headscarf who lives in the suburbs?'

'Quite a few, actually.'

'If you follow my advice you'll do fine. Otherwise I would leave it. You know nothing of what it's like to come to a foreign country. And why aren't you and Andrea having babies?'

'We're talking about it.'

'Andrea says you rarely make love these days.'

Humlin dropped the little fork that he had been using to skewer the oysters he was only pretending to eat.

'You and Andrea talk about things like that?'

'We have an open, trusting relationship.'

Humlin was shocked. Andrea had often said how overbearing and self-centred she found his mother. Now it turned out she had a completely different relationship to this woman in front of him who forced him to eat food he didn't like.

'I am never coming back here again if you and Andrea keep talking like this behind my back.'

'We simply want what's best for you.'

Humlin suddenly remembered the phone conversation he had had with his mother a few days ago. He didn't want to get drawn in any further into a meaningless debate about what exactly Andrea and his mother talked about. What he had heard was already enough.

'What was that important announcement you said you were going to make?'

'What announcement?'

'You called and told me I had to come over because you had an important announcement to make.'

'I have no recollection of doing any such thing.'

'If you have made changes in the will that leave me out I want to know about it,' he said.

'What is in my will is no one else's business.'

'If we knew we could count on some measure of economic security in the future that would really help me and Andrea make the decision to have children.'

'Are you telling me you hope I'm going to die soon?'

Humlin pushed his chair back from the table. It was late, but that seemed to have no effect on his mother.

'I have to go home now. I'm tired and I have no desire to talk finances with you in the middle of the night.'

His mother gave him a wounded look.

'Where did I get this son who always complains of being tired? It must be from your father.'

Then she started talking about how tired her husband had always been and Humlin stayed until three in the morning. In order not to be woken up by Andrea when she came home he put in earplugs and lay down on the couch in the living room. It took him a long time to fall asleep. In his thoughts he returned to the memory of the young woman who called herself Tea-Bag.

*

The following day Humlin stopped by his publisher's office. He was going to try to convince him that his new idea was worth taking seriously. He even brought a woollen cap with him since he expected to spend a long time in Lundin's ice-cold office. Lundin was rowing when he walked in.

'I'm just leaving the Åland islands,' Lundin said. 'How is that crime novel going? I'm going to need a title from you in a week. We have to start planning the marketing campaign.'

Humlin didn't answer. He sat down in the chair furthest away from the air ventilation unit. When Lundin had finished rowing he marked his position with a red pin on a map of the Baltic. He lit a cigarette and sat down at his desk.

'I take it you're here to give me a title,' Lundin said.

'I'm here to tell you I will never write a crime novel. But I have another idea.'

'It's not as good.'

'How can you say that when I haven't even told you what it is?'

'Only crime novels and certain indelicate confessional works sell more than fifty thousand copies.'

'I'm going to write a book about an immigrant girl,' Humlin said.

Lundin gave him an interested look.

'A confessional, then? How long has this little affair been going on?'

Humlin pulled on his woollen cap. He was so cold he was shivering.

'What's the temperature in here, anyway, for God's sake?'

'One degree Celsius.'

'Unbearable. How can you work in here?'

'It's good to toughen oneself up a little. Whatever happened to your tan, by the way?'

'Nothing, other than the fact that it never stops raining in this godforsaken place. Do you want to hear me out or not?'

Lundin threw out his arms in a gesture that Humlin interpreted as a mixture of openness and boredom. Humlin went on to present his idea with the feeling that he was being judged in a court of law where all those not writing crime novels were presumed guilty. Lundin lit another cigarette and measured his blood pressure. When Humlin was done, Lundin leaned back in his chair and shook his head.

'It'll sell four thousand, three hundred and twenty copies at most.'

'How can you know that?'

'It's that kind of book. But you can't write about fat immigrant girls. What do you know about their lives?'

'That's what I'm going to find out.'

'They'll never tell you the truth.'

'Why not?'

'I'm just telling you. I have experience in these matters.'

Lundin jumped up and leaned over the table.

'What you should write is a crime novel. Nothing else. Leave these fat girls alone. You don't need them and they don't need you. What we do need is a crime novel from you and then let some young immigrant talent write the great new Swedish novel. I want a title on my desk by the end of the week.'

Lundin stood up.

'It's always a pleasure, Humlin. But I have a meeting with the oil executives. They have already indicated their approval of your new crime novel, by the way.'

Lundin swept out of the room. Humlin went to the nearest cafe and drank some coffee to try to regain body heat. He wondered briefly if he should talk to Viktor Leander about his latest idea, but decided against it. If the idea was as good as he thought it was Leander would immediately use it.

He took a taxi back to his apartment and noted with relief that neither Andrea nor his mother had left any messages. After leafing through the notes he had made for his next work of poetry – tentatively titled *Torment and Antithesis* – he lay down on the bed and stared at the ceiling. Even though he was not entirely confident it still seemed that the idea he had had in Gothenburg was the strongest impulse he had to go on right now.

He lay on his bed turning his thoughts this way and that until he got up and called Pelle Törnblom. Törnblom sounded short of breath when he finally answered.

'What are you up to?' Humlin asked.

'I'm sparring with a guy from Pakistan. How did Andrea react?'

'Exactly as I had predicted. But I survived.'

'You have to agree it was a great party. The kids at the club feel very proud.'

'Has an Iranian girl named Leyla given you her phone number by any chance?'

'Her brother boxes at the club,' Törnblom said. 'He's told me what this is all about. I think it's a great idea.'

Humlin quickly rifled through the pages of his weekly planner.

'Tell her I'll come see her next Wednesday. Can we meet at your place?'

'It'll be better for you to meet here at the club. I have a large room on the ground floor that you could use.'

'I hope we'll be undisturbed there,' Humlin said.

'Of course, you realise her brother will have to be present.'

'No – why is that?'

'To make sure everything is above board, that no impropriety is committed.'

'What could possibly happen?'

'It's not proper for her to meet alone with an unknown man. We're talking serious cultural differences here, ones that need to be respected. You never know what could happen when a man and a woman are left alone together.'

'Good God, Törnblom! You've seen her!'

'She may not be the most beautiful woman on earth but that means nothing in this case. Her brother needs to be there to make sure all goes well.'

'What do you think me capable of, anyway?'

'I think it's a wonderful idea for you to stop writing poetry and write something worthwhile. That's what I think. You could really make something of yourself, you know.'

Humlin was starting to get angry. He felt insulted, but said nothing. He realised he would have to accept the fact that Leyla's brother would be chaperoning her.

He hung up and the phone rang almost at once. Humlin let the answering machine pick up. It was a reporter from one of the biggest papers in the country. Humlin answered the phone and tried to sound as if he had just been interrupted in the middle of something very important.

'I hope I'm not disturbing you,' the reporter said.

Humlin always hoped against hope that the journalists who called would be women with soft, pleasing voices. But this was a man with a rough regional dialect.

'I'm working, but I'm happy to take a moment to speak to you.'

'I would like to ask you a couple of questions about your new book.'

Humlin assumed the reporter meant the book of poetry that had come out a few months earlier.

'A few questions would be fine,' Humlin said.

'Do you mind if I turn on my tape recorder?'

'Not at all.'

Humlin waited until the reporter, whose name he didn't recognise, had turned on the tape recorder.

'First I just want to know how you feel about it,' the reporter said.

Images of the night at the Mölndal library flickered through Humlin's mind.

'I feel good about it,' he said. 'Very good.'

'Is there anything in particular that you can point to as a reason for writing this book?'

Humlin looked forward to answering this question. It was one that reporters always asked. A few days ago he had thought of a new answer as he was lying in the bathtub.

'I am always looking for ways to stray from my familiar literary surroundings and find my way along hitherto undiscovered paths. If I hadn't become a poet I would probably have gone into topology. Mapping unknown terrain.'

'I see. Could you translate that for me?'

'I have a hard time thinking of a more important task than to show people new paths.'

'Which people are these?'

'The next generation.'

The reporter coughed.

'That's a strange but interesting answer.'

'Thank you,' Humlin said.

'But you have to admit,' the reporter continued, 'it's a big step for you as a poet to be trying your hand at a crime novel.'

Humlin stiffened. His knuckles on the hand holding the receiver grew white.

'I'm afraid I don't know what you mean.'

'We just received a press announcement from your publisher that you are working on a crime novel to be published in the autumn.'

Humlin had often had reason to think badly of Lundin in the past, but at this moment – cornered without warning by a reporter – he hated him. The only plot for a crime novel he could possibly think of was that of a writer who murdered his publisher by stuffing false press announcements down his throat.

'Hello?' the reporter said. 'Are you still there?'

'I'm here.'

'Do you want me to repeat the question?'

'No need. It's just that I've decided not to answer any questions about the new book. I've only just started working on it and it's easy to lose one's sense of concentration. It's a bit like letting unwelcome guests into one's home.'

'That sounds complicated. But surely you have something to say. Why would your publisher be releasing this information otherwise?'

'That I have no idea about. But I will say that I should be ready to talk about the book in about a month.'

'Can you at least tell me what it's about?'

Humlin thought hard.

'I suppose I can say it will play out in the minefields of cultural difference.'

'Look here, Mr Humlin, I can't write that. No one will understand a word of it.'

'People from different cultures who meet and do not understand each other. Conflicts. Is that better?' Humlin asked.

'So the murderer targets immigrants?'

'I'm not going to say anything else. But you're on the wrong track.'

'You mean immigrants are killing Swedes?'

'There are no murders of any kind in this book.'

'How can it be a crime novel?'

'I will say more in due course.'

'When will that be?'

'In about a month.'

'Can you say anything else?'

'No, nothing more at this time.'

Humlin hung up. The reporter had sounded grumpy by the end. Humlin himself was furious and drenched in sweat. He wanted to call Lundin immediately, but knew that nothing would really come of it. The damage was already done. The crime novel he was thought to be writing was already the new literary sensation.

*

Andrea stopped by unexpectedly that evening. Humlin had fallen asleep on the couch, exhausted by his conversation with the reporter. When he heard Andrea at the door he jumped up as if caught in the act of doing something unlawful. But when he heard that she didn't slam the door he breathed easy. That meant she was not immediately going to attack him. If she closed the door gently that usually meant she was in a good mood.

She lay down beside him on the sofa and shut her eyes.

'I'm starting to get bitchy,' she said. 'I'm turning into an old woman.'

'It's me. I often give you reason to worry,' Humlin said. 'But I'm trying to change all that.'

Andrea opened her eyes.

'Oh, I doubt that very much,' she said. 'But maybe one day I'll get used to it.'

They cooked dinner together and drank some wine even though it was the middle of the week. Humlin listened patiently while she ranted about the increasing chaos of the Swedish medical system. At the same time he was thinking about the best way to tell her that he was going to meet with Leyla. But foremost in his mind was what his mother had told him the night before, that she and Andrea discussed intimate details of their private life.

She seemed to have read his thoughts.

'How was your visit with Märta?'

'Oh, the way it usually is. But she had bought oysters. And then she told me something I didn't like.'

'That she's going to write you out of her will?'

Humlin frowned.

'She said that?'

'No.'

'Then why would you say that?'

'For God's sake, what's the big deal?'

Humlin realised it probably wasn't the right time to talk about it. Both he and Andrea had drunk too much wine. That could lead to an explosion. But he couldn't stop himself.

'She said you two talk about our sex life. According to my mother you said we aren't sleeping with each other very often.'

'It's true, isn't it?' Andrea said.

'Do you have to tell her about it?'

'Why not? She's your mother.'

'She has nothing to do with us.'

'But we talk about everything. I like your mother.'

'That's not what you used to say.'

'I've changed my mind. And she is very frank with me. I know things about her that you could never imagine.'

'Like what?' Humlin asked.

Andrea topped up their wine glasses and smiled enigmatically. Humlin didn't like the look in her eye.

'Like what?' Humlin repeated. 'What is it I don't know about my mother?'

'Things you don't want to know.'

'How can I know if I want to know them or not before I know what they are?'

'She has a job.'

Humlin stared at her.

'What kind of a job?'

'That's what you don't want to know.'

'My mother has never worked a day in her life. She's jumped from one ridiculous artistic endeavour to another. But she's never held down a real job.'

'Well, she is now.'

'What does she do?'

'She's a phone sex operator.'

Humlin slowly put his wine glass down.

'I don't want you saying things like that about her. It's not funny.'

'It's true.'

'What's true?'

'She's a phone sex operator,' Andrea repeated.

'She's eighty-seven years old.'

'I've heard her myself. And why can't an eighty-seven year old woman be a phone sex operator?'

Humlin was starting to get the gnawing feeling that there was something to what Andrea was saying. He was just having trouble putting it all together.

'What exactly does this work involve?'

'There are ads at the back of every newspaper with phone numbers for these kinds of services. You call up to talk dirty and hear someone moan on the other end and God only knows what else. One of your mother's friends came up with the idea that there might be a market for older men who would want to masturbate to the sounds of women their own age.'

'And?'

'Well, she was right. They formed one of these services, an incorporated business, actually. It's run by four women, the youngest of whom is eighty-three and the oldest ninety-one. As it happens, your mother is the CEO. Last year, after deductions they made a profit of four hundred and forty-five thousand kronor.'

'What kind of deductions? What are you talking about?'

'I'm just telling you that your mother spends a few hours every day making sexy sounds into the phone for money. I've heard her myself and she sounds very convincing.'

'Convincing?'

'That she's horny. Don't play stupid. You know what I mean. How is your book coming along?'

'I'm going to Gothenburg next week to get things going.'

'Good luck.'

Andrea got up and started to clear the table. Humlin stayed where he was. What Andrea had told him made him both angry and uneasy. He knew deep down that what she had said was true. He had a mother who was capable of just about anything.

*

When Humlin got on the train to Gothenburg a week later he had spent most of the time in between fielding questions from more reporters wanting to know all about the crime novel he wasn't going to write but that was nonetheless scheduled to come out next autumn. He had also had a fight with Viktor Leander who called him on the phone to accuse him of being a spineless plagiarist who stooped to stealing his best friend's ideas. In exchange for the promise of total secrecy Humlin had finally managed to convince Leander that the rumour was false and no crime novel written by his hand was ever going to be published.

The man he had most wanted to speak to, Lundin, had been unreachable all week. Humlin had even called him at home in the middle of the night without receiving any answer. He had also not confronted his mother about the scandalous information he had heard. But he had forced himself to accept what Andrea had told him as the truth. One day when he was alone he had drunk two glasses of cognac and then called the number that Andrea had pointed out to him in the newspaper. The first two times he had not recognised the women's voices, but on his third attempt he was horrified to recognise his mother's – albeit disguised – voice on the other end. He had thrown down the receiver as if he had been bitten by it, then poured himself some additional glasses of cognac to calm his nerves.

Humlin sank down in his seat and wished he was on an aeroplane that was going to take him far away, rather than on a train to Gothenburg. He leaned back and closed his eyes. The previous week had exhausted him. But just as he was falling asleep someone close by started talking loudly into their mobile phone. Humlin decided to set all thoughts aside for a moment and pulled an evening paper towards him. He still felt a shiver of unease when he looked at an evening paper. After all, there was still the possibility that some reporter would find the events in Mölndal interesting enough to write about. Especially now that Humlin's name had been figuring more frequently in the media, due to the book he was not going to write.

He picked at his food unenthusiastically and spent the rest of the trip looking out over the darkening landscape. A secure foothold, he thought. Here I am in the middle of my life, of the world of the Swedish winter. And I lack a secure foothold.

*

Törnblom met him at the station in a rusty van. Once they pulled out from the station they immediately got stuck in traffic.

'Everyone's already there,' Törnblom said with satisfaction. 'They are very excited.'

'What do you mean they're already there? I'm not supposed to meet with Leyla and her brother for another four hours.'

'They have been there since this morning. It's a big event for them.'

Humlin gave him a suspicious look. Was he being serious or sarcastic?

'I don't know exactly where this is going to lead. It may end in nothing,' Humlin said.

'The most important thing is that you do something. In this country immigrants are still treated like victims. Because of their circumstances, their poor language skills, for almost any other reason you can think of. Sometimes they think of themselves as victims. But most of them simply want to be treated like normal people. If you can help them tell their stories, you will have done a lot.'

'Why do you say "them"? I'm working with Leyla, that's it.'

The traffic let up for a couple of metres, then stopped again. A wet snow began to fall.

'We'll be more than just her and her brother tonight.'

'What do you mean? How many more?'

'We had to put in a couple of extra chairs.'

Humlin put his hand on the door as if he was preparing to jump out.

'Extra chairs? How many people are we talking about?'

'Oh, around fifty, I'd say.'

Humlin really did try to open the door. The handle came off in his hand.

'What kind of car is this?'

'It normally does that. I'll fix it later.'

'How can there be fifty people coming?'

'Leyla decided to invite a couple of her friends who also want to write,' Törnblom said.

'And how does that make fifty people?'

'She has a big family. And then there are also neighbours, friends.'

'Why all these relatives?'

'I already told you. They have to protect the virtue of their daughters. I think you should be proud that they are so interested in this project.'

'I came here to talk to *one* girl. Not with any others and not with their families. I want you to take me back to the station.'

Törnblom turned to face him.

'Come on, it'll be fine,' he said. 'When the families see that you're a man who can be trusted, fewer people will come in the future.'

'I don't care how many people stop coming. I'm here to talk to *one* girl. That was the arrangement. Take me back to the station immediately. I mean it!'

'There's one other person who's coming that I should mention.'

'Who's that?'

'A reporter.'

'How did he find out about this?'

'I called him.'

'Damn you, Törnblom.'

'You can imagine what he'll write if you don't show. These girls have already been let down by society. And now you as well?'

Humlin sat silently with the car handle in his hand. Why does no one listen to me? he thought. Why do I have to talk to fifty people when I came to talk to one?

The traffic was finally starting to let up. The snow fell more heavily. By the time they reached Stensgården and the boxing club Humlin felt a strong inclination to cry. But he followed Törnblom into the fully packed room. People sat tightly pressed together along the walls of the room. They were of all ages and appearance. There were a few very old people and a few young children who were crying loudly. The room was filled with the smell of exotic spices that Humlin could not identify.

He stopped once he had entered the room and looked around. Leyla and her girlfriends sat at a table at the far end of the room. To his great surprise one of the friends was Tea-Bag.

He turned around, but Törnblom was blocking the exit.

There was only one way for him to go.

6

At a quarter past ten that evening Humlin was knocked down by a giant Finnish gypsy man by the name of Haiman. Haiman hadn't liked the way Humlin had patted his niece Sasha on the cheek. He felt it was too intimate. Sasha was not one of Leyla's girlfriends gathered around the table and why Humlin ever took it into his head to pat her cheek was never clarified. But the blow that struck Humlin was forceful. Haiman had been playing rugby with his friends on a field in Frölunda for many years. His fist hit the totally unprepared Humlin on the left cheek and sent him straight into the wall before he crumpled on the ground. According to Törnblom – who had seen many knockouts in his life – it was a thing of beauty.

When Humlin came to his senses about an hour later he was lying on a stretcher at the hectic emergency room at the Sahlgrenska Hospital. Törnblom was standing at his side. It took Humlin a few seconds to orient himself.

'The doctor said that nothing's broken. You were lucky.'

'Lucky,' Humlin spat. The pain shot all the way down into his throat.

'I can't hear you. You'll have to speak up.'

Törnblom found a piece of paper and a pencil in his pockets. He handed them to Humlin who wrote the question: *What happened?*

'It was a misunderstanding. Everyone is very sorry. There are about twenty people waiting here at the hospital to see how you are feeling. They want to come in and say hello. They're very concerned about you.'

Humlin shook his head in horror at the thought.

'They won't come in unless I tell them it's all right. It was a misunderstanding. A culture clash,' Törnblom said.

Törnblom gave him an enthusiastic pat on the shoulder. The pain in Humlin's cheek increased.

'This was exactly the kind of cultural insight you were looking for, wasn't it?'

Humlin wrote another sentence while his hand shook with fury.

I never asked to be hit in the face by a lunatic.

'Haiman is normally a very peaceful man. He just felt you were behaving inappropriately. You shouldn't pat the girls on the cheek. It can be misunderstood. But you were lucky. The doctors don't think you have a concussion. Still, they want you to stay overnight.'

Humlin kept writing.

I want to go home. I'm never coming back.

'Of course you'll be back. You're just a bit shaken up. Everyone thought you were wonderful. This is all going to work out.'

A bright light hung above Humlin's head and shone straight into his eyes. He turned away from it, looked at Törnblom and slowly shook his head. If he had been able to do so, he would have hit him. He wrote some more and said he never wanted to see any of the people waiting to see him ever again. Törnblom nodded in an understanding way and disappeared behind a curtain. Humlin fingered his cheekbone. The whole area was very swollen and throbbed with pain. Törnblom came back.

'They're happy to hear that you're fine. They all look forward to seeing you again. I told them you thought the evening had been a promising start.'

Humlin wrote furiously on the scrap of paper.

Go away.

'I'm waiting for Amanda. She's going to sit with you for a few hours. Tomorrow I'll come and get you and take you either to the airport or the train station, as you wish. And we'll have to set a date for when you'll be back.'

Humlin cursed silently and shut his eyes. He heard Törnblom leave. He tried to keep the pain at bay by thinking back to everything that had happened before the blow that had sent him into total darkness.

*

Törnblom had been blocking the exit. When the two of them entered the room a sudden silence had descended on everyone gathered there. He felt everyone's eyes on him and then the murmurs had started up again, even more loudly. Humlin tried to avoid looking at everyone as he made his way to the table where Leyla, Tea-Bag and one other girl were seated. They had pulled up a seat for him. He thought with increasing desperation that when he reached the table and sat down he would be expected to know how to proceed.

For some reason he suddenly thought of his stockbroker. Maybe it was because the noise in the room reminded him of the chaos of the various stock exchanges he had seen on TV. Or perhaps it was simply because it had been over a week since he had been in touch with Anders Burén, the broker in charge of his investments. For a couple of years these investments had been unbelievably lucrative, but lately his shares had started to plummet, like all the rest of the stocks around the world.

If I survive this I should give him a call tomorrow, Humlin

thought. He immediately started worrying that something dramatic was taking place somewhere in the world at this very moment, the effects of which would soon render all his investments as worthless as if they had been wiped out by a tidal wave. When he reached the table all chatter around the room ceased. He nodded to Tea-Bag, but it was Leyla who stretched out her hand in greeting. Tea-Bag seemed to be testing him somehow. The third girl sat with her face turned away from him.

When he took Leyla's hand it was like grasping a dead, sweaty fish. But fish don't sweat, he thought in a confused way. And girls must be allowed to sweat if they get nervous. Perhaps I can use this image in some future poem, although it seems unlikely I will publish another collection. My future right now is determined by two books I will never write. The marketing campaign for one of them is already underway.

Humlin held on to Leyla's hand, afraid that he would lose his tenuous hold on the situation if he let go of it. He greeted them all in a friendly fashion. Somewhere in the room behind him someone started clapping enthusiastically.

'I see you brought some friends with you,' Humlin said to Leyla, trying to sound casual.

'They really wanted to be here. You've already met Tea-Bag.'

Humlin shook Tea-Bag's hand. She pulled her hand back as if he had squeezed too hard. He didn't manage to catch the third girl's name. She didn't stretch out her hand and sat turned away from him. He sat down on the empty chair. At the same time a group of people in the room who had been sitting at the very back got up and made their way to the front.

'They're my parents,' Leyla explained.

'All of them?'

‘The two tallest ones are my brother and sister. The other two are my parents.’

Leyla pointed to them as she spoke. They all looked equally short to Humlin.

‘My family would like to be introduced to you.’

‘I thought only your brother was going to come,’ Humlin said.

‘I have three brothers. My grandmother is also here. And two aunts on my father’s side.’

Humlin was introduced to the family members one by one. They were friendly enough but were also clearly looking him over. Humlin heard their names but forgot them all immediately. When all the introductions were over they started their way back through the rows of other people. Humlin felt sweat running down his chest, inside his shirt. The windows looked nailed shut. He looked over at Törnblom who was standing by the door like a bouncer. Humlin felt a growing panic and cursed the fact that he had for once in his life forgotten to bring the pills he had for calming his nerves.

‘This is Tanya,’ Leyla said, indicating the girl who sat with her head turned away.

Humlin half-expected to hear a new group of family members approach the table, but heard nothing. Tanya must have come on her own.

‘Where are you from?’ Humlin asked.

‘She’s from Russia,’ Leyla answered.

‘And you are here to learn to write? To tell your story?’

‘She has been through more than any of us,’ Leyla said. ‘But she doesn’t talk very much.’

This turned out to be an accurate observation. Tanya did not say a single word all evening. Humlin looked at her surreptitiously from time to time. He assumed she was the oldest of the three, perhaps twenty-five or twenty-six. She was the complete opposite of Leyla, slender and with a beautiful oval face framed by straight brown hair that fell to her shoulders. She was very tense and stared at a fixed point on the wall. Humlin realised that he didn't have the slightest idea what she could be thinking, not even when he employed all of his imaginative powers. He also realised, with the usual mixture of anxiety and anticipation, that he was starting to feel attracted to her.

Next to Tanya was Tea-Bag, the young woman he had first met in Mölndal and who had asked him the question that was the real reason he had returned to Stensgården. That time she had struck him as outspoken and strong. Now she seemed preoccupied and insecure and never quite met his gaze.

There was a hush in the room. Humlin realised that the orchestra had arrived, and that he was the conductor. He had to think of something. He turned to Leyla.

'Why do you want to write?' he asked.

'I want to be a TV star,' she said.

Humlin was taken aback.

'A TV star?'

'Yes, to be on TV, ideally a programme that comes on every night for ten years.'

'Well, I hardly think I can help you with that goal. We're not going to be talking about the TV business.'

Humlin didn't know how to continue. The whole situation seemed preposterous. A low buzz had started up again in the room. On one side he had Leyla, who was sweating and who had just told him she wanted to be a TV star, on the other side was Tanya, who still had her face turned away from him, and Tea-Bag whom he no longer recognised. In order to buy some time he pointed to the pads of paper the girls all had in front of them, labelled 'Törnblom's Boxing Club'.

'I want you to write two things,' he said and was immediately interrupted by someone with a heavy accent asking him to speak up.

'This is not actually intended to be a lecture,' Humlin replied in a loud voice. 'What I want at this point is for the girls to write down the answers to two questions: "Why do you want to write?" and "What do you hope to do in the future?"'

A murmur of surprise and anticipation filled the room. Törnblom made his way over to the table with a glass of water.

'Can't we open a window in here? It's so hot!' Humlin asked.

'We've had too many burglaries. I was forced to nail the windows shut.'

'I'm suffocating!'

'You're just dressed too warmly. But this is going very well, I think. Keep it up.'

'It's going to hell. I'm going mad. And if I don't get any air I'm going to faint. I can't faint. What I should do is kill you.'

'I don't think you can since I'm much stronger than you are. But don't worry. Things are going well.'

Törnblom returned to his place by the door. The girls were busy writing on their pads of paper. What do I do next? Humlin thought and felt a growing sense of desperation. He decided not to do anything at all. He would just gather their answers, read them and then ask them to write something for next time – though there would be no next time – about how they had experienced this evening. After that he would be able to leave this suffocating room and maybe even make the last train or flight back to Stockholm. He was never going to return. He looked around at all the people in the room. A woman who was breastfeeding her child nodded encouragingly to him. Humlin nodded back politely. Then he gathered up the pages that the girls had written. He did not plan on reading their answers out loud. In order not to have to deal with wild protests from the crowd he turned to Leyla and whispered, 'I want you to tell these people that these answers have been written in confidence. I am not going to read them out loud.'

She looked horrified.

'I can't do that. And I don't even know all the languages these people speak.'

'Surely they understand a little Swedish?'

'You can't be too sure about that.'

'Why can't you tell them the notes are written in confidence?'

'My brothers might think I was writing a secret message to you.'

'And why on earth would you do that?'

'I don't know.'

'I can't run a writing seminar if everyone always has to know everything that's going on. To write is to tell stories from deep within yourself. It's a process of revealing your innermost self.'

Leyla thought about it.

'You don't have to read our answers out loud,' she decided. 'But you will have to give them back to us so that I can show them to my family when I come home. It doesn't matter in the case of Tanya or Tea-Bag, of course.'

'And why not?'

'They have no family. We are their family.'

Humlin saw they were not going to get any further. He stood up.

'I will not read these answers out loud,' he announced.

A grumble broke out among the crowd.

'But naturally the girls will keep what they have written.'

The protests slowly dwindled in volume. Humlin sat down again and threw Leyla a grateful glance. Then he looked through the notes. First there was Tanya's. Her page was blank except for a drawing of a little heart that appeared to be bleeding. Nothing else. Humlin looked at the image of the bleeding or weeping heart for a long time. Then he looked at Tanya. She was still staring at a point on the wall opposite her and seemed to be somewhere far away from this stuffy room. He folded her note, realising it had moved him, and handed it back to her.

Next he looked at Leyla's note. She wrote that she wanted to be an author so she could tell people what it was like to be a refugee in a country like Sweden. But she had also added an honest addendum: *I want to write so I can be thin*. Humlin wondered if this was perhaps the most honest answer he had ever received to the question of why someone wanted to be a writer. She had also written that she dreamed of one day becoming a talk-show host or actress.

The last page was from Tea-Bag. *I want to write about what happened on the beach*. In answer to the question of her future she had also written that she wanted to be a talk-show host.

The answers were interesting but also confusing. Humlin searched his increasingly weary mind for a good way to round off the evening. He looked at the three girls, and then at the ever more impatient crowd. I'm just going to lie, he thought as he stood up. I'm going to lie and I'm going to do it well. Not because I'm mean-spirited or full of disgust, but because this whole project has stalled before it even got off the ground.

'I'm not going to keep you here any longer this evening. Now we know a little bit more about each other and I have a better idea of what you would like to get out of the writing seminar.

I will be in touch to arrange our next meeting. Thank you very much for coming here tonight.'

There was a second of confused silence, then someone started to clap. Humlin felt a huge wave of relief that it was all over. He started making his way towards the exit and stopped to shake the many outstretched hands along the way. That was when the seventeen-year-old girl Sasha had smiled at him and he – without ever knowing why – patted her on the cheek. Then everything went black.

*

Now he was lying in a hospital bed. The left side of his face was extremely swollen. Pulses of pain came and went. A harried doctor pushed aside the curtain and looked in on him. He did not speak Swedish very well. From his nametag Humlin assumed he was Polish or Russian.

'The X-rays look good,' he said. 'How are you feeling?'

'It hurts.'

'Take some painkillers. You will feel much better in a few days. Were you intoxicated when this happened?'

'Are you asking me if I was drunk?'

'That is the normal reason for fights.'

'I don't appreciate your insinuations. I was not drunk, as it happens. Someone attacked me.'

'Then you should report it to the police,' the doctor said.

Törnblom came in through the curtain at that moment and heard the last thing the doctor said.

'There's no need to fill out a police report. It was just a family dispute that got out of hand.'

The doctor left. Humlin forced himself to sit up with the intention of telling Törnblom what he thought of him once and for all, but the pain was too great. He was forced to lie back down again.

'What do you mean by a "family dispute"?' he whispered.

'We feel like one big family out in Stensgården. Or should do. You're becoming part of it now.'

Humlin gestured towards the curtain.

'They've left,' Törnblom said. 'They wanted me to tell you that they all look forward to seeing you again. Haiman is very sorry. He's going to give you a present next time you meet.'

'There won't be a next time. What kind of a present?'

'He said something about a rugby ball.'

'I hate rugby. I don't want a rugby ball. I'm never coming back here if I can help it.'

Then Humlin thought of something. It had slipped his mind.

'What about the reporter? You said you had talked to somebody. Was he there? Did he see what happened?'

'He was very enthusiastic about it. He's going to give you a good write-up.'

'The only thing he's going to write about is that I was knocked out. It'll be in all the tabloids. And the guy who hit me will claim I was sexually harrassing his daughter or cousin or whatever the hell she was. How am I going to be able to defend myself? I'll look guilty before I even have a chance to say anything.'

'He's not going to write anything about all that, I promise. He's actually more interested in your writing seminar.'

Humlin looked sceptically at Törnblom but decided in the end to believe him.

'I'm going now,' Törnblom said. 'Amanda will stay behind for a while. I'll take you to the station tomorrow morning so we can agree on a date for your next visit.'

Humlin didn't bother answering. Amanda went to get him a glass of water. Humlin looked admiringly at her backside, then thought about Tanya and immediately felt a little better. That bleeding heart had touched something in him. He had also been affected by her looks. But then he pushed these thoughts aside. He wasn't coming back. The whole idea behind this writing seminar was ludicrous. Or at least he was the wrong man to do it. For the first time it seriously occurred to him that maybe he should try to write this crime novel. Maybe there had been something to what Lundin had said, and that he might actually be able to come up with something unexpected, something innovative that would leave all the conventional crime thrillers dead in the water.

*

Törnblom drove him out to the airport the following morning. Humlin still had a great deal of pain in his left cheek and the swelling had not yet started to go down.

'That was a very interesting evening last night,' Törnblom said. 'People have already been asking me when you'll be back.'

'I'm never coming back.'

'In a few days everything will look different. You'll realise what an important experience this was. When is the best time for you?'

'Wednesday. But only on one condition.'

'What's that?'

'That the girls only have *one* chaperone each.'

'That's a tough one.'

'It's non-negotiable.'

'I can ask them to cut the numbers down.'

'I'm taking it for granted that the man who hit me will not be there again.'

'I can't do that. He'll be insulted.'

Humlin was outraged.

'*He'll* be insulted! What about me? I wasn't only insulted, I was injured!'

'He wants to give you the rugby ball to make up for it.'

'I don't want a rugby ball.'

'Just take it. You can always get rid of it later. But you have to accept his apology.'

'What if he hits me again?'

'You are filled with prejudice, Humlin. You really don't know much about this country and the people who live here.'

'Why was he there in the first place?'

'He's considering sending his daughters to your next seminar.'

'What next seminar? There will not be a next time.'

The pain in his cheek had increased while he talked. Humlin sat quietly for the remainder of the trip. He was also unsure of how to counter the accusation that he was filled with prejudice, since it was probably true. Törnblom dropped him off at the airport in the wet snow. Humlin hoped no one recognised him. His cheek had turned purple and blue.

*

When he got home he went straight to the bedroom, shut the curtains and crawled into bed. The phone woke him up a few hours later. He hesitated before answering, but picked up on the seventh ring. It was Törnblom.

'The reporter wrote great things about you.'

'Nothing about the fight?'

'There was no fight. You received a blow to the face that can only be described as a perfect uppercut. But he didn't say a word about it. He writes about "an admirable initiative by one of our leading poets".'

'He wrote that?'

'To the letter.'

Humlin sat up.

'What else did he write?'

'That other writers would do well to do the same. "Why write crime novels when one can engage with reality?"'

'Really – he said that?'

'I'm quoting straight from the article.'

For the first time in many days Humlin felt the relief of feeling like a real person again.

'Next time he wants to interview you. I've also had some calls from TV.'

'Which channel?'

'Two different ones.'

'I'm happy to speak to them.'

'See, I told you this would all start falling into place once you felt better.'

'I don't feel better.'

'Let me know when you've booked your flight or train and I'll arrange to come and pick you up.'

Humlin hung up and stretched out between the cool sheets. Even though he was still troubled by the situation in Stensgården and was not sure how to get out of it he was pleased that he was finally getting some media attention that did not simply paint him as a respectable but boring poet. The most pleasing aspect was how this news would affect Lundin and Viktor Leander. Lundin would most likely break the oars of his rowing machine in a fury over the fact that one of his authors had not taken his good advice.

Humlin recalled a time when he had been invited to Lundin's apartment on the exclusive Strandvägen. Expensive art filled the walls. Late that evening, when Lundin had had more than a little to drink, he had wobbled around with an equally unstable Humlin and told him which authors had made him the profits to buy which paintings. They finally stopped in front of a miniature watercolour landscape by a lesser-known west-coast artist in one corner of the hallway which Lundin announced – with a certain measure of needling disapproval – that Humlin had managed to scrape together the money for.

As Humlin now lay in bed he relished the idea that Lundin's blood pressure was about to shoot up to new heights. But he was not completely able to banish the thought that Lundin was in fact a big player in the world of publishing and one who had the power to slam many doors in his face.

Viktor Leander's reaction was easy to imagine and it provided him with a less ambivalent pleasure. Leander would lie sleepless for a number of nights and worry that Humlin's idea would prove better than the number of lemming-like attempts by contemporary authors to jump on the crime novel bandwagon. In the on-going power struggle between Humlin and Leander the chief motivation was to cause sleeplessness in the other. This time it would be Leander's turn to lie awake.

*

Humlin spent the rest of the day in bed. In the evening he took a taxi to Andrea's apartment. There he explained what had happened. He changed some details, however, and omitted the fact that he had patted a girl on the cheek. He claimed instead that an unstable gypsy man had become violently upset when Humlin decided not to let him into the seminar.

'Why couldn't you have let him in? Gypsies have always been discriminated against in our society.'

'I decided to restrict it to girls.'

'Couldn't you make an exception?'

'Then I would have had at least ten boxers lining up.'

'Why boxers?'

'Törnblom has a boxing club. I can't tell you anything more. It hurts to talk.'

That night they had sex for the first time in three weeks. The next day, when Andrea had left for work, Humlin immediately opened her diary to check what she had written. He knew she always wrote in the morning. *What is going on with him? He comes so fast I hardly have time to feel anything.*

Humiliated, Humlin took his revenge by imagining a night of passion in a Gothenburg hotel with the beautiful and mysterious Tanya. There was more than one reason for him to return to Stensgården and continue this unruly mess of a class that he had not organised so much as landed in the middle of.

He went home. He spent the afternoon trying to find ways of concealing his bruise with self-tanning lotions. Whenever the phone rang he stood over the answering machine and let it pick up. Both Lundin and Leander called. Humlin didn't take either call, nor did he call either of them back. His face hurt when he smiled.

Shortly after five o'clock he decided to take a walk. When he opened the front door he saw that someone was sitting in the stairwell. It was dark enough that at first he didn't recognise who it was. Then he saw that it was Tea-Bag.

7

A door slammed shut several flights up. Since Humlin didn't want a curious neighbour to catch him in conversation with an exotic-looking woman, he quickly ushered her into the apartment and shut the door. At the same time he started worrying about the possibility that Andrea would come by and fall into a jealous rage. He led Tea-Bag into the kitchen and asked her if she wanted a cup of tea. She shook her head energetically.

'I don't drink tea,' she said.

Humlin thought about her name and was surprised.

'Is there anything you would like?'

'Coffee.'

She sat down on a chair and watched him as he brewed the coffee. Every time he looked over at her she smiled. He thought to himself that she was probably one of the most beautiful women he had ever seen. He still couldn't decide how old she was. She could be anything from seventeen to twenty-five. She was very dark. Her skin was so black it almost looked blue. She had long beautiful braids woven into her hair. She wore no make-up. She was wearing a puffy down coat that she didn't remove even in the warmth of the kitchen. She had tennis shoes on her feet, with different-coloured laces.

When the coffee was done he sat down across from her. She was sitting where Andrea normally sat. The thought both worried and excited him. He had the constant urge to touch her face, to feel with the tops of his fingers if she was warm or cold.

'How did you find out where I live?'

'It wasn't very hard.'

'Did Törnblom tell you?'

She moved her lips but didn't answer.

There was a sudden sound at the front door. Andrea, Humlin thought with horror. All hell is about to break loose. But no one came in. Later, when Tea-Bag had left, Humlin saw that someone had slid a notice through the mail slot. *Annual check of ventilation systems in rental units.*

'You've clearly gone to a great deal of trouble to find me, and you've travelled all the way from Gothenburg. You must want something.'

Tea-Bag seemed to hesitate for a moment and pulled at her fingers. Then she said something in a foreign language.

'Sorry, I didn't quite catch that,' he said.

'I have to speak my own language before I can speak yours. I am unlocking a door.'

'What did you say?'

'Once when I was a little girl a monkey cling on my back.'

Humlin waited but she didn't elaborate.

'Could you repeat that?'

'You heard what I said. "Once when I was a little girl a monkey cling on my back."'

'Not "cling". It should be "clung".'

'But it didn't cling. It did something else.'

'It jumped on you?'

'No.'

'It attached itself to you?'

'No.'

Humlin searched among the verbs at his disposal.

'Perhaps it just climbed onto your back?'

Tea-Bag smiled, drained her cup and got up.

'Are you leaving already?' he asked with surprise.

'That was all I wanted to know.'

'What?'

'That the monkey climbed.'

Suddenly she seemed anxious, but Humlin couldn't stop himself from asking more questions.

'You have to understand my curiosity,' he said. 'You travel all the way from Gothenburg to ask me about this one word?'

She sat down again, hesitantly, still without unzipping her thick jacket.

'Is your name really Tea-Bag?' Humlin asked.

'Yes. No. Does it matter?'

'It's certainly not without significance.'

'Taita.'

'Taita. Is that your first or last name?'

'My sister.'

'Your sister's name is Taita?'

'I don't have a sister. Please don't ask any more.'

Humlin didn't pursue it. Tea-Bag looked into her empty coffee cup and he suddenly sensed that she was hungry.

'Would you like something to eat?'

'Yes.'

He got out some slices of bread and some butter, jam and cheese. She threw herself at the food. Humlin said nothing while she ate, but tried to recall what hours Andrea was working this week. The whole time he was expecting her key to sound in the lock. Tea-Bag kept going until all the food was gone.

'So you live in Gothenburg?' he asked.

'Yes.'

'Why did you come here?'

'To ask you about that word.'

It's not true, of course, Humlin thought. But I won't press her any further. The real reason will come out sooner or later.

'Where do you come from?'

'Kazakstan.'

Humlin furrowed his brow.

'Kazakstan?'

'I am a Kurd.'

'You don't look like a Kurd.'

'My father was from Ghana but my mother was a Kurd.'

'Are they dead?'

'My father is in prison, and my mother is gone.'

'What do you mean "gone"?'

'She went into a container and disappeared.'

'She did what? She entered a container?'

'Maybe it was a temple. I don't remember.'

Humlin tried to interpret her strange answers, to get the different pieces to hang together, but he couldn't make any sense of it.

'Are you here as a refugee?'

'I want to live here with you,' she said.

Humlin jumped.

'You can't.'

'Why not?'

'You just can't.'

'I can sleep on the stairs.'

'That won't work. Why can't you keep living in Gothenburg? I thought you had friends there. Leyla is your friend.'

'I don't know anyone called Leyla.'

'Of course you do. She was the one who took you to the boxing club that night.'

'No one took me. I went alone.'

Her smile died away. Humlin was starting to feel uncomfortable. She couldn't have travelled all the way to Stockholm just to ask him about a Swedish word. He found no connection in what she had told him, between her words and the big smile that came and went on her face like waves breaking on the shore.

'What are you thinking about?' he asked.

'I'm thinking about the boat that sank. Everyone who drowned. And my father who sat on the roof of our hut and wouldn't come down.'

'Is that hut in Ghana?'

'In Togo.'

'Togo? I thought you were from Ghana?'

'I come from Nigeria. But that is a secret. The river brought us cold and clear water from the mountains. One day a monkey climbed onto my back.'

Humlin was starting to wonder if the girl was sane.

'What else did this monkey do, apart from climb onto your back?'

'It disappeared.'

'And then?'

'Isn't that enough?'

'Probably. But I don't understand the significance of this monkey.'

'Are you stupid?'

Humlin looked narrowly at her. No little African hussy, however beautiful, was going to sit in his kitchen and tell him he was stupid.

'Why did you come here?' he asked.

'I want to live here.'

'You can't. I don't know who you are or what you do. I can't have any Tom, Dick or Harry moving in here.'

'I'm a refugee.'

'I hope you've been well treated by the authorities.'

'No one knows that I am here.'

Humlin looked back at her in silence.

'Are you here illegally?' he asked finally.

She got up without answering and left the kitchen. Humlin expected to hear the front door slam shut. Then he wondered if she had locked herself in the bathroom. But everything was quiet. Too quiet, he thought, getting up. Maybe she was looking for things to steal. He walked into the living room, it was empty but the bathroom door was ajar. He continued on into the study but she wasn't there either. Then he opened the door to the bedroom.

She had finally taken off her puffy coat. It lay on the floor with the rest of her clothes. Her head looked very dark against the white pillow. She was on Andrea's side of the bed. Humlin felt a chill. If Andrea came home at this moment there was no way he could make her believe that he had had nothing to do with the fact that an illegal alien now lay in his bed. On her side.

Humlin saw scandalous newspaper headlines in his mind. First he had stroked an immigrant girl's cheek and been knocked out. If Tea-Bag started screeching that he had forced her into his bed then all the country's journalists would come after him like a pack of wolves and rip him to shreds. He walked over to her. She lay with her eyes closed.

'What do you think you're doing? You can't lie in my bed! And you're lying on Andrea's side. What do you think she's going to say about that?'

There was no answer. He repeated his question and noticed that he was starting to sweat. Andrea could appear at any moment. Her work schedule was always changing. He grabbed Tea-Bag's shoulder and shook it. No reaction. He wondered if it was even possible to fall asleep as soon as one put one's head down on the pillow. But she didn't seem to be trying to trick him, she had actually fallen asleep. He shook her harder. Irritated, without waking up, she threw out her arm and hit the side of his face that Haiman had earlier visited with his fist.

The phone rang. Humlin flinched as if he had received an electric shock. He ran into the living room and answered it. It was Andrea.

'Why are you out of breath?' she asked.

'I'm not out of breath. Where are you?'

'I just wanted to tell you I'm going to a lecture tonight.'

'What lecture? How long is it?'

'Why do you want to know how long it is?'

'I want to know when you're going to come. If you're coming. I don't like to be here all alone, you know that.'

'I don't know anything of the sort. I'm going to a reading by some young poets. You should be going too. I'm hoping to get inspiration for the book I'm writing.'

'I don't want you to write a book about us.'

'I'll be coming when it's over.'

'And when is that?'

'How should I know?'

Humlin heard that she was starting to get suspicious.

'I thought maybe we could eat together,' he said. 'If I know when you're coming I'll have dinner ready.'

'Not before nine.'

Humlin breathed a sigh of relief. That gave him three hours to get Tea-Bag out of the apartment. He didn't like Andrea listening to the work of other poets, but for once his young rivals had actually helped him out. He hung up and returned to the bedroom.

She still refused to wake up when he shook her. He sat down on the edge of the bed and tried to understand what was happening. Who was she and why had she come here? What was the monkey she had talked about? He looked down at her puffy coat and her trousers on the floor. He had a sudden impulse to lift the covers and see if she was naked underneath them, but resisted.

He searched all her pockets. There were no keys or money. It was a mystery to him that anyone could get by without keys or money. He found a little plastic sleeve in the inside pocket of her coat. It contained a Sudanese passport in the name of Florence Kanimane, with a photograph of Tea-Bag. Humlin flipped through it but did not find any stamps or visas. Not even for Sweden. But she had talked of Ghana and Togo. And Kazakstan. Hadn't she claimed to be a Kurd?

The only other thing he found in the passport was a dried insect – large and rather frightening – as well as a pressed yellow flower. The flower looked like a heart, a compressed heart. He thought about the heart that Tanya had drawn. There was also a black-and-white photo in the plastic sleeve, showing an African family with a mother, father and six children. The picture had been taken outside with a hut in the background. There were no shadows so the sun must have been very high at the time. The picture was a bit blurry and even with good lighting Humlin could not tell if one of the children was Tea-Bag. Or Taita. Or Florence, as the name she apparently also went by.

The plastic sleeve also contained a scrap of paper on which someone had written 'Sweden' and the name 'Per'. There was nothing else. When he held the scrap of paper up to the light he saw that it had a watermark that said 'Madrid'. He frowned. Who was she, this woman who had asked him a question in Mölndal, then turned up on his doorstep and ended up in his bed?

He searched her clothes again but didn't find anything except sand. What I have in my hands is a story, he thought. A girl who most probably has entered Sweden illegally and who talks about a monkey, a girl whose name I can't be sure of and who has neither money nor keys. He sat down closer to her. She was sleeping deeply, peacefully. He carefully brushed her cheek with his fingers. She was very warm. He looked at the time. It was ten to six. He could let her sleep another hour, then he had to get her up and out of the apartment.

The phone rang. He walked out into the living room and listened to the answering machine. The caller was Viktor Leander. 'I'm just calling to see what you're up to. We should get together. Call me, or better yet, pick up if you're there. I think you are.'

Humlin did not pick up. He sat down and tried to imagine what it would be like to have a monkey jump onto his back. But he couldn't do it, his imagination failed him.

*

He didn't hear her come out of the bedroom. She moved soundlessly.

'Why did you go to bed?' he asked when he saw her.

'I was tired. I'm going now.'

'Who are you?'

'Tea-Bag.'

He hesitated.

'Your passport fell out of your pocket while you were sleeping,' he said. 'I couldn't help seeing that your real name is Florence.'

She laughed heartily, as if he had told a good joke.

'It's a fake,' she said.

'Where did you get it?'

'I bought it in the camp. On the beach.'

'What camp? Which beach?'

That was when she started telling him her story. How she had crawled up onto the Spanish shore and been caught by armed guards and albino German shepherd guard dogs.

*

Even the tongues hanging out of their mouths were white. I don't know how long I was in the camp. It may have been many years, perhaps I was even born there, perhaps the beach beyond the barbed-wire fence was the sheet on which my newborn body first felt the earth and sand. I don't know how long I was there and that is something I don't even want to know now. But finally one day, when my desperation was greater than it had ever been, I walked down to the fence and threw away all of the stones I used to count the days. I saw how they fell in a large fan shape of lost days and nights, and then they were washed away by the waves.

I had given up all hope of ever being allowed to leave the camp. The beach onto which I had crawled no longer meant freedom to me, it was a bridge to death and I was only waiting for the day when a finger would point at me and I would have to wade out into the water and join those who were already dead at the bottom of the sea. Every day was like the space of time between two heart-beats. But suddenly there was a tall thin man who stood in front of me, a man who swayed like a palm tree, and then I heard for the first time about Sweden. I decided I had to go there because there there were people who cared about the fact that I existed.

There was a black market in false papers in the camp. Sometimes passports had been falsified several times over. An old man from Sudan felt that his time was near and that he would never leave the camp alive. He gave me his passport on the condition that I go to a church or mosque or temple once a month and think of him for exactly one minute. That was what he wanted in return, a reminder of his existence even though he had long ago left the land he came from. I had a photograph of myself that I had kept safe in waterproof waxed paper. With the help of a Malaysian refugee who was very good at falsifying stamps and seals although he had almost no tools, he removed the old man's photograph and affixed mine in its place. The name was changed to Florence. It was like a holy ritual to give the passport with a dying man's picture a new life. I blew my soul into the passport and helped the soul of the old man to free itself. I will never forget the moment the passport changed. It was one of the most important turns my life has taken.

I found Sweden on an old and torn map from a Moroccan man who was fleeing to Europe for the ninth time, trying to get to his brother who lived somewhere in northern Germany. I realised it would be a long journey, but I never understood how long. Or perhaps I realised but did not want to accept it. I don't know. Since I never let my expectations get the better of me I decided simply to concentrate on getting out of the camp.

I made friends with some young men from Iraq. In secret they had been constructing a ladder made of bits of rope, branches and plastic that they tore off from the tables in the camp mess hall. When I sought them out they did not at first allow me to join them in their escape attempt since they were worried that a black girl would not manage very well on a flight through Spain. But my loneliness must have touched them because they gave me permission to use their ladder if I waited one hour after they had gone.

One dark night when there was no moonlight the three Iraqi men took off. After exactly one hour – I had no watch but counted the seconds and minutes by tapping against my wrist – I climbed the fence and disappeared into the night. I followed the first path I found, then turned off on another as if I had an inner compass directing me. I walked in darkness without knowing where I would find myself in the morning. I slipped and fell several times. Tree branches and thorns cut my face, but I continued towards Sweden and the memory of that tall swaying man who was the first to show an interest in my story.

By the time the sun came up I was exhausted. I sat down on a rock and all I remember is that I was very thirsty. I discovered that I had climbed up through a rocky and mountainous landscape with many steep cliffs that could have sent me to the death I escaped once in the sea. On a field in the distance I saw people. The sun reflected off the windshield of a car in the distance. I started walking due north, avoiding civilisation and people as much as I could. I ate fruits and nuts, drinking rainwater in crevices. The whole time I kept walking north. Every morning when the sun came up I oriented myself to the north and kept walking.

How long I kept going, I don't know. But one day I couldn't do it any more. In the middle of taking a step I sank to the ground. Despite what my father had taught me about keeping my feet firmly planted on the ground I was close to giving up at that moment, lying down and crumbling into the burned earth. If I had been walking for a week or a month I couldn't tell. But I knew I had to find out where I was. I forced myself to get up and keep going until I came to a small town that lay exposed on a great plain.

I walked into the town. I had come during the worst of the midday heat. The town lay still like a parched corpse. I read on a sign that the name of the town was 'Alameda de Cervera'. On another sign I read 'Toledo 111 kilometres'. All of the shutters on the whitewashed houses were closed, some dogs lay panting in the shade but I did not see a person anywhere. I walked along the empty streets, blinded by the strong light, and found only one shop that was open. Or perhaps it was closed but the door was open and I walked into the dim interior.

In the corner there was a man sleeping on a mattress. I tried to move as quietly as possible; I had removed my tattered shoes and I still remember how cool the stone floor felt against the soles of my feet. I was holding my shoes in my hand when I realised that I had walked into a shoe shop. Shoes were stacked up on shelves along the wall. On another wall I found what I was looking for: a map. I found Alameda de Cervera, then traced my way to Toledo and realised that I had only come a short distance from the camp, even though I thought I had been walking for ever. I started crying, silently so that the sleeping man wouldn't wake up.

What I then did I can only recall in unclear images. The heat, the dogs, the sharp white light that was reflected on the whitewashed walls. I walked into a church, it was cool in there, and I drank the stale water in the baptismal font. Then I forced open the cash box sitting on a table for people to put money for postcards that they bought. There was not much money, but I thought it was enough to cover a bus ticket.

'Toledo,' I said to the driver who looked at my dark skin with distaste and desire.

But my smile did nothing for him. Somewhere inside me a deep rage was born at these stolid European men who were not able to appreciate my beauty. I don't remember much from the bus trip. I slept and was woken up by the driver who shook my shoulder abruptly and told me we were there. The bus was parked in an underground garage. I walked through the fumes, through the people who were crowding to get on and off the buses and at last found myself out on a street with so much traffic I became afraid. It was evening and I took shelter in a park. Suddenly I became convinced there were wild animals in the park. I don't know where this feeling came from but it was very strong, stronger than the rational part of my mind that said there were no dangerous animals in Europe.

I stayed awake until dawn with fear beating in my chest. It was only when the first light of morning came that I saw a drunk man come stumbling down one of the paths. He sat down on a bench, leaned forward and threw up, then fell asleep. I crept towards him, stole his wallet and then ran away. Then I hid again, this time in a thicket that stank of urine. I found to my surprise that the wallet was full of cash. I put the money in my pocket, threw the wallet away and left the park. I ate breakfast in a cafe and realised I would not have to walk any more. I had money. I could buy a map and take the train to the border and then continue as long as the money lasted.

I made my way into France by crawling through a ditch at the border. In the distance I heard dogs barking and whining exactly like the albino dogs in the camp. The money that was left I changed in a small town. I still had enough to eat regular meals and buy train tickets. But as I was leaving the bank I was stopped by a policeman who demanded to see my identification. I got out my

Sudanese passport, then changed my mind and ran away. I heard the policeman shouting behind me but he was not able to catch me. At that moment I understood that I had been given magic powers. When I had crawled through the ditch my fear had made me invisible and when I was pursued by the policeman I moved as fast as one of the birds I had seen gliding on the warm air streams over the valley on the other side of the river next to the village where I was born. Now I knew I would make it to Sweden as long as I did not try to thwart my fear. It was my most important guide. It helped me to discover powers I did not know I had.

During the next few days I was so excited I ran all night, towards the north. Sometimes I followed paths that snaked along roads with cars speeding by. But I moved just as fast and my eyes could see in the dark as if there had been strong lights posted nearby. If there was a rock or a hole in front of me I knew it was there even though it was completely dark.

One morning I came to a large river filled with brown, slow-moving water. A rowing boat was pulled up on the shore and chained to a tree. I smashed the lock with a rock and pushed the boat into the water. That day I did not lie low during the day and wait for darkness. I let the boat drift along and stretched out along the bottom that smelled like tar and looked up at the clouds far above my head and noticed that I had started to breathe easily again. It was as if I had been short of breath ever since I climbed the fence in Spain and disappeared into the dark. I slept and dreamed that my passport was like two doors that opened into landscapes that I recognised from my childhood. I could see my father there, how he came towards me and lifted me like a feather he wanted to toss up towards the sun and then catch me again in his warm arms while I slowly floated back towards the ground.

I woke from the dream when the boat started swaying. A barge had passed me. Shirts were hung out to dry from a line aboard the vessel. I waved even though I didn't see anyone.

*

Tea-Bag stopped abruptly as if she had said too much and should never have revealed her secrets. Humlin waited for her to continue but she didn't. She zipped up her jacket and pulled her chin down towards her throat.

'Then what happened?' he asked.

She shook her head.

'I don't want to tell more. Not now.'

'How are you going to get back to Gothenburg? Where are you going to stay? You can't stay with me. Do you have any money?'

She didn't answer.

'I don't know what your name is,' he said slowly. 'Maybe your name really is Tea-Bag. I don't know where you live. I don't know why you came here. But I suspect you are in this country illegally. I don't know how you manage.'

She still didn't answer.

'I'm going back to Gothenburg in two days,' he said. 'There I will meet with Leyla and Tanya again, and hopefully with you. Why don't you take the train with me then? You can tell me the rest of your story. Meet me at the Central station at a quarter past two the day after tomorrow. If you aren't there then I'll assume you're not coming. But if you do come I'll pay your ticket. Do you understand?'

'I understand.'

'You have to go now.'

'I know.'

'Do you have anywhere to stay tonight?'

She didn't answer. He gave her two hundred kronor in notes that she pocketed without even looking at them.

'Before you go I would very much like to know your real name,' he said.

'It's Tea-Bag,' she answered.

For the first time since she had left the bedroom she smiled. Humlin escorted her to the door.

'You can't sleep in the stairwell.'

'I'm not going to sleep,' she said. 'I'm going to visit my monkey.'

He watched her – suddenly filled with energy – dance down the stairs until she was out of sight. While he smoothed the sheets in the bedroom and checked to make sure she hadn't left any traces of herself, he only thought of one thing.

Shirts hung out to dry on the line.

A dark-skinned girl in a rowing boat waving to a boat where there was no one to be seen.

8

When he woke up the following morning Humlin felt more refreshed than he could remember being for a long time. It was as if his meeting with the smiling girl named Tea-Bag or perhaps Florence had allowed him to access some hidden energy reserves. He got out of his bed as soon as he woke up instead of lying in like he usually did. He decided that this was the day to confront his mother. He was also finally going to get in touch with his investment broker.

The latter was easier than he had imagined. His broker picked up one of his mobile phone lines.

'Burén.'

'Do you have any idea how many times I've tried to reach you during the past week?'

'Nineteen, I think.'

'Why in God's name can't you return a call?'

'I don't like to trouble my clients unnecessarily.'

'But I told you I wanted to speak to you.'

'You're speaking to me now.'

'I'm coming by your office in half an hour.'

'By all means. Let's talk if I'm still here then.'

'Why wouldn't you still be there?'

'Something might come up. You never know.'

Humlin called a taxi immediately since he suspected a moment's delay would allow Burén to disappear into any one of the labyrinths of his financial world from which it would be impossible to retrieve him.

The taxi driver wore a turban and had loud reggae music playing on the sound system. Burén's office was on Strandvägen which was easy to find. Humlin became increasingly more irritated by the music as the trip wore on. What irritated him the most was his own inability to ask the driver to turn it down. Why can't I make a simple request, he thought. Do I think he'll assume I'm racist just because I'd like for the music to be turned down during a ride that I'm paying for? When the taxi pulled up outside Burén's building Humlin was still irritated and compensated by tipping the driver way too much.

*

Humlin always felt uncomfortable when he entered Burén's office. He had often asked him why the curtains always had to stay drawn.

'I think it creates a cosier atmosphere,' Burén said.

'I think it creates the feeling of sitting in a cellar.'

'When talking about money I find one needs to stay completely calm and rid oneself of all extraneous thoughts.'

'The only thought I have when I come to see you is that I want to get out of here as soon as possible.'

'That is also the point.'

'What do you mean?'

'That I don't like for my clients to stay longer than necessary.'

Burén was all of twenty-four years old, but looked closer to fifteen. He had had a skyrocketing career within the financial world, beginning when he borrowed money in school to make a couple of extremely lucky investments in the growing Internet business. He had made his first million before he even graduated. For a few years he worked for one of the largest investment firms in the country, then he had broken off to start his own business in this dim office. Humlin sat down in the uncomfortable wooden chair Burén had bought for an outrageous sum of money at the Bukowski auction house.

'I just want to know how my investments are doing,' Humlin said.

'Everything is fine.'

'What about the recent stock-market fluctuations?'

'What fluctuations?'

'Every paper in the country has been running this as front-page news! The market has lost fourteen per cent of its value.'

'An excellent development,' Burén said.

'How can you say that?'

'It just depends on what perspective you use to look at it.'

'I can only see it this way: how are my stocks doing?'

When Humlin started investing a few years ago, he decided to follow his mother's advice to be conservative and not put all of his 250,000 kronor in one basket. He had insisted that Burén – whom Viktor Leander had recommended – buy shares in a variety of companies and industries. But after about a year Burén had convinced him that it was time to make a concerted investment in some extremely promising Internet company. Burén had suggested White Vision, a company that apparently made 'cloned accessories', which was a phrase Humlin still did not understand. The company was being praised to the skies in the media and the founder was a nineteen-year-old student at Chalmers Business School who was considered a brilliant innovator. She was also a beautiful woman whose private life was often the subject of extra press coverage.

At first the new strategy had been extremely profitable. Humlin's initial investment of 250,000 had risen in just a few months to three times his original stake. Every time he suggested selling and pocketing the profits Burén had convinced him the stock had not yet peaked. Now Burén was looking at his computer screen in an inscrutable, thoughtful silence. Humlin's stomach was starting to hurt.

'Your shares are doing just fine,' Burén said finally.

Humlin felt a wave of relief. He had been worried about the market for several weeks now and had not been able to make himself follow the numbers in the papers.

'So they're still going up?'

Burén looked again at his screen.

'They're not going up. But they're fine.'

'You sound as if you're talking about an unruly group of schoolchildren. When we bought those shares they were worth a hundred and twenty kronor per share. Last time we talked they were up at almost four hundred. What are they today?'

'Their recent fluctuations have been negligible.'

'Is that up or down?'

'Both. Sometimes mostly up, sometimes mostly down.'

Humlin's worry was starting to return.

'And where are they right now, exactly?'

'They appear to have stabilised.'

'Can't you give me a straight answer?'

'I am giving you straight answers.'

'What are they worth?'

'Right now: nineteen fifty.'

Humlin stared with horror at the man he only saw dimly on the other side of the desk. In his mind he saw all his savings turning from a mountain of gold to a heap of ashes.

'But that's a catastrophe. I bought shares for two hundred and fifty thousand kronor. What would I get today if I sold everything?'

'About thirty-five thousand.'

Humlin gave a bitter roar.

'You mean to tell me I have lost two hundred thousand kronor?'

'As long as you don't sell you haven't lost anything.'

Humlin's heart was starting to beat irregularly.

'Do you think they will go back up?'

'Of course they will.'

'When?'

'In all probability they will go up shortly.'

'How can you know that? How soon?'

'White Vision is a well-run company. If they don't declare bankruptcy they will almost certainly grow strongly over the next few years.'

'Bankruptcy?'

'And in that case we can deduct your losses against the profits you've made in other deals.'

'But I have no other shares!'

Burén looked at him sternly, and with a certain amount of pity.

'I have been trying to tell you this for a long time,' he said. 'You should have diversified earlier. Then you would always be able to counter losses.'

'I had no more money!'

'You can always borrow.'

'So I should have taken out a loan to buy shares that will be profitable so that I can deduct the losses of the shares I have that I lost everything on?'

Humlin felt completely crushed. Suddenly he wanted nothing

more than to beat up the spotty young man on the other side of the desk.

'You need to keep a cool head in these situations,' Burén said.

'What I have is a pain in my head.'

'The market always bounces back. Your shares have stabilised at a very satisfactory number. The company has already alerted investors about anticipated losses and cash-flow strain in the next quarter. But these things are never written in stone. How are the poems coming along?'

'At least they haven't lost all their value yet.'

Suddenly Burén leaned across the desk.

'I should perhaps tell you that we will become colleagues soon.'

'I will never set foot in the world of finance.'

'That's not what I mean. I'm writing a novel.'

For a split second Humlin imagined Burén publishing a book and being welcomed by the critics as the new hope, as Humlin himself was sidelined and forgotten.

'What about?'

'It's a crime novel. It will centre on a terrible financial crisis.'

'Will you figure in this novel?'

'Not at all. The murderer is a woman. She is a ruthless investment broker who doesn't simply stop at fleecing her clients.'

'What else does she do?'

'She literally skins them. I plan to finish the book next month.'

Humlin felt outraged that a man like Burén assumed he could master something as complicated as writing a novel. He wanted to protest, but of course said nothing.

Burén glanced at the computer screen.

'They're very stable. Nice and easy. Just levelling out at seventeen kronor.'

'Five minutes ago they were up over nineteen, you said.'

'These are negligible fluctuations. You bought for one hundred and twenty. What do you care if they are at nineteen or seventeen?'

Humlin was almost at the point of tears.

'What is your professional advice?' he asked.

'To sit tight.'

'Is that it?'

'I'll be in touch when things look better again.'

'And when will that be?'

'Shortly.'

'How soon is that?'

'In a few weeks. Ten years at most.'

Humlin stared at him. The chanting of Franciscan monks was coming from somewhere. Burén must have turned it on without him noticing. The music swelled to a deafening roar inside his head.

'Ten years?'

'That is the outer margin. Not more than that.'

Burén stood up.

'I have to leave now. But please don't worry. I'll send you a copy of the manuscript when I finish. I look forward to getting your feedback.'

*

Humlin returned to the street in a daze. He searched in his head for some reassuring and calming thoughts but found nothing until he saw Tea-Bag's smiling face. Then he started to come back to life, freed from the chill that had followed him from Burén's dimly lit office. He wondered again if he should write that crime novel after all, if for no other reason than to make some money. The nagging thought that Burén would prove to be the more successful author wouldn't leave him.

Humlin visited his mother that evening. He squirmed at the thought of having to confront her. When he called her to let her know he was on his way he sensed that she knew what he was planning.

'I don't want you to come over this evening,' she said curtly.

'What about the fact that I'm supposedly always welcome?'

'Not tonight.'

Humlin immediately became suspicious. He was convinced there was a hint of a sexual moan in her voice even now.

'Why exactly is this not a good evening for you, Mother?'

'I had a dream last night that I shouldn't have any visitors tonight.'

'But I need to talk to you.'

'What about?'

'I'll tell you as soon as I come over.'

'I have already told you that's not possible.'

'I'll be over around eleven.'

'On no account are you to come over before midnight.'

'I'll be there at eleven-thirty, not a minute later.'

When he stepped into the apartment at exactly eleven-thirty he was assaulted by the smell of strong spices and smoke.

'What is that smell?' Humlin asked.

'I've made a Javanese bamboo dish.'

'You know I prefer not to eat in the middle of the night. Why do you never listen to what I say?'

His mother opened her mouth to say something and fell onto

the floor. For a few paralysing seconds Humlin assumed that what he had always feared had finally come to pass, that she had suffered a heart attack and died. Then he realised she had simply executed one of her well-practised fainting manoeuvres.

'There's nothing wrong with you. Why are you lying on the floor?'

'I won't move until you've apologised.'

'I have nothing to apologise for.'

'You can't treat your ninety-year-old mother like dirt. I have taken the trouble to search for a good recipe, carry home exotic foods, and then stand in front of the stove for four hours and only because my son insisted on carrying on with an unwanted visit.'

She pointed to a stool in a corner of the hall.

'Sit down,' she said.

'Are you going to stay on the floor?'

'I may never get up again.'

Humlin sighed and sat down on the stool. He knew his mother was capable of staying on the floor the whole night if he did not follow orders. Her methods of emotional terrorism were tried and tested.

'There's something I've been meaning to speak to you about,' she said.

'I'm the one who came to speak to you. Can't you at least sit up?'

'No.'

'Do you want me to bring you a pillow?'

'If you can bring yourself to do so.'

Humlin stood up, went into the kitchen and opened a window. Every time his mother cooked the kitchen was transformed into something that resembled the remains of a bloody battle. On his way to the bedroom to fetch a pillow he stopped and looked angrily at the phone. He had the sudden inspiration to lift up the phone book; underneath it lay an advert for 'the Mature Women Hotline'. As he was carrying the pillow back to his mother he wondered if he should use it to suffocate her instead of helping to make her stay on the hall floor more comfortable.

'What was it you wanted to tell me?' he asked.

'I want to inform you of my activities.'

Humlin stiffened. Was she a mind reader? He decided on a counter-attack.

'I know what you're doing,' he said.

'Of course you don't know.'

'That's why I came here to talk to you. You do realise how upsetting this is for me, don't you?'

His mother sat up.

'Have you been snooping in my private papers?'

'If anyone in this family roots around in other people's papers, it's you. I don't.'

'Well, then you can't know what I've been up to.'

Humlin shifted around on the stool trying to find a more comfortable position. It reminded him of the chair he had sat on in Burén's office. I'm going to wait her out, he thought. I won't say another word, I'll just wait.

'Let's just agree on that then. I have no idea what you've been doing and I don't know what it is you want to tell me.'

'I'm writing a book.'

Humlin stared at her.

'What kind of a book?'

'A crime novel.'

For a moment Humlin felt as if he was going insane. He was the victim of a great conspiracy, the extent of which he was only now beginning to realise. All of the people around him seemed to be working on crime novels.

'Are you happy for me?'

'Why on earth would I be happy for you?'

'You could be happy that your mother's creativity has remained intact into old age.'

'Everyone is writing a crime novel these days. Except me.'

'From what I read in the papers that's not true. You are working on one, but I can't imagine it'll be any good.'

'Whatever the papers have been saying it isn't true. But why wouldn't mine be any good?'

His mother lay back down on he floor.

'It's good to know you won't be competing with me.'

'I'm the writer in this family, not you.'

'In a few months that won't be true. I hope you realise what a sensation it will be when an eighty-seven-year-old woman makes her debut with a crime novel of international stature.'

Humlin felt an impending catastrophe speeding towards him. The final defeat would be when his own mother was hailed as a more accomplished writer than himself.

'What's it about?' he finally made himself say.

'I'm not going to tell you.'

'Why not?'

'You'll steal my ideas.'

'I have never in my life stolen anyone's idea. I happen to be an artist who takes his work seriously. Just tell me what the book is about.'

‘A woman who kills her own children.’

‘How original.’

‘She also eats them.’

Even with the window in the kitchen open the smoke from the food started to make him feel sick.

‘That’s what you’re writing about?’

‘I’m already on chapter forty.’

‘So it’ll be a thick book?’

‘I’m assuming it will be around seven hundred pages. Since books are so expensive these days I think it’s only right to write books that last longer.’

‘Tell that to my publisher.’

‘I already have. I told him about the book and he was very interested. He is planning to market us as the “Literary Family”.’

Humlin was at a loss for words, the same way he had felt when Burén told him what his shares were actually worth. His mother got up, picked up the pillow and went into the living room. Humlin stayed on his stool. I lost my footing, he thought. Again. Then, in a series of brief but sharply focused images he saw in his mind Leyla, Tanya and Tea-Bag. Tea-Bag and her smile, Tanya with her face turned away from his, Leyla with her ungainly body. Maybe helping these girls tell their stories is actually something worthwhile, he thought. A good deed, when all is said and done.

*

Humlin forced himself to swallow a few bites of the tangy Javanese dish that his mother had prepared. He also drank a few glasses of wine in preparation for what was to come. During the meal they did not mention the crime novel Märta Humlin was writing nor the crime novel Humlin was not writing. They avoided all topics that could lead to dramatic conflict, since they both needed to rest up for the one that would soon take place.

Humlin pushed his bowl away from him, even though it was still filled with food.

'You have never understood fine cooking,' his mother remarked.

'You have never understood that I'm not hungry at midnight.'

'If you don't learn to appreciate fine food, let alone get your sex life in order, you will come to a bad end, mark my words.'

Humlin was taken aback by her frankness, but it also gave him the opening he needed.

'I don't think it's my sex life that needs discussing. What about yours?'

'I have no sex life.'

'That's your business, but what I do know is you spend your time on revolting and most probably highly illegal phone sex conversations.'

She looked at him with surprise mingled with amusement.

'You sound like a policeman. I've always known that about you, that there wasn't a poet's soul in you but a policeman's.'

'What would people say if this came out?'

'That you have the soul of a policeman?'

Humlin banged his fist on the table.

'We are not talking about me, we are talking about you. I am not acting like a policeman, I am telling you that I want this disgusting phone business of yours to stop. I don't understand how you can live with yourself. Don't you have any principles? You are denigrating and humiliating yourself.'

'There's no need to get so worked up over it. The old men who call are very nice. Many are interesting people. A famous author is one of my most faithful customers.'

Humlin couldn't help his curiosity.

'Who is it?'

'I would never dream of telling you, of course. Discretion is the foundation of this business.'

'But you get paid for this, don't you? Your business is nothing more than common prostitution.'

'I have to pay my phone bill somehow.'

'I take it you make a lot of money?'

'Not a lot.'

'How much?'

'Between fifty and sixty thousand kronor a month. Of course there are no taxes to pay in this line of work.'

Humlin couldn't believe his ears.

'You make fifty thousand a month by moaning into the phone?'

'Basically.'

'What do you do with all the money?'

'Make Javanese bamboo dishes. I buy oysters to offer my children.'

'But you're doing something illegal! And you aren't paying any taxes.'

His mother looked worried for a moment.

'We have discussed the question of taxes in our board meetings. We have come up with a solution we find satisfactory.'

'And what is that?'

'We have written a will for all profits made by our company. All remaining profits will go directly to the state. That should be more than enough to take care of all back taxes.'

Humlin decided to hit as hard as he could.

'If you and your girlfriends don't stop with this at once I will anonymously inform the police of your activities.'

The intensity of her anger surprised him.

'Didn't I know it! There it is again, the policeman in you. I want you to leave my apartment this instant and never return. I am cutting you out of my will and I never want to see you again. I even forbid you to attend my funeral!'

When she finished she tossed the contents of her wine glass in his face. That had never happened before, in all of their most heated discussions. He was temporarily thrown and simply watched as his mother refilled her glass.

'If you do not leave this apartment at once without making any further comments I will throw another glass of wine in your face.'

'Mother, we need to talk about this. Please calm down.'

This time most of the wine landed on his shirt. Humlin realised the battle was lost, at least for the moment. He wiped off his face and shirt with his napkin and stood up.

'We'll talk about it when I get back from Gothenburg.'

'I am never speaking to you again in my life.'

'I'll call you when I get back.'

His mother lifted her wine glass again. Humlin ran out of the apartment.

*

A mixture of snow and rain was falling outside. He did not manage to hail a taxi. Two drunk Finns begged a few cigarettes off him and then followed him in a threatening manner for several blocks. When he got home he was wet through and freezing. Andrea was sleeping. He had been hoping he would be alone. In order to avoid her sharp questions he buried the soiled shirt in the bottom of the rubbish. Looking at it, it occurred to him that the wine stains looked curiously like blood.

Since he was still worked up he decided against trying to sleep immediately. Instead he sat down in his study and tried to prepare for his second meeting with the girls in Gothenburg. Suddenly he was not so sure that Tea-Bag would meet him at the station and this made him disappointed, almost sad. He thought about what she had told him, the unfinished story. How much of what she had said was true? He couldn't know, but as he sat there he started working on what she had said, filling in the blanks. In a way he felt he was taking her by the hand and leading her into her own story. He had never been to Africa but now it was as if he could finally go there in his imagination because he had found someone who made it come alive for him.

He walked into the kitchen and got a tea-bag that he put on his desk in front of him. It seemed to him that the small black specks behind the thin paper were letters, words, sentences, perhaps even songs that all told the real story of the girl with the big smile . . .

*

'Why are you sleeping with a tea-bag in your hand?'

Andrea was bent over him. He had fallen asleep at his desk. He tried to get up but fell back into his chair. One of his legs had fallen completely asleep.

'I'm asking you why you have a tea-bag in your hand.'

'I was going to make myself a cup and fell asleep.'

Andrea shook her head as if he were a hopeless case. He massaged his leg until he heard the front door slam shut behind her. He could see through the weak dawn light that it had stopped snowing outside. He crawled into bed on the side that was still warm from Andrea's body. He slept heavily without dreaming.

*

He was at the Central station at exactly a quarter to two. He looked around but saw no one who smiled at him, everyone seemed despondent as if on their way to undesirable destinations. He was just about to give up when someone touched his arm.

Tea-Bag was smiling.

The train left the station with a jerk just after they had stepped on board.

9

Everything was going well until they reached Hallsberg. There Tea-Bag disappeared without leaving a trace. But before she left, she had continued to tell the story she had abruptly cut short in Humlin's apartment. There was something so unbelievable about her narrative that Humlin started to think it was probably true. She had told him – in her broken but clear Swedish – how she had managed to reach Sweden from the internment camp in Spain. Humlin wondered if there could be anyone quite as alone as a young refugee on her way through a Europe that was as forbidden to those without legal access as if it had been fenced off with high walls and barbed wire.

As far as Södertälje she had sat motionless in her seat and had not even – this irritated him since he felt she should have shown more gratitude – reacted when he bought a ticket for her from the conductor. She had simply sunk down into her thick jacket and stared out of the window. Humlin tried to poke a hole in her silence by asking her a number of essentially meaningless questions but she had not answered, and after a while he wondered what he thought he was trying to achieve. They went through a series of tunnels in Södertälje and when they were back in daylight it was as if the darkness of the tunnels had inspired her. She removed her jacket and he couldn't help but notice that she had a very beautiful body.

'Do you want me to tell you about the monkey?' she asked.

'Please,' he said. 'But why don't you finish the other story first. You were in the rowing boat that had started swaying from the wake of the barge. There were shirts hanging out to dry. You waved even though you didn't see any people.'

'I'd rather tell you about the monkey.'

'You should always finish the stories you tell. Unfinished stories are like restless ghosts. They will continue to haunt you.'

She looked at him attentively.

'I assure you I know what I'm talking about. Unfinished stories can become one's enemies.'

Slowly, hesitantly, she started up her narrative again. At points she spoke with a certain amount of reluctance, as if she wanted to smash parts of her story because it caused her too much pain.

*

I continued to drift in that boat. Time was no longer of any importance. I think the boat trip lasted three days and three nights. I only rowed in to shore the few times I passed a small village and wanted to buy some food with the last of my money. In one of the villages there was a black man in the market that I had decided looked as if it sold the cheapest food. This was the shop I always looked for, the one with the dirty façade and the broken sign. He looked at me with serious eyes but when I smiled he smiled back. He said something to me that I did not understand. But when I answered him in my own language, the language that was already beginning to feel foreign to me, he jumped up from his rickety chair and answered me in the same language.

'My daughter!' he said. 'You come from my country. What are you doing here, who are you, where are you going?'

I thought it was best to be careful in my answers. This man was one of my people, but he sat on a strange chair in a foreign land. Perhaps he would contact the police who would come down with their dogs and make sure I was thrown in jail. I did not know. But it was as if I had no more energy for subterfuge. I couldn't run away or even give false answers. All of my lies felt meaningless, as if they were simply going to bounce back into my mouth and choke me. I decided to tell this man the truth.

'I have escaped from a Spanish refugee camp.'

He frowned. I could see in his face all the lines and scars he had received from many dangers and sorrows.

'How did you get here?' he asked.

'I walked.'

'My God! You have walked from Spain?'

'I have also drifted along the river in a boat.'

'How long have you been travelling?'

When he asked me that question, I suddenly knew the answer. I thought I had lost all sense of time, but suddenly I could see the long line of white stones in my head. I counted them all.

'Three months and four days,' I said.

He shook his head in disbelief.

'How have you managed? Where have you found food? Have you been alone? What is your name?'

'Tea-Bag.'

The man was tall and strong, but his hair was already starting to turn white. He leaned forward and looked me in the eyes.

'You have been alone for a long time but now you are my daughter. At least for a while. Soon Monsieur Le Patron will be back and then you can't stay, since like the white man that he is he has explained to me he can only tolerate one black person at a time.'

I still did not trust him. Even though he looked me straight in the eyes, allowing me to see deeply into him, I never forgot that I was trespassing on forbidden territory.

'What is your name?' I asked him.

'Zachary. But in our language my name is Luningi.'

My father's name! Now I was the one who opened my eyes wide and hoped he could see through my eyes to the village where my father had lived until he was one day taken away.

'My father's name was Luningi.'

'I have my name after an uncle who dreamed of a mountain. He set out to find it and never returned. We think he found the mountain and decided to stay because it was so beautiful. Perhaps he is still there deep inside it. What do you and I know, what does anyone really know? Where is it you are going, my daughter?'

'To Sweden.'

Luningi frowned again.

'Is that a city? I have heard the name before.'

'It is a country, to the north.'

'Why are you going there?'

'Someone is waiting for me there.'

Luningi looked at me for a long time with his wide eyes. The silence around him was heavy with thought. There was a sharp smell in the shop from the cheese counter that I found calming. The smell of the cheese and the man's white hair were real. I had hardly spoken to a person for three months. My tongue had started to feel swollen and stiff, as if it was suffering from being used so little.

'Who is waiting for you?'

'The country. The people who live there know who I am.'

Luningi nodded slowly.

'It is good to have a goal. You should hold on to it. People who

have lost sight of their goal often begin to live in a careless manner. I had a goal once. It was to travel to Europe and work for ten years. Nothing else, only that. I wanted to live as cheaply as possible, save my money and then return home in order to fulfil my dream.'

'What was that?'

'To build a mortuary.'

I had never heard that word before. 'Mortuary'. Was that a cheese shop? Brightly coloured cloth for dresses? Or was it a restaurant with food so spicy that one started to sweat after the first bite? I didn't know.

'Perhaps you don't know what that is,' he said. 'Or perhaps you don't want to know. Are you afraid of death?'

'Everyone is afraid of death.'

'Not me. A mortuary is a place where the dead rest before their burial. It is a room full of ice where the sun never reaches in. The dead have time to cool after their battle with death, before they are placed in the earth.'

'Why do you want to build a mortuary?'

'When I was young I travelled around our country with my father. He was helping people look for water. He was not a shaman, he did not look for it with a wooden stick. He simply saw the water in his mind. But what I saw were big cities where there were so many people crowded together they almost stuck to one another, and villages where the sense of desolation was so strong it made people silent. I saw that we were slowly losing our ability to die a slow and thoughtful death. An African who loses the ability to die with dignity is a lost man. He loses the ability to live, just like the people in this country. I want to build a mortuary where dignity is intact. In my mortuary the dead will be able to rest in the cool air before they bow one last time to the earth and disappear.'

'I think I understand.'

'No, you don't. One day perhaps you will, if you are not eaten alive by the country that is waiting for you. Countries can be like hungry animals with a thousand mouths. They eat us up when their need is great and they spit us out when they are done. I sell some cheese in this shop every day, but I am never able to save any money. The only thing I fear is that when I feel my death approaching I will not have enough money or strength to return to the place where I was born. One can live a rootless existence but one cannot die without knowing where one should plant one's last and most valuable roots.'

Luningi walked to the door and squinted in the light out into the street. There were church bells pealing in the distance.

'Now it is best that you leave. Monsiuer Le Patron will soon be back.'

Luningi put some cheese in a plastic bag for me. I saw that his back was bent as if under a great weight. His left leg dragged slightly behind him when he walked.

'Cheese will fill you up,' he said.

Then he handed me some wrinkled banknotes from his pocket but I would not take them.

'They are for your mortuary,' I said.

'Other people will build it. It is too late for me.'

'But what about your trip home?'

'It is not as important as your trip to the north.'

We stood there silently in the dim light of the shop. Luningi stretched out his hand and stroked my cheek.

'You are very beautiful, my daughter,' he said. 'When I remove my hand I can no longer protect you. Many men will desire you, perhaps hurt you, because you are so beautiful. The only one who can protect you is you.'

'I am not afraid.'

Luningi pulled back his hand and looked at me with sudden disapproval.

'Why do you say you are not afraid when that was the first thing I saw in you? I have also been on the run. I know what it is like not to be welcome anywhere, always to be hunted, surrounded by people who want to catch you. Don't stand there and say you are not afraid. I am too tired to listen to lies.'

'I am afraid.'

'Yes, you are afraid. Go. I will try to see in my dreams if you reach the goal you have set for yourself. To arrive. To become visible. But don't forget that you live in a world where thousands of unwelcome refugees are streaming across the globe. The ones who have already made it to the other side will do all in their power to make sure that you do not make it. Now you should go.'

'What is wrong with your leg?'

'I only have enough energy to give to one leg. Go.'

He pushed me to the door, caressed my face a last time with his fingers, then forced me out onto the street. I tried to remember the feel of that push for the remainder of my journey, to try to capture the strength he had tried to give me along with the cheese and the money. In my thoughts I spoke to him every day. I could always ask him for advice. Every time he answered me it was as if the energy it required made his hair grow more and more white.

When I was tired the images of Luningi and my father were joined together into a new face that I had never seen before but that still seemed familiar to me. In my dreams, often as I was just falling asleep, I saw the two of them, Luningi and my father, deep in conversation in a secret language I had never heard. From time to time they would turn to me and smile. They were discussing how best to help me, what advice to give, which prayers to say and which gods would best protect my venture. Sometimes I was angry at their inadequacy. Neither one of them was a very powerful protector. I was always running into bad luck and the only one who helped me out was me.

*

Many weeks after I had met Luningi I crossed the border into Germany during a terrible storm. It was a time when heavy rain fell regularly from the sky. It gave me constant colds and fevers and forced me to hide out under bridges and in abandoned houses. One time I was in a service station by one of the big motorways where there was always traffic regardless of the time of day. I was looking for food in a rubbish bin when a truck driver who was urinating against the wall suddenly spotted me. He was dirty and smelled like the rubbish bin. His big stomach hung over his belt. He asked me if I wanted to hitch a ride in his truck and although I knew what situation it could lead to I said yes. But not before I had checked that he was headed north.

I don't know why but I still remember the name of the town where he was headed. Kassel. I thought it sounded like the name of an insect, perhaps one of the bugs that used to crawl on me when I was a child playing in front of our hut. A kassel, a little creature with thousands of tiny legs, a bug that never bit me but crawled all over my skin just as I was now crawling across that part of the Earth's skin called Europe.

I climbed up into the cab and he steered out onto the road. I knew I should be on my guard but the warmth made me drowsy and I fell asleep. When I woke up the truck had stopped and he was on top of me, an enormous weight that I was sure would crush me. I ripped at his throat with my nails and somehow managed to get away. The last I heard of him was his panting giving way to a roar of curses. Then the engine started, the strong headlights came on and I saw him drive off.

Even after this I courted other pissing truck drivers. My smile worked on all of them, and every time I had to scratch my way out of their grip with my nails. All except once, when the driver let me out at a rest stop because he was no longer going my way. He invited me to breakfast and we ate together. He didn't ask me any questions, just finished his coffee, shook my hand and returned to his truck.

At last I stood by the sea. It was cold, the wind stung my face, but I was not going to give up. I was determined to keep going. I sneaked aboard a ferry and hid under some seats in a cafeteria. The ferry swayed and rolled out at sea. I threw up several times but knew – because I had looked at a map – that I was almost there. The white stones in my head were now so many I could almost not count them. But time was like something I shed every morning. I simply left it behind and forced myself to look forwards.

At dawn I crept out of the cafeteria and looked for a toilet. I washed my face and looked at the person in the mirror. I only partially recognised the person I saw there. I had lost weight and had a strange rash on my face. But the biggest difference from the person I had been before were all the furrows that had been carved into my forehead. There I saw all the roads, rivers and rubbish bins that marked the miles of my journey. It was as if the map had been silently imprinted on to my face. I would never be allowed to forget.

When I left the bathroom and walked out on deck I suddenly saw a person I recognised. He was curled up under an awning in a lifeboat and he was shaking with cold. He was one of the young men who had built the ladder in the camp, one of the men who had left an hour before I was allowed to. He flinched when he saw me. I smiled but he did not recognise me. Fear shone out of his eyes. I walked over to him. The wind was bitingly cold.

'Don't you know who I am?'

He shook his head.

'I was the one who climbed the fence after you had left.'

'What fence?'

His voice was hoarse and faint, his face covered with dirty stubble. When I reached for his hand he pushed me away.

'Where are the others?' I asked.

'What others?'

'The ones you left with.'

'I am alone. I have been alone the whole time.'

'Where are you going?'

'Home.'

'Where is your home?'

He mumbled something I didn't understand. I tried to take his hand again to calm him but again he resisted, then he got up and wove down the deck. I started following him but then I hesitated and stopped. He wanted to be alone. He walked as if he were drunk, wobbling and tripping as he made his way along the deck. I saw him hide behind a chimney.

It was full daylight now, the sea was grey and spiked with foamy waves. Far away I saw the dark contours of land. Suddenly I knew what I should do. I pulled away the fluttering awning and climbed into the lifeboat where the young man had been. I had seen madness in his eyes. Fear had eaten him up inside, as if it were an invisible parasite that had bored a hole through his skin. I curled up inside the damp boat and tried to stay warm. I called out for my father but he didn't answer. My mother was an uneasy spirit who was somewhere far away. I called out to her too but she also did not hear me. I had reached the end of my strength, I could not have felt more alone. I knew it was only a short time before the madness would shine from my eyes. But I had not yet reached the land where I knew I would be welcome. Again I was in a boat drifting towards an unknown shore.

How long it took me to travel through Denmark I do not know. But one day I was on a beach with rotting seaweed looking out over the water and I saw Sweden on the other side. I used a bike for long stretches of the trip. I stole bikes at night when I wandered around in residential areas like a stray dog. I had learned how to cycle from my mother's cousin Baba. He had lived in a city and had learned many things. He had an old bike with him when he first came back to the village and he taught me to ride it.

At last I was standing in front of the final border I needed to cross. Standing there on the beach was also my first encounter with snow. It had started to snow and it was as if a blanket was slowly spreading across the beach. At first I thought there was something wrong with my eyes and then I realised frozen water was falling on me, like white flowers from an icy garden among the clouds. I stood there motionless and saw how my jacket became white . . .'

*

At this point the narrative was once again torn from Humlin's hands. Tea-Bag had been telling him her story with an undertone of urgency but had sometimes fallen silent, deep in thought. When she reached the part about standing on the Danish beach she leaned back and shut her eyes as if the telling had finally sapped her strength. Humlin had also shut his eyes for a moment and when he opened them again as they reached Hallsberg station, she was gone.

The train was already leaving the station when he started seriously wondering where she had gone. Since he had dozed off for a while he had at first assumed she had gone to the toilet but when he looked at the signs he saw that they were unoccupied. This was also true in the next carriage. He walked through the entire train, checking the toilets and waiting for the person to come out if they were occupied. But Tea-Bag was gone. When he had been waiting for her at the Central station and became convinced she wasn't going to show he had been overcome by a feeling of despondence. Now that she had disappeared from the train he only felt concern for her well-being. It was as if he had started reading a book – for the second time – and had become gripped by the narrative only to have some invisible force rip the book out of his hands. He didn't understand why she had left. She had not shown any signs that something was amiss. But they must have been there, he thought. I just couldn't see them.

Just north of Herrljunga the train suddenly came to a standstill. After thirty minutes Humlin finally asked the conductor what the problem was.

'Why aren't we moving?'

'Temporary loss of power.'

'Why aren't we being given any information over the loudspeakers?'

'I'm informing you now. Loss of power.'

'How long will it take to restore?'

'We'll be on our way again shortly.'

Humlin tried to call Törnblom on his phone but naturally the train had malfunctioned in an area where his mobile was out of range.

The conductor returned after an hour.

'I thought you said we would be on our way shortly,' Humlin grumbled.

'We will. It won't take long.'

'How long?'

'A few minutes.'

'We've already been delayed an hour.'

'The engineer thinks he'll be able to make up ten minutes.'

'Then we'll still be fifty minutes delayed.'

'These things happen. It won't be much longer now.'

*

The train was delayed for three hours. Then the loudspeakers announced that all passengers would be transferred to buses. Humlin was close to breaking down at this point, partly from worry about Tea-Bag, partly by the fact that the meeting in Stensgården would have to be cancelled.

Once he had climbed onto the overfull bus he went to call Törnblom again. He looked through his briefcase and all his pockets, but to no avail. He must have left his phone on the train.

It was a quarter to eleven when the bus pulled up to the Central station in Gothenburg. Humlin looked around for Törnblom but, of course, no one was there to pick him up.

10

Humlin took a deep breath.

It was all over. The best thing he could do now was simply to get himself out of the project he had started with Leyla and her friends, a project that he had lost control of almost immediately.

Standing there in the slushy snow outside the train station he saw the entire situation with excruciating clarity. The whole idea had been misguided from the start. He had imagined that a literary adventure awaited him. But a chasm separated him from the people of Stensgården. He would never be able to bridge it, however well-meaning his intentions. The latter he wasn't even entirely sure of, to be honest. He thought that Leyla's desire to be a TV personality was actually not so different from his own ambitions. He wanted to be rich, famous, always mentioned in the papers and with a string of great international successes.

He stepped into a taxi and asked to be taken to the hotel he normally stayed in when he came for the annual book fair. But just as the cab was pulling up to the kerb outside the hotel he changed his mind and asked to be taken out to Stensgården. The driver turned around and looked at him.

'But this was where you wanted to go, right?'

'I've changed my mind.'

The driver did not speak Swedish fluently, but his Gothenburg accent was unmistakable.

'Where in Stensgården?'

'Pelle Törnblom's boxing club.'

The cab pulled away from the kerb with great speed.

'My brother belongs to that club,' the driver said. 'I live in Stensgården.'

Humlin sat back so his face would be cast in shadow. The driver was going way too fast on the empty city streets.

'I'd be grateful if you kept the speed down,' Humlin said. 'I was planning to arrive at my destination alive.'

The taxi slowed down, but after the first light the driver resumed his previous speed. Humlin decided it was hopeless to get him to drive any slower.

'My cousin is at the club tonight,' the driver volunteered.

'Is he a good boxer?'

'My cousin is a she. She is meeting with an author tonight.'

Humlin tried to make himself even smaller.

'That sounds interesting.'

'Leyla is going to be very successful. This author is going to teach her what she should do to write a bestseller. Leyla has calculated that she can write four books per year. If they sell one hundred thousand copies per book she will be a millionaire within a few years. Then we will open an institute.'

'Who is "we"?'

'Leyla, me and my brother and her other cousins. Also, two uncles who are still in Iran. But they are on their way, probably with Turkish passports. We haven't decided yet. Altogether we will be eleven part-owners.'

'And what is this institute? Is it really so easy to emigrate to Sweden? Don't they check the passports?'

'The institute is for dieting. And yes, it is very hard to gain residence visas for Sweden. You have to know what to do, then it's easy.'

'And you know what to do?'

'Everyone knows.'

'How do you do it?'

'You should come here first. Either they let you in, or they deport you. If you are in, you're in. But if you are deported you are also okay.'

'How is that?'

'You refuse to leave.'

'And that works?'

'It works very well. You can escape from the refugee camp, for example. Maybe you change names with someone. Or else you disappear. There are churches that harbour refugees.'

'That sounds too good to be true,' Humlin protested. 'I feel like I read articles every day about people with desperate stories who fight their deportation. Some of them try to kill themselves and they are still deported.'

'It is unfortunate that the Swedish authorities have not yet understood the way things work. We have tried to tell them how refugees think, but they don't want to listen.'

Humlin was starting to feel like an enraged conservative. In his mind he saw a Sweden with completely porous borders over which people from all over the world cheerfully crossed at will.

'I thought our government was supposed to set rules for immigration, not the other way around.'

'You don't think that is undemocratic? Refugees know so much more about their situation than any public servant. Like what it is like to travel through Europe in a locked container, for example.'

Humlin thought about this in silence, not only what the driver had told him about immigration, but also Leyla's real motives for learning to write. He had the feeling there was more to the story.

Was her desire to write really motivated by superficial motives? Was there no deeper reason, a need to find a form of self-expression? Humlin simply couldn't believe that all she wanted to do was make money and run a diet institute with her relatives.

The taxi slowed down in front of the boxing club. The windows and outside lights were dark.

'They have probably gone home. It's half past eleven.'

Humlin leaned forward to pay. He still didn't know what had made him change his mind and ask to be driven out here, nor did he have a phone with him to order another taxi and get back. I never know why I do things, he thought despondently. It's that damned foothold again, I've lost my foothold. The best thing I could do would be to go back to the hotel. But I'm determined to get out here.

'Are you sure you want to be dropped off here?' the taxi driver asked.

'Yes, I'm sure.'

Humlin stepped out of the car and watched it drive off at breakneck speed in the snow. What the hell am I doing here, he thought angrily as he pulled at the locked door. Then he flinched and turned around. He saw someone come out of the shadows at him. I'm going to be robbed, he thought. Robbed, stabbed and left for dead in this slush. Then he realised it was Tanya. Her long hair was wet and she was shivering. But unlike last time she was not staring off at the horizon, she was looking into his eyes. And she smiled. It suddenly dawned on Humlin that she had been waiting for him all this time. When everyone else had given up on him and gone home, she had stayed there in the cold.

'I'm so sorry I'm late,' he said. 'There was a problem with the train. And Tea-Bag disappeared. Do you know where she lives?'

Tanya did not reply. I wonder if she even understands what I'm saying, he thought. But she must speak some Swedish. Does she just not want to talk about Tea-Bag?

'It's locked,' he continued. 'We can't get in. Everyone has gone home, it appears. I can't blame them since I'm so late.'

The next moment Humlin realised Tanya understood him very well. She took out a collection of skeleton keys and a small torch and went to work on Törnblom's door. After a while she gave up, pulled out a small crowbar that had been hidden in her boot and forced it into the door. Before he had a chance to react, Humlin found himself pulled into the dark hallway while Tanya closed the broken door behind them.

'This is breaking and entering!' Humlin hissed.

Tanya did not answer. She was already on her way to the room where they had met before, the one with the boarded-up windows. The light from her torch danced over the walls with their old boxing posters. He followed her in. She found the light switch and turned it on.

'Someone will see the light,' he said.

'Even in Sweden light cannot pass through boarded-up windows,' she said.

She spoke slowly, searching for each word like a blind person trying to find their way down an unknown path. He thought her voice sounded something like a small clear bell, delicate and definite at the same time.

'Nonetheless someone might have seen us,' he said.

'No one saw us.'

Humlin thought about the impressive collection of keys she had hauled out, not to mention the crowbar.

'Do you do this a lot?' he asked.

He heard how silly the question sounded, but it was too late to take it back. Tanya sat down on the chair she had used last time. She removed her jacket and the backpack he only now saw she was carrying. She pulled her wet hair out of her face and placed a notebook and pen in front of her. She's ready to start, Humlin thought. What do I do now?

Then it occurred to him that these events could be used as the start of a narrative. He quickly made some notes in his head. *Darkness, taxi, boxing club, Tanya, break-in, empty room with boarded-up windows. Start of story about contemporary Swedish life.* He removed his overcoat and sat down on the chair that he had used before. She was watching his every move.

'You drew a picture of a heart last time,' he said. 'Whose heart was it?'

Instead of answering, she picked up her backpack and emptied the contents on the table. In the resulting jumble he could see everything from icons to pine cones, old cinema ticket stubs, a baby's dummy, a tin opener, a piece of cut crystal and two brown envelopes. Tanya pushed the envelopes towards him. When he picked up the first she gestured to him in an irritated manner to take the other. He opened up the second envelope and saw that it contained a letter from the immigration authorities. *Application for asylum and permanent residence in Sweden denied as of this 12th of August, 1997.*

The letter was addressed to someone named Inez Liepa and the reasons given for the denial of her application were that she had given false information about her name and nationality, as well as the reason for her application for asylum. In the margin someone had doodled in a number of hearts from which drops of blood seeped down the page. Humlin assumed the latter had not been added by the immigration authorities.

Humlin picked up the first envelope. It was from the local police authorities in Västerås. This letter was also addressed to Inez Liepa, a Russian national, and it stated that she was to be deported from Sweden on the 14th of January 1998. Humlin put down the letter. She was still watching him very carefully. Do none of these people ever use their real names, he thought. First there's Tea-Bag/Florence, now Inez/Tanya. He found it impossible to hide his disapproval.

'We have laws and regulations in this country,' he said, 'in case you hadn't noticed. How do you expect to be granted permanent residence if all the information you use has been falsified? Why can't you simply tell them the truth?'

'What truth?'

'Your real name, for a start. Is it Inez or Tanya?'

'Natalia.'

'Natalia? Now you have a third name?'

'I only have one real name. Natalia.'

'And are you from Russia, Natalia?'

'I was born in Smolensk.'

'Liepa sounds Estonian. With a name like that people assume you come from a place like Riga.'

'But Riga is in Lithuania, not Estonia.'

'That was what I meant. Lithuania.'

'There are so many countries in this world. It is easy to make mistakes.'

He looked at her searchingly but couldn't tell if she was being ironic. He grew more irritated.

'Can't you just answer my question? What is your real name

and what is your nationality? I would also like to know where Tea-Bag lives. I'm worried about her.'

She didn't say anything. He looked at the objects that were still lying on the table.

'You can of course also tell me why you decided to come to Sweden,' he said. 'In particular I'm rather curious to know how you have managed to dodge the police for so long. But most of all I want to know why you came. What made you leave your home? That is what you are here to write about. It is your story. I promise to listen, but I want to hear the truth. Nothing less. I am tired of this never knowing who you really are.'

Humlin waited. Inez/Tanya/Natalia was silent. Well, we have the whole night, he thought. She has to say something sooner or later.

But he was wrong. She had still said nothing after half an hour. The silence was finally broken by the sound of the front door being thrown open by a barking police dog. The dog was quickly followed by three armed officers.

'Hands in the air where we can see them!'

Humlin felt like he was in a bad dream. But the fear was real.

'I can explain,' he said. 'There's nothing illegal going on here, I promise.'

Tanya was frozen in her chair. Her gaze was once more fixed on some point far away. But Humlin was sure she was following everything that went on in the room.

'Please call Pelle Törnblom who owns this building.'

'His alarm system indicated that the front door had been opened and the door does show signs of force.'

'I can explain. My name is Jesper Humlin and I am an author. I take it none of you officers is a fan of poetry but you may have heard my name. My name appears in the papers with some regularity.'

'We'll get to the bottom of this at the station. Come with us.'

Tanya gathered her things together and put them in her backpack. Humlin saw that she intentionally left the two envelopes behind.

'I protest!' Humlin said. 'I demand to be allowed to call Pelle Törnblom.'

One of the police officers grabbed his arm. Humlin could already see the next day's headlines.

*

Humlin did not manage to convince the officer who filed the report to let him call Pelle Törnblom until four o'clock in the morning. Before then he had managed to spend a few moments alone with Tanya.

'I'm going to tell them the door was already open when we arrived,' he said. 'And I won't tell them anything about who you are. How did you learn to break open doors anyway?'

'My father was a burglar. He taught me.'

'Is that what you do, then? Are you a thief?'

'How would I manage otherwise?'

'Is that why you keep a crowbar in your boot?'

Her eyes glinted angrily.

'I hate being poor. Do you even know what that is? To be so poor you start to despise your own existence? Do you know? No, how could you know.'

'Is that why you left? You wanted to escape the poverty?'

'I did not try to escape anything. I left Smolensk in order to become rich. I was tired of breaking into houses where there was nothing left to take. I wanted to come to a country where there was something to take behind the doors I was going to break open. And it happened to be Sweden.'

At this point they were escorted to different rooms. Humlin was placed in a room with a drunken ice-hockey fan who had thrown up on the floor and whose right eye had swollen shut. During the half-hour that followed, Humlin was forced to listen to a completely incomprehensible account of the brawl that had taken place at the Scandinavium arena. It was only when the ice-hockey fan was taken away that Humlin was able to gather his thoughts. What could he do? When Törnblom finally turned up at dawn Humlin had prepared an explanation that shielded Tanya. Törnblom stood and glared at him for a long time before speaking.

'Why didn't you just call me and ask me to come down and unlock the door?'

'I left my phone on the train. Didn't you ring to check what time the train was coming in and hear it was delayed?'

'I was waiting for your call, you know. It was damned difficult to stand there and explain to everyone that you had simply stood them up.'

'The train was delayed,' Humlin repeated in hurt tones. 'I didn't let them down.'

'Haiman had brought a rugby ball to give to you. When he realised you weren't coming he said he regretted not having hit you even harder. Everyone was very disappointed.'

'The train lost all power just outside of Herrljunga! How many times do I have to say this?'

'Why didn't you call?'

'The phone was out of range.'

'I hope you realise I find this all a bit hard to believe. There are a few too many convenient coincidences in your story.'

'Every word I'm telling you is true. What happened anyway? I mean, when I didn't show up.'

'I had to explain that unfortunately you had revealed your true colours as a fundamentally unreliable person. We decided to cancel the whole thing.'

'Cancel?'

'I hope you realise how disappointed the girls are.'

'This is ludicrous. You've heard my explanation. I haven't let them down.'

'Where did you find Tanya anyway?'

'She was waiting for me outside your club.'

'Why was she still there?'

It was at this point that Humlin used his newly fabricated story.

'She was guarding your door since there had been a break-in.'

'There was no break-in. Nothing was stolen.'

'I wouldn't know about that.'

Humlin was completely unprepared for Törnblom's next reaction which was to reach out and grab Humlin by his shirt.

'I don't know what the hell you're up to or what you're thinking. But you leave my club alone!'

He slowly let go. Humlin was speechless. They were alone in the room. Humlin had to wait for the report to be completed before the police could let him go. He had no idea where Tanya was.

'How many times do I have to tell you that I had nothing to do with your club being broken into?'

'You're probably enough of a worm to pin this on Tanya, aren't you?'

'I told you she was just guarding the door. I'm not pinning anything on her.'

Törnblom pulled out a pack of cigarettes although a sign clearly stated that all smoking was forbidden.

'You can't smoke here, you know.'

Törnblom calmly lit his cigarette and sat down.

'This isn't good enough. You're not good enough.'

'What do you mean?'

'You aren't man enough to help these girls start to believe in themselves.'

'And how could I do that? You just cancelled everything.'

'I was humiliated when you didn't show. Leyla was close to tears and all her relatives were upset. Even if you don't care about them you don't have to treat them like shit. You'll have time to regret you did.'

'I assume you mean Haiman is going to come looking for me.'

'We don't use violent methods. That's part of the stereotype of immigrants people like you help to perpetuate.'

'I'm not perpetuating any stereotypes. I'm just trying to understand what you're saying.'

'The reporter was also very disappointed. He said he was going to study your poetry for signs of a mindset that despises weakness in people. Even if you try to hide behind pretty words he'll find you out. He'll crush you.'

Humlin's stomach started to hurt.

'This is unfair. I don't deserve this kind of treatment.'

Törnblom threw his cigarette on the floor and crushed it with his foot.

'There's no point in continuing this conversation. I still don't understand how you can claim one of the girls was with you on the train only to disappear in Hallsberg. It sounds implausible. I take it for granted you understand that we will have no contact after this. You should also avoid Stensgården, at least for the next few years. The people out there have their pride, however humble their circumstances.'

Törnblom left. Humlin searched desperately for a solution to what he now viewed as his greatest problem, the fact that a reporter was going to write an article with the intention of crushing him. But he was also hurt and saddened by Törnblom's words.

The door opened and a police officer looked in.

'You are free to go,' he said. 'We just need you to sign a couple of papers.'

'I'm not signing anything.'

'It's just a document stating that you are not accused of having committed any crime.'

Humlin signed it.

'What happened to the girl who was brought in with me?'

'Do you mean Tatyana? Tatyana Nilsson?'

Humlin wasn't surprised by anything at this point.

'Yes. Where is she? We arrived at the boxing club at the same time. The door was already broken in.'

'We know that.'

'So I'm assuming that means she is also being released now?'

'We can't release her.'

'Why not?'

'She escaped through a window in the bathroom. We're still not sure how she actually opened it and got herself out.'

'Is that a crime?'

'Not in itself. But we have been checking her driving licence in our registers and there's something fishy about the information she gave us. We haven't got to the bottom of it yet.'

'There are few things that make any sense in this life,' Humlin said. 'But can I go now?'

It was a quarter past five. Before Humlin left the station he called his mobile phone number. He was surprised to hear that someone answered.

'Who am I speaking to?' he asked.

'Who's asking?'

'The phone you're using actually belongs to me.'

The man who had answered Humlin's phone sounded sleepy and not completely sober.

'I bought this phone yesterday for one hundred kronor.'

'I'm going to block the account as soon as this conversation is over. If you really did buy the phone you bought stolen property.'

'I don't care about that. But you can get it back for five hundred.'

'Where can I meet you?'

'I'll think about it. Call back in an hour. What time is it anyway? Who the hell calls people at this hour?'

'I'll call back in quarter of an hour.'

Humlin's head was throbbing. During the last few years he had become increasingly convinced that he was going to develop high blood pressure, just like Olof Lundin. But his doctor had patiently explained to him that his blood pressure was completely normal. He had bought a blood pressure cuff in secret since he always suspected she didn't tell him the truth. When the cuff showed the same results as the doctor's, he immediately suspected that it had malfunctioned.

Every morning he spent the first few minutes of his day going through his various body parts to see how he felt. He was rarely sick but often felt bad. If he discovered some little thing that seemed amiss it could ruin his whole day. A few weeks earlier he had found a strange rash on his leg and right arm. He immediately suspected it could be the sign of serious illness and asked Andrea about it as soon as he had a chance. She glanced at his arm.

'That's nothing,' she said.

'You can see this, can't you? How can you say it's nothing?'

'Because I am a highly qualified nurse and because I can see with my own eyes that it's nothing.'

'But I'm completely red here!'

'Does it itch?'

'No.'

'Hurt?'

'No.'

'Then don't worry about it.'

Then, he was temporarily assuaged by Andrea's words. Now he massaged his aching head and wondered if he should call his doctor, even though it was only half past five in the morning.

After fifteen minutes he called his mobile again. It had been turned off. He slammed the phone down in a fury and left the police station. It was still dark outside. He was tired and hungry and his head still ached. He was worried about what Törnblom's reporter was going to write. When he walked past the Gothenburg football stadium he suddenly had the feeling that someone was following him. He turned around but there was no one there. He continued on towards the Central station. It was windy and icy cold. He thought he felt a sore throat coming on. When he reached the station someone appeared at his side. He jumped. It was Tanya. Or Inez/Natalia/Tatyana.

'What are you doing here?'

'I wanted to see how things went.'

'Neither of us is accused of any crime, but they did find something wrong with your licence. Is your name really Tatyana Nilsson?'

'Of course not. It's a fake ID.'

Humlin looked around nervously. He felt additional problems growing up around him. First Tea-Bag had disappeared. Now Tanya had escaped from the police station. He pulled her over to a cafe that had just opened.

She looked curiously at him.

'Why are you so worried?'

'I'm not worried. Do you by any chance have a mobile phone I could borrow? I left mine on the train and now someone has stolen it. Probably one of the cleaners. Who then sold it.'

'Is there any particular brand you want?'

'What?'

Tanya got up. Some businessmen in expensive winter coats were leaving a table nearby. She walked past them, then returned. When the men had left she handed him a phone. Humlin realised she had somehow managed to steal it from one of the men.

'I don't want it.'

'They can afford to buy new ones.'

'I can't understand how you managed to take it. Was it lying on the table? Didn't he notice that you took it?'

'He had it in his pocket.'

'His pocket?'

'Is that so strange?'

'I don't understand how you could get it.'

She leaned forward and patted his arm.

'What do you have in your pocket?' she asked.

'Some change. My keys. Why do you ask?'

'Can you show me your keys?'

Humlin reached for his keys but couldn't find them. Then she opened her hand and showed them to him.

'When did you take them?'

'Just now.'

Humlin stared at her.

'Who are you? *What* are you? A burglar, a pickpocket?'

The door to the cafe opened and one of the businessmen hurried in. He looked at the table he had been sitting at, then went up to the counter and asked if anyone had found his phone. The server behind the counter shook her head. Humlin crouched down. The man shook his head and walked out again.

'Didn't you have to make a call?' Tanya asked.

'I don't think I'm quite up to it.'

Tanya got up again.

'I have to do something. I'll be back.'

'How do I know that?'

'I will be back. An hour at the latest.'

'I might be gone by then.'

'No,' she said, 'you can't go until I've answered your question.'

'Which one?'

'The one about if I'm a thief or a pickpocket.'

Tanya left. Humlin had another cup of coffee, then tried to gather his thoughts. The phone felt heavy in his pocket. He forced himself to take it out and call Andrea.

'Why are you calling so early?' she said.

'I haven't slept all night.'

'I can hear that.'

'How can you hear it?'

'You sound like you always do when you've been up drinking all night. Have you had a good time?'

'I've been holed up in a Gothenburg police station accused of breaking and entering.'

'Did you do it?'

'Of course not. It has not been an enjoyable evening. I just wanted to tell you I'll be home later today.'

'Good,' she said. 'Because I want us to have made a decision about our future together in exactly forty-eight hours.'

'I promise.'

'What do you promise?'

'That we'll talk about this.'

'It's for real this time. Also, you should call Olof Lundin.'

'What did he want? When did he ring?'

'He called last night. He said you could call back any time. I also should tell you that your mother called.'

'What did she want?'

'She said you had attacked her.'

'I never laid a finger on her!'

'She said you hit her so hard she ended up lying on the floor in the hallway for several hours.'

'It's not true. She's losing her mind.'

'She always sounds coherent and clear when I talk to her.'

'She's senile. She just puts on a good act.'

'I have to go. But I'm counting on the fact that we're going to have a serious discussion tonight.'

'I'll be there. I miss you.'

Andrea hung up without commenting on the last thing he said. Humlin sighed and wondered if Andrea was plotting to leave him. He also wondered what new dramas his mother had up her sleeve. In order to distract himself from these concerns he called Lundin.

'Lundin here.'

'It's Jesper Humlin. I hope I didn't wake you up.'

'I've been up since four. Where are you?'

Humlin decided to make something up on the spot.

'In Helsinki.'

'What are you doing there?'

'Preparatory research.'

'So you've decided to go ahead with the crime novel. Excellent. Then we can market your book alongside your mother's.'

'There will be no team marketing strategy. And my mother is never going to write a book.'

'Never say never. I've read a draft.'

Humlin felt a stabbing sensation in his stomach.

'She sent you a manuscript?'

'One page, to be more precise. Handwritten. She summarised the plot in a few paragraphs, something about cannibals and civil servants I think. I couldn't read all of it since her handwriting is somewhat difficult but one has to have patience with ninety-year-old first-time authors.'

'I'm telling you you'll never see a book from her.'

'I've been worried about you. Are you done with that crazy stuff in Gothenburg?'

'No. And it's not crazy.'

'As long as I get my crime novel you can spend your time however you please. I'd like it to be three hundred and eighty-four pages.'

'I was thinking of something more like three hundred and eighty-nine.'

'No can do. We've already informed the book binders and ordered the paper. How far along are you? Why is the book set in Helsinki? It's too easy for it to degenerate into a cold war spy thriller. Brazil is better.'

Humlin was taken aback.

'Why is it better?'

'It's warmer.'

Humlin thought about Lundin's ice-cold office and wondered if there was a connection.

'I'm just joking with you,' Humlin said. 'I'm not in Helsinki, I'm in Gothenburg. I'm not planning to write a crime novel. I don't know what I'm going to write next. Maybe a story about a young pickpocket, or a book about a girl who has a monkey on her back.'

'Are you ill, Humlin?'

'No.'

'You are talking very strangely.'

'What was it you wanted to talk to me about when you called yesterday?'

'I just wanted to reassure myself that the news in the paper wasn't true. I await your crime novel with pleasure. So do the oil executives.'

'There's not going to be a crime novel.'

'The line's breaking up. I can't hear you.'

'I said, there's not going to be a crime novel.'

'I can't hear anything now. I'm going to hang up. Come up and see me when you get back. We need to talk. And the marketing department want to meet with you to present their ideas for your next book campaign.'

He hung up. Humlin was exhausted. The feeling of having lost his foothold in life returned like a great weight. It was as if someone had blocked all the exits out of a burning house.

*

An hour went by. He had just started to gather up his things, assuming that Tanya was not going to return, when the door to the cafe swung open.

Tanya was back. With Leyla.

11

When Humlin sat up in bed he had no idea where he was. He had just had a series of disconnected dreams in which he was strangling his mother. Slowly his memory of the recent past returned. He looked at the time. It was a quarter to eleven. Tanya had left shortly after eight and he had immediately fallen asleep since he was exhausted from his long night at the police station. His head was still throbbing; sleep had not helped that. All of the events since he had arrived by bus in Gothenburg the night before seemed painfully clear. Most of all he wanted to dive back into sleep, back into the unfamiliar bed in an unfamiliar apartment in Stensgården, to try to forget. But he knew it wouldn't work.

He tiptoed out into the kitchen and drank some water. Then he walked around the apartment and tried to identify any objects that looked like they belonged to Tanya. She had claimed that she lived here, if only temporarily and in secret. He found no traces of her. In one of the kitchen cabinets that was filled with, to him, unknown spices, he saw a brand of coffee he recognised. He boiled some water, trying not to make any noise that would draw unwanted attention from the neighbours and then sat down on a chair by the window in the living room with his cup of coffee. A wet snow was falling onto the uniform rows of apartment buildings outside. In the horizon he saw an expanse of forest, then some exposed granite bluffs and the sea.

He thought back to the moment when the girls had walked

into the cafe. He had got up and started walking towards them when Tanya motioned for him to stop.

'I just wanted to say hello,' Humlin said when Tanya pushed him back down in his chair.

'You can't.'

'Why not?'

'Someone who knows her might see you. And that wouldn't be good.'

'I was just going to say hello. That was all.'

Humlin watched as Tanya returned to Leyla. The girls sat down at a table in the corner. From time to time they looked over at him but without interrupting their conversation. Leyla was wearing a thick shawl over her head.

Humlin was confused and this irritated him. Finally Tanya returned to his table like a messenger.

'Why did she come here if I can't even go over and say hello to her?'

'Leyla wanted to see with her own eyes that you were here. That you came back.'

'Törnblom said you had all decided to cancel the whole thing.'

'What else could we have done when you didn't turn up? We're used to disappointments.'

'I just want to state for the record that the only person to disappear in this context was Tea-Bag. No one else.'

'She must have had her reasons. It's always best to be careful in a country like Sweden.'

'Why Sweden?'

Tanya shook her head impatiently.

'We want to hold another meeting tonight to make up for the missed one last night.'

Humlin thought about the phone call with Andrea.

'I can't.'

Tanya's eyes flashed with anger.

'Are you backing out on us again?'

'I thought we had agreed that there was no backing out on my part.'

'If you want us to believe in you, you'll come to the meeting tonight.'

'I have plans.'

Tanya got up.

'Leyla won't be very happy when I tell her what you just said.'

Humlin desperately searched for a way out.

'Can't we have the meeting now, before my train leaves?'

'No.'

'Why not?'

'Leyla has to go to school.'

'Why isn't she already in school then?'

'She'll be in trouble if anyone finds out she isn't there.'

'I'll be in trouble if I'm not in Stockholm this evening. What about having the meeting this afternoon?'

'I'll ask.'

Tanya went back to the other table. Humlin thought of her as a messenger sent back and forth between two warring camps. He then thought that Sweden had turned into a country he really knew very little about.

Tanya returned.

'Five o'clock,' she said.

Humlin revised the schedule in his head.

'We can meet for up to two hours,' he said. 'Then I have to go. Where shall we meet?'

'At my place.'

'I'd be grateful if Haiman were not invited this time.'

'He won't be there.'

'How can I be sure of that?'

'No one is going to know about this meeting. Leyla will take care of it.'

Humlin became concerned.

'How will she do that?'

'She'll say she's over at Fatima's.'

'Who is that?'

'A Jordanian friend of hers. If Leyla's parents call to check up on her they'll get the message that Leyla and Fatima have gone to see Sasha. And if they call there they'll hear they're all over at my place. And if Leyla's parents do start calling it's okay because Fatima's brother will call us to let us know. That way she'll have time to go home without being found out.'

Humlin sensed but did not quite understand what Leyla's life must be like. Leyla left the cafe. She smiled briefly at him, a secret sign that no one else saw. Shortly afterwards Tanya got up and gestured for him to follow her. They took a tram out to Stensgården. When they arrived Tanya escorted him to one of the apartment buildings at the edge of the isolated housing project. They took the lift to the seventh floor. Humlin expected to see 'Nilsson' on the front door but he realised the situation was a bit more complicated when she told him to keep his voice down and then proceeded to use one of her skeleton keys to open the front door.

'Take off your shoes,' she told him once they were inside. 'Don't turn on the TV or the radio.'

'Isn't this your apartment?'

'I live here when it's unoccupied.'

'You have no key?'

'I don't need keys.'

'I know. Who lives here?'

'Some people by the name of Yüksel.'

'Are they related to you?'

'I have no relatives.'

'Then how come you are allowed to live here?'

'They're in Istanbul right now.'

'And they have no idea that you're living here.'

'Right.'

'I thought you said we were going to have this meeting at your place?'

'This is my place. I find out which apartments are going to be empty and when. People who are away or who have moved. Then I move in for a while. I leave before anyone comes back or the new people move in.'

'How do you know which apartments are going to be empty?'

'Leyla knows everything about everyone around here. She lets me know if someone is going away.'

Humlin thought for a moment.

'You don't have a place of your own?'

'How could I if I don't even exist?'

'What do you mean "don't exist"?'

'You saw the deportation notice. The police are after me. Now that I was forced to show them the ID with Tatyana Nilsson on it it's only a matter of time before they put two and two together.'

'So who are you?'

Tanya flinched.

'You know who I am. I'm not answering any more questions.

Don't open the door if anyone knocks. Don't answer the phone. I'll be back in a few hours.'

'Wait, I can't stay in an apartment where the owners could come back at any moment!'

'They won't be back until next week. Leyla has a cousin who works at the travel agent where they booked their tickets.'

'This whole thing makes me very nervous.'

'How do you think I feel knowing that the police could find me at any time and throw me out of the country?'

Humlin couldn't think of a good answer.

'Is there anywhere I can lie down and take a rest?' he asked.

'There are beds in every room. It's a large family.'

Tanya left. Humlin walked around the apartment very carefully and lay down on a bed in a room that – by the looks of the football posters on the wall – belonged to a teenage son. He pulled the blanket up to his chin and thought about the fact that he was in the middle of something he would never have been able to imagine even in his wildest dreams. Then he fell asleep.

*

The coffee cup was empty. He carried it out into the kitchen and returned to the living room. He looked around. There were a number of photographs in gilt frames on one shelf. They depicted children of various ages, a wedding couple, a man in a uniform. Above the shelf there was a flag that he assumed must be Turkish. I am in the middle of a story, he thought. Everything that is now happening to me, everything that the girls tell and don't tell, what they do and don't do, I may be able to shape into a narrative that has not been related before. Tea-Bag disappears God knows where; police dogs burst into the room at the boxing club.

I am currently camping out in an apartment that belongs to a Turkish family. The girl who lives here for the moment is a person who doesn't exist. She hides out in caves, behind borrowed identities. A girl whose real name may or may not be Tanya, and who supports herself by committing burglaries and picking pockets.

He gingerly started opening drawers around the apartment looking for a pen and some paper. So much had happened during the past week that he wanted to make some notes. He found a pad of paper and a pencil, then sat down at the kitchen table. He decided it was probably best to call and reassure Andrea that he was coming home this evening even though he would be quite late. He left a message on her answering machine, this time not even thinking about the fact that he was still using a stolen phone. Before he returned to his notes he called his investment broker.

'Burén here.'

'How come you're suddenly always there when I call nowadays?'

'Have you changed phone numbers? I thought you were someone else.'

Humlin frowned.

'You mean you wouldn't have answered if you saw the call was from me? I thought I was one of your clients!'

'You are.'

'It doesn't seem like it. I'm borrowing the phone of a friend of mine. You don't need to keep this number. I won't be using it again.'

'I save all phone numbers. My computer stores them automatically. What was it you wanted?'

'I don't want you to store this number. Is that understood?'

'I heard you. What was it you wanted?'

'I want to know how my shares are doing.'

'If they don't go down I think we can reasonably expect them to go up.'

'Please give me an honest answer. Will I ever recoup the money I invested?'

'In time.'

'"In time." How long is that?'

'Five to ten years. By the way, I've just started the middle section of my novel.'

'I'm not interested in your novel. I'm interested in my investments. You have swindled me.'

'It is always risky to let one's greed get the better of one.'

'You were the person who talked me out of selling.'

'It is my duty to give you the best advice at my disposal at any given moment.'

Humlin felt that he was simply getting snared by Burén's avoidance strategies. He hung up without saying anything else. Anders Burén himself would be a good subject of a novel, he thought angrily. The distance between his world and Stensgården is like an expanding universe. The distance is increasing every second. If I brought the girls and him together, what would they talk about?

He bent over his notes. There was a sound at the front door. He held his breath and felt his heart start beating faster. It's the Yüksels, he thought. Soon a large Turkish family will pour in and they are going to want to know what a strange man is doing in their apartment.

But it was Tanya who had come back. She looked questioningly at him. She sees my fear, Humlin thought. If there's anything she knows all about it's insecurity since she lives with it constantly.

Tanya emptied the contents of her backpack on the table. Apart from the now-familiar icons, pine cones and baby's dummies there were mobile phones. Seven, to be precise.

'You can choose the one you want.'

'Where did you steal these?'

'At the police station.'

Humlin stared at her.

'The police station?'

'I didn't like being kept there overnight. I wanted to revenge myself a little. I went back there and picked up a few phones.'

'These phones belong to police officers?'

'Only the commanding officers. And a prosecutor. Take them all. If we're lucky they won't be blocked until tomorrow.'

'I don't want a stolen phone. Particularly not one that belongs to a policeman.'

He saw that she was hurt. Then there was that angry glint in her eye again. Before he said anything she shoved one of the phones in his hand.

'Take this one. Answer it when it rings.'

'Never. How would I explain who I was?'

'Do as I say. If you really want to know who I am.'

She left the kitchen. The front door was closed quietly. Shortly afterwards the phone rang. He hesitated, then answered it. It was Tanya.

'This is Irina,' she said.

'Why are you calling yourself Irina? Where are you?'

'You can see me from the windows in the living room.'

He walked over to the windows and looked out. Tanya was standing in the middle of a muddy patch of land that was supposed to be a lawn.

'I see you. Why are we talking on the phone?'

'It's easier for me.'

'Why are you calling youself Irina?'

'That's my name.'

'What about Tanya? And Natalia, Tatyana and Inez?'

'I like to think of them as my stage names.'

'Actresses have stage names. Not pickpockets.'

'Are you making fun of me?'

'I'm just trying to understand why you go by so many names.'

'How are you supposed to make it in this world if you aren't prepared to sacrifice something like a name?'

'I still don't know which is your real name.'

'Do you know how I came to Sweden?'

He was surprised by her question. Her voice sounded different, less hard and remote.

'No, I don't know that.'

'I rowed.'

'How do you mean "rowed"?'

'It means what you think it means. I rowed to Sweden.'

'From where?'

'From Tallinn.'

'From Estonia to Sweden? That's impossible!'

*

I'm here, aren't I? I was forced to row, I had no choice. I would not have dared to try to get through the passport check in customs after the ferry from Tallinn to Sweden when I was escaping from those who had kept me imprisoned. I walked away and came to a small fishing dock. There was a boat pulled up on the shore. I knew I had to get away from the city or I would die. I sat down in the boat and rowed out of the bay. There was no wind. I had no idea how far it was. I rowed all night. The only thing I had with me was some water and a few sandwiches. When dawn came I was surrounded by ocean on all sides. I didn't even know which way to row, but then I tried to orient myself by the sun. I steered west. I rowed straight into the sunset.

The second day I saw a passenger ship in the distance. I thought it was probably headed for Sweden. I kept rowing. My back and arms had lost almost all feeling, but I had to keep rowing to keep my panic at bay. I was rowing away from the hell I had been in since leaving Smolensk. It is still hard for me to think about that time. It was much worse than having the Swedish police on your heels. I can really only think of it if I turn it into a story about someone else. I can still see him clearly, the man I met in Smolensk who promised me that I could have a bright future in Tallinn if I came and worked in his friend's restaurant. Every morning I pray that he has died, that the world has become rid of him, been rid of the burden that an evil man is.

That second night at sea the wind picked up. I don't know if it was a real storm but I had to continually scoop water out of the boat. It was like that for two days. I don't remember anything except that I was cold and I had to keep scooping. I fainted several times, but I had bound the oars to my belt because I knew I would never make it without them. I loved those oars, they were what kept me alive. It wasn't the boat, it was the oars. If I ever build a temple there will be two oars by the altar. I could start my own religion where I pray to two old oars that smell of tar.

I think it took about four days to row to Sweden. I never turned around as I was rowing because I didn't want to feel the disappointment of not seeing land. Therefore I never realised how close

I was. Suddenly the boat hit something. It was stuck. When I turned around it almost scared me because I was so close to the bottom. I had hit a small sandbank and was so close I could wade to shore. It was evening. I wandered around on the beach. I saw lights in the distance but did not dare go closer since I didn't know where I was. I lay down by a big rock and even though it was cold I slept until the sun came up.

The boat had disappeared in the night. It must have floated back out to sea. My oars were gone and I was so upset I started to cry. Then I started walking. I passed a house with a flagpole and the blue and yellow flag on top. That's when I knew I was in Sweden. It was a childish thought, but I was sad that the oars were not with me and that we could not celebrate our success together.

When I was imprisoned in the brothel in Tallinn with Inez, Natalia and Tatyana the only thing we had with us was a book about all the flags of the world. We learned them all. You can ask me about Cameroon or Mexico. I can describe them all in detail. This is the story of how I came to Sweden.

*

Humlin waited to see if she would continue but she did not. While Tanya had told her story he had been watching her from the window. He wondered if he would ever have a phone conversation like this again.

'Where was it you had landed?'

'The island of Gotland.'

'Incredible. What did you do then?'

'I don't have the energy to tell any more.'

'What was it that had happened in Tallinn?'

'You can't use your imagination?'

'It's your story. I don't want to put my own thoughts in it.'

'I can't say anything more.'

'You must have been lured to Tallinn. There was no restaurant. You met some other girls who were in the same situation as yourself. One was Natalia, one was Tatyana. But who is Inez, and Tanya? And Irina?'

'I'm not going to answer your questions. I'm getting cold.'

'Why can't you come back up?'

'I don't have time. I put a bag of food by the door.'

The connection was broken. Tanya waved at him. He watched her leave. You didn't row from Estonia, he thought. You borrowed that story from Tea-Bag, in the same way that you borrow identities and phones. But on some level there was also some truth to what you told me.

Humlin opened the front door and saw that she had brought him a hamburger and a Coke. He went back to the Yüksel family kitchen table and ate. He thought about the story he had heard related from one stolen phone to another. He again felt that he was in the middle of a strange story, or rather, that he was jumping from story to story as if from ice floe to ice floe. None of them had a real beginning and an end. For the first time in a long time he felt that he was involved in something important.

He pulled the pad of paper towards him and continued making notes. But the stories had already begun to take on new life. He added details and saw many new stories about a kind of life he had know nothing about before he came to Stensgården.

I don't even know what I'm doing, he thought. My main concerns are still that Viktor Leander will sell more copies than I will, that my shares are worthless, that my mother is going crazy, and that Andrea will leave me if I don't agree to having a child. Perhaps I should be more concerned about these girls and what they have told me. But isn't what they have told me also something that is as much about me?

*

Humlin heard Tanya's soft knock on the door at exactly five o'clock. Leyla was with her.

They sat down in the living room because Tanya felt it was the safest room in the apartment and the place they were least likely to be overheard. They had to speak with low voices, leaning towards each other, as if they were conspiring together. Humlin decided he should probably start by saying a few words about the chaos that had erupted at their first meeting.

'Naturally, I should never have touched that girl's cheek. But it was an innocent mistake. I like to touch people.'

Leyla looked closely at him.

'You've never tried to touch me,' she said.

'It's a spontaneous impulse.'

'I think you're lying. I think you think I'm too fat.'

'I don't think you're too fat.'

Tanya shifted uncomfortably on her chair. Leyla had a defiant look.

'Let's see,' he said. 'I'm not quite sure how we should begin today.'

'Shouldn't you ask us about what we've written?' Leyla asked.

She was starting to irritate him. She really was quite obese.

'Of course we'll get to that. But first I want to know why you all wrote that you wanted to be talk-show hosts.'

'I didn't,' Tanya said.

'No, you didn't. And why didn't you write that? Don't you want to be a talk-show host?'

'Of course I do. I want to host a show that is about confronting men.'

'Explain that to me.'

'The programme would be a forum for women to revenge themselves on the men in their lives.'

'I've never heard of a show like that,' Humlin said.

'It's an original concept.'

Humlin didn't say anything. He looked over at Leyla.

'I want my show to be nice,' she said.

'And how is that?'

'Guests would be able to just sit there, if they felt like it. They wouldn't have to talk all the time, just have a nice time. There's always so much conflict on TV.'

Humlin tried to imagine a show where the guests were quiet and intent on relaxing, but couldn't. He asked them to show him what they had written.

First he read aloud what Leyla had written. Her handwriting was childishly neat and round.

'*I would like to write about what I know of life, of what it is like to be fat and dream each night of being thin only to wake up disappointed the next morning. Actually I want to write something that makes me famous so I can stay in fancy hotels and have breakfast in bed. But actually I don't know why I'm doing this at all. Or anything, for that matter. Why do I bother to live at all? Sweden is like this rope I cling to. However hard I try I can never reach the floor with my feet. I want the answers to all my questions. And I want to be able to write to my grandmother and tell her what snow is. When can I start working in TV? If you touch me like you touched that girl, Haiman or someone else will wrench your head from your shoulders and then I'll keep it at home in a flower pot. Is this enough? Leyla.*'

'A good start,' Humlin said. 'You should develop this a little further for our next meeting.'

Tanya gave him a small packet.

'I don't want you to open it now,' she said.

'What are you giving him presents for?' Leyla asked angrily, grabbing the package.

'It's not a present. It's what I wrote.'

Leyla took it back. Humlin was worried they were going to start fighting. He raised his arms and tried to calm them.

'I will bring both texts home with me and read them carefully. Next time we'll talk about what you wrote, Tanya. I promise not to show it to anyone.'

*

They decided to meet the following week. Leyla promised to speak to Törnblom and explain that the writing seminar was going to continue as if the delay with the train and the resulting disaster had never happened. Humlin promised to be punctual.

'Törnblom may not believe you,' he said. 'It may be hard to convince him.'

'Everyone believes me,' Leyla said. 'I look harmless.'

'I have to go now,' Humlin said. 'But I also wanted to give you a moment before I left to ask me about my own work, if there's anything you want to know.'

'I tried to read one of your books,' Leyla said. 'But I didn't understand a thing. I hate feeling stupid. When do we get to meet someone who writes for a soap opera?'

Humlin was starting to get used to the rapid changes of subject matter.

'I'll see what I can do.'

'What does that mean exactly?'

'That I'll think about whether I know or know of anyone who has anything to do with soap operas.'

'I want a good part.'

'I'll see what I can do,' Humlin said.

'I want a big part with lots of lines.'

'I may be able to think of someone you can talk to.'

Leyla did not seem satisfied with his vague answers, but her phone rang. She listened without saying anything.

'My dad has called,' she said. 'I have to go.'

She left very quickly, before Humlin had a chance to really say goodbye.

'I can walk you to the tram,' Tanya said.

'I think I can manage to find my way,' Humlin said.

'It's better if I go with you. You might be attacked.'

'Who would do that? I didn't think Haiman knew I was out here?'

'I'm not talking about someone like Haiman. He's nice. I wish I had had a friend like Haiman in Tallinn. But there are gangs out here, guys who aren't used to people like you. They could get angry.'

'Why would the mere sight of me anger them?'

'You make them feel like they're nothing. Like they're black and you're white.'

Tanya escorted Humlin to the tram stop.

'How do you think it went?' he asked her.

'Fine,' she said.

'I was very moved by what you told me on the phone.'

'What does that mean, "moved"?'

'I was touched.'

She shrugged.

'I just told you what happened, that's all.'

'I think there was a lot you didn't tell me.'

'There's your tram.'

She turned her back and started walking away. Another unfinished story, he thought. I can only see the back of it. She's going back to the Yüksel apartment to sleep, unless she's got some robberies planned. He put his hand in his pocket to make sure he still had his keys, then got on the tram and went down to the Central station.

*

He was home by ten-thirty. Humlin unlocked the front door and was prepared for the fact that Andrea might still be awake and ready for a fight. She walked out to meet him in the hall. He noticed to his relief that she did not seem angry.

'Sorry I'm home so late,' he said.

'That's all right. We have company.'

'Company? In the middle of the night? Who is it?'

Humlin thought with horror that perhaps his mother had dropped by.

'Is it Märta?'

'No. Come out to the kitchen,' Andrea said.

Humlin did not want company in the middle of the night. What he wanted was sleep.

He went out to the kitchen. A girl was sitting across from Andrea, with a cup of coffee in front of her. She was smiling.

Tea-Bag had returned.

12

Humlin was upset to find Tea-Bag in his kitchen. How long had she been there? What had she told Andrea? What would he tell Andrea about why he hadn't mentioned Tea-Bag's previous visit when Tea-Bag left? He foresaw a whole host of difficult questions.

'This is unexpected,' he said carefully.

'Tea-Bag has told me quite a remarkable and shocking story,' Andrea said.

I don't doubt it, Humlin thought. If her name really is Tea-Bag and not Florence. At this point I don't believe much of what people tell me, particularly not if they are young female refugees.

Andrea frowned at him.

'Why don't you say hello and sit down? I thought you two were friends?'

He sat down and nodded kindly in Tea-Bag's direction without looking at her.

'Why have you never talked about her brother?' Andrea continued.

Warning bells went off in his head.

'Her brother?'

'Why are you giving me such a funny look?'

'It's not a funny look. I just don't know what you're talking about. I'm tired.'

'Adamah? Who has the restaurant where you often eat lunch? I've never heard of either one of them, of course. I don't know why you are always so secretive about your life. I would think you would have enough of being mysterious with your poetry, but you insist on weaving these inexplicable subtexts into your life as well.'

'You've never told me you thought my poetry was mysterious before,' Humlin said.

'I've only used that word every time you publish a new collection. But we'll talk about your poetry another time. I just want to come with you next time and have some African food. Adamah seems to be quite something, both as a chef and a person.'

She's probably not the only person who's never heard of Adamah or his restaurant, Humlin thought. I just hope Tea-Bag didn't say anything about having slept in our bed.

'It was nice of you to let her sleep here since she had lost her ticket and couldn't get back to Eskilstuna.'

The phone rang and Andrea left the kitchen. Humlin leaned over to Tea-Bag – who was still smiling – and quietly shot a string of questions at her.

'When did you get here? What have you said? Why are you going to Eskilstuna? Why do you disappear the whole time? What happened in Hallsberg? Why do you come out to Stockholm when we have arranged to meet in Gothenburg?'

The questions just poured out of him. She didn't answer, just took his hand as if to calm him down. He pulled it back.

'Don't do that! Andrea is insanely jealous.'

Tea-Bag looked affronted.

'I just wanted to show you I was happy to see you. Why would she be jealous of me?'

'That's beside the point. Why did you come? What have you said? Why did you disappear? You have to answer these questions.'

'I always tell the truth.'

'Who is Adamah, and what restaurant is she talking about? I never eat African food.'

'You should.'

'I should do many things. Why did you say you were going to Eskilstuna?'

'That's where I live.'

'You live in Gothenburg.'

'Have I ever said so?'

'That was where we met. In Gothenburg, or more precisely Mölndal and Stensgården. That's where your friends live. You can't turn up at a reading in Mölndal or Stensgården if you live in Eskilstuna.'

'I never said I lived in Eskilstuna.'

'You just did. What happened in Hallsberg anyway? Why did you leave the train? Can't you understand that I was worried?'

But Humlin had to wait for his answer. Andrea came back.

'That was Märta.'

'What did she want?'

'She's coming over.'

'I don't want to see her.'

'That's not going to be a problem.'

'What do you mean?'

'She doesn't want to see you either. She's coming over to see me. She made a point of saying that she'll leave at once if she sees you.'

'Then why does she have to meet you here? Can't you go over to your place?'

'She needs some advice for the book she's writing.'

'She's not going to write a book. What kind of advice?'

'She wants suggestions for how a nurse could use her expertise to kill people.'

'And why does she need to know this in the middle of the night?'

'Anything your mother does normally happens after midnight.'

Andrea changed the subject by turning to Tea-Bag.

'Jesper will help you make up the sofa bed in the study. I was planning to go home to my place tonight but now I'll be staying after all.'

I don't even count, Humlin thought. She's not staying for my sake but for the sake of my crazy mother.

Tea-Bag got up and went to the bathroom.

'Why does she have to spend the night?' Humlin asked.

'There are no trains to Eskilstuna at this hour.'

'She doesn't live in Eskilstuna. She lives in Gothenburg.'

'Her brother Adamah lives in Eskilstuna.'

'I want to know what happened. Did she knock on the door?'

'Why are you so nervous all of a sudden? What have you been getting up to in Gothenburg?'

'I've already told you everything.'

'Everything you've told me has been completely disjointed and incomprehensible. She was sitting in the stairwell when I came back from work. She asked about you. She wondered if you were back from Gothenburg yet. She told me she was forced to cancel her plans and get off in Hallsberg.'

'Did she tell you why?'

'No, just that it was necessary. But I imagine you probably said something objectionable. She's very sensitive.'

'So am I.'

'What did you say to her?'

'I didn't say anything. She told me her story of how she came to Sweden. Then I closed my eyes for a while. She disappeared.'

'Think of cycling across all of Europe.'

'Cycling?'

'I thought you said she told you how she managed to get to the border through northern Finland?'

Humlin realised there was no point in asking more questions. Tea-Bag's story was as full of contradictions as Tanya's. He wondered more than ever which story really belonged to whom. If anyone could have cycled over the border at Tornea it was Tanya and not Tea-Bag.

'Help her make up the bed. Märta will be here soon. We'll sit in the kitchen and I'll keep the door closed. I'll tell her you're sleeping.'

'And how am I supposed to sleep knowing that my mother is sitting in the kitchen with you plotting how best to kill me?'

'You silly man. She loves you. Why would she want to kill you?'

'Because she's off her rocker.'

'She's writing a book. I think it's wonderful that a person her age has that kind of energy and drive.'

*

Humlin brought sheets and a blanket to the study and made up the sofa bed. Tea-Bag came in wearing his robe. He turned away while she removed it and crawled into bed. That was when the front doorbell rang. Tea-Bag made a startled sound and seemed frightened.

'It's just my mother.'

Humlin closed the door to the study and sat down in his chair.

Tea-Bag lay in bed with the covers pulled up to her chin. He saw her gaze travel over the wall-to-wall bookcases.

'This is where I write my poetry,' he announced.

'You don't happen to have a book about monkeys?' she asked.

'Not that I can remember.'

She seemed disappointed.

'What are most of these books about, then?'

'People, I guess.'

Then he took the plunge.

'What happened that made you get off that train?'

Tea-Bag didn't answer. She started to cry. Humlin felt like an oaf.

'Shall I leave you alone?' he asked.

She shook her head and Humlin stayed put. It was as if he were holding her book in his hands again, waiting for it to be opened.

'I got scared.'

'Were you scared of me?'

'Nothing from the outside frightens me any more. My fear comes from inside. I heard my father's voice. He told me to run. I couldn't see him, but I knew I had to do as he said. I ran as fast as I could and I didn't look back.'

'Then what?'

'The fear went away. I hitched a ride all the way back to Stockholm.'

'And what's all this talk of a brother?'

'Who?'

'You say you have a brother by the name of Adamah. He has a restaurant where I often eat, apparently.'

She turned her back to him and curled up so that all he could see was her braided hair against the pillow. In a few seconds she had fallen asleep. He looked at the contours of her body under the covers and thought about what she had said: *My fear comes from inside. I heard my father's voice. He told me to run*. Humlin turned off the light and carefully opened the door. He tiptoed over to the kitchen door. His mother's voice was loud and authoritative. He fled to the bedroom.

*

When he woke up in the morning the other side of the bed was empty. It was half past seven in the morning. Andrea had already left. He got up and walked to the study. Tea-Bag was also gone. The train ticket he had bought her was lying on the floor. She's disappeared again, he thought. I still don't know why or where she's gone.

The phone rang and when he heard on the answering machine that it was Anders Burén he picked up.

'I hope I'm not calling too early?'

'Writers work best in the morning.'

'I thought you said writers worked best at night. But that's not why I'm calling. I've just returned from my monastery. For a meditation retreat.'

Humlin knew that Burén went out to some monastic health spa in the archipelago about four times a year. Rumour had it that the place was run like a private club and cost a small fortune in membership fees.

'And did you think of a way to raise the prices of my White Vision shares?'

'White Vision is unimportant.'

'Not for me.'

'I have had a brilliant idea. We are going to make you an incorporated company.'

'What are you talking about?'

'It's very simple. We start a company and call it "Humlin Magic". I own fifty-one per cent, you forty-nine. The company consists of your publishing contracts and copyrights.'

Humlin interrupted him.

'For an author to even try to present himself as an investment opportunity he surely has to be someone who actually makes money. The only incorporated authors I know are ones who write crime fiction. Which I do not.'

'You didn't let me finish. Your contracts and the like are negligible in this context.'

'Thank you.'

'What I mean is that *you* will be the company's biggest asset.'

'And how does that work?'

'We divide you up into shares and sell you. It's the same principle as selling timeshares in a mountain retreat.'

'I'm not sure I enjoy being compared to a holiday rental.'

'Where's your sense of imagination? I thought writers had imagination.'

'I use my imagination to write books.'

'Don't you see what a brilliant idea this is? People buy shares in you, in your future books. I'm thinking the first public offering will bring in around fifty million. We'll divide you into a thousand shares. People with money like new ideas. Then the board of directors will meet once a year to decide what you should write. If the worst comes to the worst we'll declare bankruptcy, liquidate the company, wait until you write something good and then try again.'

'When I hear the word "liquidate" I think of the Mafia and tough guys executing unpopular members by shooting them in the neck. I take it all this is your idea of a joke?'

'On the contrary, I am already drafting the first mission statement for "Humlin Magic".'

'You can go ahead and stop wasting your time right now. I have no plans to sell my soul.'

'No one wants your soul, Humlin. I am simply suggesting a way to make the most of your value as a writer. Nothing more. Think about it. I'll call you back in a few hours.'

'I won't be here. How are my shares?'

'They are wonderfully stable. At yesterday's closing they were at fourteen fifty.'

Humlin slammed the phone and held his receiver down against the base as if he were drowning it, foreswearing any future calls from Burén. He finally let go and it remained silent.

*

The small amount of light coming in from the windows was grey. The noises from the street were soft and muffled. Humlin stood frozen on the spot and held his breath. He felt he was going to have a dizzy spell. All these damned problems, he thought. An investment broker who wants to turn me into an incorporated company and a girl called Tea-Bag who sleeps on my couch and only fears the nightmares she carries on the inside. Where do my fears come from? From the knowledge that my shares are losing value and that Andrea places demands on me I can't meet. I fear my mother will write a masterpiece. I am afraid that my publisher is going to drop me and that my next book will only sell a thousand copies. I'm afraid of scathing reviews, and of losing my tan. In short, I am afraid of anything that will reveal that I am a person devoid of passion and true character.

Humlin tried to shake off all these unpleasant thoughts and went to get a cup of coffee from the kitchen. He sat down in the study and looked at the two texts that the girls had given him last night. He had been meaning to read them on the way home but had been too tired.

He reread Leyla's short text, then reached for Tanya's packet and opened it. Inside was a photograph wrapped in a piece of cloth. It was a picture of a girl. The name 'Irina' was written on the back. A picture of Irina as a child, he thought. Or Tanya or Inez, whatever her name really is. He thought he could recognise her face even though the girl in the picture was hardly more than three. He lay down the photograph and leaned back in his chair. She presents her life as a puzzle, he thought. She carefully gives me one piece at a time, never turning her back to me, never taking the chance that I may betray her. She shows me pine cones and pieces of crystal, she lets me know she is a skilled pickpocket, that she is not afraid, that she is alone. And now she shows me a picture of herself as a child.

During the next few hours Humlin sat in front of his computer and entered in everything he could remember about his first encounters with Tea-Bag. Although he was simply making notes for himself, he felt that he could already feel a book starting to take shape. The various stories dovetailed into each other. When he finally turned off the computer he felt satisfied for the first time in a long while. There is something here, he thought. So far I have only been allowed to browse through their stories, but if I keep going out to Gothenburg I will one day have something to write about. I don't have to concern myself with their dreams for the future. I doubt any one of them has the necessary talent to become a writer. If they can make it in TV I have no idea. But I won't leave this project empty-handed.

*

When he was done he called his doctor. He had begged his way to a weekly phone appointment with her.

'Beckman.'

'This is Jesper Humlin. I don't feel well.'

'You never do. What is it this time?'

Anna Beckman, who had been his doctor for ten years, had a somewhat brusque manner that he had never completely been able to get used to.

'I think it may be something with my heart.'

'There's nothing wrong with your heart.'

'I've had palpitations.'

'I do too sometimes.'

'Who are we talking about here? Me or you? I am telling you I'm concerned about my heart.'

'I'm concerned about wasting my lunch hour. You are of course welcome to come in on a drop-in appointment.'

'Yes, is that possible?'

'As luck would have it I have a cancellation. Two o'clock.'

She hung up before she had received his reply. Immediately the phone rang. It was Andrea.

'Is she gone?' she asked.

'She's not here. What did my mother have to say?'

'She's worried about you. She thinks you should re-evaluate your life.'

'What did she mean by that?'

'You'll just get angry if I tell you.'

'I'll be angry if you don't tell me what she said.'

'She thinks your last book stank.'

Even though Humlin had decided a long time ago not to care what his mother thought of his work, he still felt a pain in his stomach at these words. But he said nothing about it to Andrea.

'That's enough. I don't need to hear any more.'

'I knew it would make you angry.'

'I thought she wanted to know how nurses can kill people.'

'That was just an excuse. She wanted to talk about you.'

'I don't want you two to talk about me.'

'But *we* need to talk. Soon. Is that understood?'

'I'll be here.'

'That's all I wanted to know.'

Humlin put the phone down, his head empty. Then he walked out to the mirror in the hall and looked at the remains of his rapidly fading tan. Luckily he had an appointment at the tanning salon tomorrow.

He ate lunch at a small restaurant around the corner, read the paper and then caught a taxi to the doctor's office. His driver was from a small town on the island of Gotland and still wasn't sure of his way around town.

*

Dr Anna Beckman was almost six foot tall, very thin and with short spiky hair. She also had an earring in one eyebrow. Humlin had heard that she had broken off a promising research career because she had become tired of the intrigues that went on behind the scenes in the constant battle for research funds. She pulled open her door and stared at him. The waiting area was full of people.

'There is absolutely nothing the matter with your heart,' she shouted as she pushed him into the examination room.

'I would be grateful if you announced your diagnosis in a quieter voice so not all of your patients hear it.'

She listened to his heart and checked his pulse.

'I can't understand why you insist on bothering me with these things.'

'Bother you? You're my doctor.'

She looked at him critically.

'Are you aware of the fact that you're putting on weight? And I'm sorry to say your tan is pathetic.'

'No one could call me fat.'

'You have gained at least four kilos since you were here last. When was that? Two months ago? You were afraid you were going to catch some intestinal bug in the South Pacific and shit your pants, if I recall correctly.'

As usual her way of expressing herself irritated him.

'I think it's only normal to consult one's doctor before setting out on a long international journey. And I have not gained four kilos.'

Dr Beckman checked his chart and then pointed at the scales.

'Take your clothes off and get on.'

Humlin did as he was told. He weighed 79 kilos.

'Last time you were here you weighed 75. Isn't that four kilos?'

'Then prescribe something for me.'

'What kind of thing?'

'Something to help me lose weight.'

'You'll have to deal with it yourself. I haven't got time for this.'

'Why do you always have to get so pissed off when I come to see you? There are other doctors I could go to, you know.'

'I'm the only one who can stand you and you know it.'

She reached for her prescription pad.

'Is there anything you need?'

'Some more calming pills for my nerves would be nice.'

She looked in his chart.

'You know I keep an eye on these things. I don't want this to become a habit.'

'It's not a habit.'

She threw the prescription at him and got up. Humlin stayed in his chair.

'Is there anything else?' she asked.

'Yes, actually. You're not by any chance writing a book, are you?'

'Why would I be doing that?'

'No crime novel in the works?'

'Can't stand them. Why do you ask?'

'Oh, nothing. I was just wondering.'

Humlin left Dr Beckman's office and was at first unsure of where he should go. In his pocket he felt Tea-Bag's used ticket stub. He was about to throw it in a rubbish bin when he saw that there was an address written on it, some place way out in one of Stockholm's less attractive suburbs. After a moment's hesitation he started walking to the nearest station. He was forced to ask at the ticket booth which station he should get off at. The clerk inside was African but spoke excellent Swedish. To his surprise Humlin saw that the man had been reading a poetry collection by Gunnar Ekelöf.

'He's one of our greats,' Humlin said.

'He is good,' the clerk agreed while stamping Humlin's ticket. 'But I'm not sure he really understood much of what the Byzantine empire was all about.'

Humlin was immediately insulted on Ekelöf's behalf.

'What do you mean by that?'

'It might take too long for us to straighten this out now,' the clerk said. Then he pushed a card over to Humlin.

'You can call me if you want to discuss his poetry some time. Before I came to Sweden, I was an associate professor of literature at a university. Here I stamp tickets.'

The clerk gave him a searching look.

'Is it possible that I have seen you before?'

'It's not impossible,' Humlin said, somewhat encouraged. 'I am Jesper Humlin. A poet.'

The clerk shook his head.

'You write poetry?'

'Yes.'

'I'm sorry.'

Humlin took the escalator down into the underworld. When he arrived at the station where he was supposed to get off he again had the feeling that he was crossing over an invisible threshold into another country, not into a suburb of Stockholm. He walked across a main square that resembled the one in Stensgården. To his surprise he discovered that the address on Tea-Bag's ticket was for a church. He walked in.

The pews were empty. He went up and sat down on a brown wooden chair and stared up at the stained-glass window behind the altar. It was a picture of a man rowing a boat. There was a strong, blue-coloured light on the horizon. Humlin thought about the boats he had heard of in Tea-Bag's and Tanya's stories.

One had drifted down a river in the middle of Europe, the other had rowed from Estonia to Gotland. Suddenly, as if in a vision, he imagined thousands of small boats across the world filled with refugees on their way to Sweden.

Maybe this is the way it is, he thought. We are living in the time of the rowing boat.

*

He was about to get up when a woman came around the corner from the altar. She was wearing a minister's collar, but the rest of her clothing did not make her look like a member of the clergy. She was wearing a short skirt and high heels. She smiled at Humlin, who smiled back.

'The church doors were open. I came in.'

'That's how it's supposed to be. A church should always be open.'

'At first I thought this was a residential building.'

'What made you think that?'

'Someone gave me the address.'

She looked searchingly at him. He sensed that something was not quite right.

'Who was that?'

'A black girl.'

'What was her name?'

'Florence. But she calls herself Tea-Bag.'

The minister shook her head.

'She has the biggest, most beautiful smile I have ever seen,' Humlin said.

'I don't know her. It doesn't sound like anyone who comes here regularly.'

Humlin realised at once that she was not telling the truth. Ministers don't know how to lie convincingly, he thought. Perhaps when they are talking about the gods above and our inner spirits, but not when it comes to earthly matters.

'No one by that name belongs to our parish,' she continued.

She picked up a psalm book that had fallen on the ground.

'Who are you?' she asked.

'A visitor,' he said.

'Your face seems familiar.'

Humlin thought of the clerk at the subway station.

'I don't think we've met.'

'But I feel sure I've seen your face. Not here. Somewhere else.'

'I'm afraid you're mixing me up with someone else.'

'But you're here looking for someone?'

'You could say that.'

'There's no one else here apart from me.'

Humlin wondered why she wasn't telling the truth. She started walking towards the exit and he followed her.

'I was about to lock up,' she said.

'I thought you said a church should always be open?'

'We always lock up for a few hours every afternoon.'

Humlin walked outside.

'You are always welcome,' the minister said before she locked the doors behind him.

Humlin walked across the street, then turned around. She wanted me to leave, he thought. But why? He walked around to the back of the church. There was a little garden. It was empty. He was about to leave when he thought he saw something moving in one of the windows. Whether it was a person or a curtain he couldn't say.

There was a door in the back. He walked over and tried the doorknob. It was unlocked. When he opened it he saw a staircase leading down to the basement. He turned on the light and listened. Then he started walking down. It led to a corridor with a number of doors leading off on either side. On the floor were some toys, a plastic bucket and a little shovel. He frowned. Then he opened the closest door and found himself staring at a woman, a man and three small children sitting on a couple of mattresses. They gave him frightened looks. He mumbled an apology and closed the door. He understood. The church was sheltering refugees in its basement, like a modern-day catacomb.

Suddenly the minister turned up behind him. She had taken off her high-heeled shoes and approached him without making any sound.

'Who are you?' she demanded. 'Are you from the police?'

She is the second woman in the space of a few days to compare me to a policeman, he thought. First my crazy mother, then a minister wearing high-heeled shoes. No Swedish minister should be dressed like she is. No minister should be dressed that way, full stop.

'I'm not from the police.'

'Are you from the Department of Immigration?'

'I'm not going to tell you who I am. Do I have to show my ID in this church?'

'The people who live down here live in fear of deportation. I don't think you know very much about that kind of fear.'

'Perhaps I do know a little about that,' Humlin said. 'I'm not completely without feeling.'

She looked at him in silence. Her eyes were tired and worried.

'Are you a reporter?' she asked finally.

'Not exactly. I'm a writer. But that's neither here nor there. I'm not going to tell anyone that you harbour refugees in your basement. I don't know if I think it's right or wrong – we do have laws and regulations in this country that ought to be followed. But I won't say anything. The only thing I want to know is if the girl with the big smile lives here.'

'Tea-Bag comes and goes. I don't know if she lives here right now.'

'But she does sometimes?'

'Sometimes. Other times she stays with her sister in Gothenburg.'

'What's the name of that sister?'

'I don't know.'

'Do you have her address?'

'No.'

'How come she lives here when she spends so much time in Gothenburg?'

'I don't know that either. She just turned up one morning.'

Humlin was more and more confused. She's lying, he thought. Why can't she just tell me the truth?

'Which room does she stay in?'

The minister pointed it out to him. She told him her name was Erika as she walked over and knocked on the door. A hotel of the underworld, Humlin thought. Erika tried the door handle, then let him into the room. There was a bed, a table and a chair inside, nothing else. He thought he recognised the jumper hanging on the chair. It looked like the one she had been wearing on the train.

Erika shook her head.

'Tea-Bag comes and goes. I never know when she's here. She keeps to herself and I let her be.'

They walked back up the stairs and into the garden. Humlin watched with fascination as she put her high-heeled shoes back on.

'You have beautiful legs,' he said. 'But maybe that's not the kind of thing one should say to a minister?'

'People should feel free to say what they want to a minister.'

'Who are the people down there right now?'

'Right now we have a family from Bangladesh, two families from Kosovo, a single man from Iraq and two Chinese men.'

'How did they all get here?'

'All of our guests simply turn up at the door, either early in the morning or late at night. They hear rumours that they can stay here.'

'Then what happens?'

'They move on. They find other places to hide. A good friend of mine is a doctor. She comes to help out when we need her. A few parishioners help with food and clothing. Do you know that there are close to ten thousand people hiding illegally in Sweden today? They are here with no legal rights. It is a blot on our conscience.'

They walked out to the street together.

'Don't tell her I was here. I'll see her later anyway,' Humlin said.

Erika went back into her church. Humlin found a taxi and was taken back to his own world. When he came home he went to his desk and sat down. The picture of Tanya as a little girl was lying in front of him. Suddenly a new thought came to him. He found a magnifying glass and looked at the back of the photograph again. He thought he could see a faint imprint on the photographic paper of the year 1994. He turned the picture face up again. The little girl stared up at him with serious eyes.

It's not a picture of Tanya, he thought.

It is her daughter.

13

After his appointment at the tanning salon, Humlin went to see his publisher. He didn't really want to see Olof Lundin, but couldn't bring himself to stay away. The thought of the profit-hungry oil executives wouldn't leave him. For once Lundin's office was at a normal temperature. But it was thick with cigarette smoke.

'The air-conditioning unit is broken,' Lundin said bitterly. 'The repairmen are on their way.'

'I suppose you can imagine you're caught in a fog bank on the Baltic.'

'That's just what I'm doing. I should have caught sight of the lighthouse on Russar Island, at the entrance to the Finnish Bay, but right now I'm left unsure of my exact coordinates.'

Humlin decided to go on the attack immediately rather than risk being pulled into a conversation led by Lundin.

'I hope you have finally accepted the fact that I am not going to write a crime novel.'

'On the contrary. The PR department has come up with a brilliant marketing plan for your book. They are talking about pictures of you holding a gun.'

Humlin shivered at the thought. Lundin lit another cigarette from the stub of the one he had been smoking.

'I am, however, seriously concerned about your lack of focus,' Lundin continued. 'Do you want to know how many copies of your poetry book have sold in the last two weeks?'

'No thank you.'

'I'm going to tell you anyway. You need to take this seriously.'

'How many?'

'Three.'

'Three?'

'One in Falköping and – strangely enough – two in Haparanda.'

Humlin was reminded of his Chinese letter-writing fan who lived in Haparanda and who would probably be sending him another lengthy missive soon.

'It is a very serious situation. I understand that you are experiencing some form of writer's block right now and that it suits you to hide out among these immigrant girls in Gothenburg, but you have to leave it at that. I am convinced that you can write a first-class thriller.'

'I'm not hiding out. I wish I could get you to understand what it is they have been telling me. These are stories that haven't yet been told in Swedish. Did you know that there are ten thousand illegal immigrants in Sweden?'

Lundin's face brightened considerably.

'That's a wonderful idea for your second thriller. The investigative poet who roots out illegal immigrants.'

Humlin realised that the conversation was already out of his control. He was not going to be able to make Lundin understand. He changed the subject.

'I hope you have also realised by now that my mother will never write a book.'

'I've seen stranger things happen, but of course I'm going to wait and see if she delivers a manuscript.'

'She claims she's going to write seven hundred pages.'

Lundin shook his head.

'We've just decided not to publish books over four hundred pages,' he said. 'People want shorter books.'

'I thought it was the other way around.'

'I think it's best you leave the publishing business to me. There's a great deal of talk about the creative genius and all that. Who talks about the genius in publishing? But I assure you it exists nonetheless.'

Humlin drew a deep breath.

'I was going to suggest an alternative,' he said. 'No book of poetry, no thriller: an exciting book about the underworld. About these girls in Gothenburg. I'm going to weave their stories together, with me as the main protagonist.'

'Who would read it?'

'Many people.'

'What makes it exciting?'

'The fact that no one has heard stories like these before. It is a book about what is happening in this country. Real voices.'

Lundin waved away the smoke in front of his face. Humlin suddenly felt as if he were on a battlefield where an invisible cavalry, tucked away somewhere behind some trees, had just received the signal to attack.

'Here's my counter-offer,' Lundin said. 'First you write the thriller, then we can talk about this immigrant book.'

Humlin was enraged by Lundin's complete lack of vision.

'No,' he said. 'First the immigrant book. Then we'll talk about the thriller.'

'The oil executives are not going to be pleased to hear that.'

'Quite frankly I don't give a damn what they say. I just don't understand what makes you so cynical.'

'I'm not cynical.'

'You despise these girls.'

'I don't even know them. How could I despise them?'

Two men carrying a ladder entered the room at this point. Lundin signalled that their conversation was at an end.

'I will think this over since you are so stubborn about it. Call me tomorrow.'

Humlin got up.

'There's nothing to think about. We do as I say or we don't do anything.'

He left Lundin's office and walked down the hall with the soft red carpet and stepped into an office where an older man by the name of Jan Sundström worked. He handled international sales. One of Humlin's earliest works had been translated into both Norwegian and Finnish. Then there had been nothing for nine years until one book was translated into Egyptian and naturally did very poorly. Sundström was an anxious man who viewed it as a personal victory every time he managed to place a book abroad.

'Norway has shown some interest,' he said when he saw Humlin. 'There's no need to abandon hope just yet.'

Humlin sat down across from him. He respected Sundström's opinion.

'What do you think of a book about immigrants? A novel about some immigrant girls and their – in my opinion – rather remarkable stories?'

'That sounds like a wonderful idea.'

Sundström got up nervously and closed the door.

'I must say I was rather surprised when I heard all this about you writing a murder mystery. What's happening to the world of Swedish literature?'

'I don't know. I'm not writing a murder mystery.'

'But I spent all morning in a long marketing meeting about it. They're counting on huge international sales. I have to say I think you could have spelled out a little more of the plot.'

Humlin stared at him.

'What plot?'

Sundström dug around in the mass of papers on his desk and pulled out a piece of paper. Humlin read the text with a rising sense of desperation.

'Jesper Humlin, one of the most important poets of our time, has taken on the task of renewing the crime novel and giving this genre a deeper philosophical bent. The plot takes place in Sweden with travels to a dark and cold Helsinki as well as bright and warm locales in Brazil. No more shall be said about the actual details of the novel here, but it may be assumed that the protagonist bears a striking resemblance to the author himself . . .'

Humlin was so furious he started to shake and turn red.

'Who the hell has written this?'

'You did.'

'Me? Says who?'

'Olof.'

'I am going to kill him. I haven't written this. I don't understand where this came from.'

'It was Olof who gave us a copy of the text. He said it had been dictated to him by you over a mobile phone line. Apparently it was a little hard to hear what you were saying.'

Humlin was so angry he couldn't sit still. He left the office, ran through the hallway and threw open Lundin's door. But the workmen were the only people still in there. At the reception downstairs Humlin was told that Lundin had just left the building for a meeting and was not expected until the following day.

'Where is he?' Humlin demanded.

'He is in a closed meeting, sir.'

'Where?'

'That is classified information. Is it important?'

'No,' Humlin said. 'I'm just going to kill him.'

*

The same evening Humlin finally had a long conversation with Andrea about their relationship. He was still fuming over the text he had read at the publishing house. He had left a number of irate messages on Lundin's voice mail. Now he forced himself with some difficulty not to think about the thriller he was never going to write and to focus on Andrea. He immediately felt pressed into a corner.

'You aren't listening to me,' she began.

He stared at her.

'What do you mean? You haven't said anything yet.'

'You're not listening.'

'That's exactly what I'm doing.'

'Well, how is it going to be?'

'What do you mean?'

'You know what I mean. We have a relationship. It's been going on for many years. I want to have a child. I want you to be the father of that child. If you don't want a child I have to ask myself if I should look around for another man.'

'I want to have children too. I just don't know if now is the right time.'

'For me it is.'

'But I am in the middle of changing my authorial profile right now. I'm not sure I can combine that with the responsibilities of fatherhood.'

'You are never going to change anything about your profile,' she said. 'You are always going to be how you are right now. And important decisions regarding anyone but yourself will always be very low on your list of priorities.'

'I don't think this will take more than a year.'

'That's too long.'

'At the very least I need a few more months.'

'Are you going away again?'

'I'm trying to write a book about those girls in Gothenburg.'

'I thought the whole point was that they were going to do that for themselves? Why else are they doing this writing seminar?'

'I'm not sure they're up to the task of doing it themselves.'

'Why are you doing this then?'

'I'm trying to get the stories out of them, help them. You aren't listening to me.'

'It sounds to me like you're stealing something.'

'I'm not stealing anything. But one of the girls is a pickpocket.'

'You're still stealing their stories. But that's not what we were talking about. I can't wait for you to make up your mind. Not for ever.'

'Can't you give me a month?'

'I want us to settle this now.'

'I can't.'

Andrea got up from the kitchen table.

'Then as far as I'm concerned our relationship looks like it's ending.'

'Do you always have to be so dramatic? Every time we have a

serious talk it's as if I've been thrown into a play where I haven't even picked my own part.'

'I am not particularly dramatic. In contrast to you I simply say what's on my mind.'

'So do I.'

Andrea looked down at him.

'No,' she said. 'I'm beginning to wonder if you've ever really said what you think. I don't think there's room for anyone in your head except yourself.'

She left the kitchen and slammed the door. In her anger and disappointment she also turned off the light. Humlin was left in the dark. He pushed aside all thoughts of Andrea and the child she wanted to have and wondered what Tea-Bag was doing right now. He tried to imagine ten thousand people hidden in church cellars and the like, but without success. He lay down on the couch in the study where Tea-Bag's sheets were still bundled. It was as if everything inside him had stopped. Thoughts of Lundin kept him from sleeping.

*

The following day Andrea called him with an ultimatum.

'One month,' she said. 'Not a day more. Then we have to decide if we have a future together or not.'

The rest of the morning he walked around the apartment and worried about what was going to happen. Later in the afternoon he went out to buy the evening papers.

*

Tea-Bag was sitting in the stairwell when he opened the door. He frowned at her.

'Why don't you ring the doorbell?' he asked. 'I don't want the neighbours to see you. They will start to wonder.'

Tea-Bag walked straight to the kitchen and sat down in her thick coat. She shook her head when he asked her if she wanted some coffee.

'If you ask me anything I'm leaving,' she said.

'I'm not going to ask you anything.'

'When are you going back to Gothenburg?'

'I haven't decided yet.'

Tea-Bag was restless and clearly worried. She stood up and Humlin thought she was going to take off.

'Where can I find you?' he asked.

'You can't.'

She hesitated. Humlin sensed that he could use the moment to ask her one of the most pressing questions he had.

'You tell me I'm not allowed to ask you anything,' he said. 'But I'm not sure that's completely true. Maybe you actually want me to ask you questions. There is one thing I'd like to know. And after all you have spent the night here. You and I were on our way to Gothenburg when you left the train. You had been telling me about how you came to Sweden. You told my girlfriend a slightly different story. But they are probably connected somehow. I know this is hard for you.'

She flinched as if he had hit her.

'It's not hard,' she said.

Humlin took a few steps back.

'But things haven't been easy for you.'

'What do you mean?'

'It can't be easy living under a church.'

Her smile died away.

'You know nothing about me.'

'You're right.'

'Don't feel sorry for me. I'm not a victim. I hate pity.'

Tea-Bag took off her thick coat and laid it on the ground. Her movements were very slow.

'I have a brother,' she said. 'I had a brother.'

'Is he dead?'

'I don't know.'

Humlin waited. Then the words started coming, finding their way with care, as if the story she had to tell could only be told slowly and with the utmost care.

*

I have a brother. He is dead, but I have to think of him as if he is still alive. When he was born I was old enough to know that babies didn't simply arrive in the middle of the night; that babies were not simply old people who had gone into the forest, spoken with a god and returned as newborns. He was the first sibling that I understood had come from my mother's body.

My brother was given the name Mazda. Two days before he was born a truck branded with that name had overturned outside the village, spilling its contents, and my father had carried home two big bags of cornmeal. Mazda, who started crying every morning at dawn just like a cockerel, learned to walk when he was only seven months old. He had crawled earlier and faster than any other child my mother had had or heard of. He had crawled over the sand as fast as a snake. Then at seven months he got up and ran. He never walked. It was as if he knew even then that his time on earth would be limited. His feet could move like no one had seen before.

Everyone knew there was something special about Mazda. He

wasn't like other children. But no one knew if his life would turn out well or not. The year he was six there was no rain. The earth turned brown and my father spent a lot of time shouting to his unseen enemies from the roof. My mother stopped speaking and we often went to bed hungry.

It was then, one morning when we had looked in vain for signs in the sky that promised rain, that the woman with the blue hair came walking into the village. No one had ever seen her before. She smiled and her body rocked as she walked, as if she had an invisible drum inside that beat a rhythm for her to dance to. She must have been a stranger from very far away; no one recognised the dances she did. But she could speak our language and glitter fell from her hands and she stopped in the middle of the village. Right by the tree where my father and the other men held their meetings to decide important matters about the problems that inevitably arise when people live so close to one another.

She stood there and simply waited. Someone ran off and told my father and the other men that a strange woman with blue hair had come to our village. My father was the first to arrive. He stood some distance from her and looked her over. Since she was very beautiful he went home and changed his shirt. The chief of our village, called Mbe, did not have good eyesight and did not like strangers turning up in our village. My father and the other men tried to explain to him that glitter fell from this woman's hands and that her hair was completely blue and it was probably wise to find out why she had come. So Mbe reluctantly allowed himself to be led over to her and asked the woman to approach him. Then he smelled her.

'Tobacco,' he announced. 'She smells of cigarettes.'

The woman understood him. She took out a packet of thin brown cigarettes and gave them to Mbe, who immediately had one lit for him. Then he asked her who she was, what her name was and where she was from. I was hovering in a group with the other children, as curious as they were, and I heard her say that her name was Brenda and that she had come to help us. Then Mbe shouted out – and he had a strong voice although he was nearly blind – that all women and children should leave at once. He wanted to listen to what Brenda had to say in the company of wise men alone.

The women did as he asked but hesitantly and with grumbles. Afterwards, when Brenda was resting in one of Mbe's huts, my father came back and whispered things to my mother for a long time. Mazda seemed restless. It was as if he knew that their conversation had to do with him. We became quiet and fearful when we heard them quarrelling. I still remember all that was said.

'You cannot know who she is.'

My mother was the one who said that, and her voice was filled with a despair I had never heard there before.

'Mbe says we can trust her. A woman with blue hair is special.'

'How can he know she has blue hair? He's blind.'

'Don't shout. We told him about it so he can see what he cannot see.'

'Maybe she eats children.'

This remark I remember especially well. Mazda stiffened and was so afraid that he bit my hand.

*

Tea-Bag held out her hand. Humlin saw the scars from a bite on her wrist.

*

It hurt so much I hit him. He curled up in the sand with his head buried in his hands. Shortly afterwards my father came over and said that Mazda had to go with him. Brenda was gathering children from the poverty-stricken villages so that they could go with her to the city and go to school. She paid in cash – father had seen the money himself. What he had first assumed was a drum strapped to her waist had turned out to be a crocodile skin filled with money. After Mazda went to the city he would be able to send money home each month. After going to school he would be able to get a job so good that no one in the family would ever need to worry again about rains that didn't come and rivers that dried up.

*

Tea-Bag stopped her storytelling abruptly, got up and left the kitchen. It was as if she was running from the shadows of her parents' house, Humlin thought. He followed her out into the living room, but when he saw that she had gone to the bathroom he returned to wait for her in the kitchen. After a while Tea-Bag came back.

'Why do you follow me?' she asked.

'What do you mean?'

'You were following me when you went to that church in the Valley of the Dogs and you were following me just now when I went to the bathroom.'

Humlin shook his head, but felt as if he had been found out.

'The Valley of the Dogs?'

'That's where the church is.'

'Why do you call it the Valley of the Dogs?'

'I saw a dog there one time. A lone dog. It was as if I was seeing myself. It didn't have anywhere to go. It had not come from anywhere. You followed me there. And just now you were standing outside the bathroom door.'

'I was worried that you weren't feeling well.'

She looked at him incredulously. But then she picked up her story as if nothing had happened.

*

A few years later, when my mother had had another son that she had also named Mazda since she was certain that the woman with the blue hair had eaten him up, a man came to the village. His name was Tindo. He told us what had really happened. Tindo was tall and had a beautiful face. All the girls in the village immediately fell in love with him. He came to help us plant our crops in the fields. Mbe had died by then and we had a new chief by the name of Leme. In the evenings I would hide in the shadows and listen to the elders talking. That evening I was hiding behind Leme's hut. The conversation turned to the woman who had called herself Brenda and who had collected children to take to the city.

'She probably ate them,' Leme said without trying to hide the fact that he was upset. 'She gave us money. When one is poor even a little money is a lot.'

'No one in this country eats children,' Tindo said.

When Tindo spoke it was as if he was singing. Even when he told them about the pain that Mazda had endured. Tindo knew about the men without conscience who sent out women to collect children from the poorest and most desperate villages. They offered money and promises of schooling and an end to poverty. But no schools awaited the children who were taken to the city. There were simply dark containers where the air was as hot as fire, there were dark stinking cargo holds in rusty ships that left the harbour with the lights turned off. There were long marches where the children were whipped if they tried to run away.

'Leme, I know how much what I am telling you will haunt you,'

Tindo said finally. 'Especially the question if and how you should tell the parents that they will never see their children again. But nothing is ever improved by concealing the truth. These children were taken away in slave caravans. Long lines of frightened children were herded over the mountains to the lands on the other side where the delicate and most valuable crops grow. There they were locked in huts and kept under constant surveillance. They worked at night and received only one small meal a day. When they no longer had the energy to work they were thrown out onto the city streets to beg for subsistence. No one has ever heard of any one of these children returning. Ever.'

*

Tea-Bag finished her story and left the kitchen. When she didn't return he walked out to see where she had gone. She was standing by a window looking down into the street. There were tears in her eyes.

'What kind of crops were they, do you think?'

'Chocolate. Cocoa.'

She got her jacket from the kitchen and left the apartment without another word. He watched her walking along the street. Suddenly he saw something that made him jump. He squinted to see better. There was something attached to her jacket. A backpack? But he was sure she had had no bag with her when she came. He trained his eyes on the object. But he refused to accept what he was seeing.

There was a little monkey on her back. A little monkey with brown-green fur.

14

Two days later they made the trip to Gothenburg for a second time. Humlin had no idea where Tea-Bag had been in the meantime. She had simply called him on a line full of static and asked him what time the train left. Like last time, she had simply appeared at the station. He had tried to convince her to continue telling her story but she had not cooperated, burrowing down into the thick jacket she wouldn't take off. He had surreptitiously looked for claw marks on her back as they were getting on the train. There were some tears in the fabric, but it was impossible for him to verify if they were inflicted by a small monkey with brown-green fur. By the time they were passing Hallsberg, Tea-Bag was asleep. Humlin was forced to shake her when they finally pulled into the station in Gothenburg. When he touched her shoulder her arm automatically shot up and hit him in the face. The conductor, who happened to be nearby, stopped in his tracks.

'What's going on here? Is there a problem?'

'Nothing. I was just trying to wake her up.'

The conductor gave him a sceptical look but continued on his way.

'I don't like it when people touch me,' Tea-Bag said.

'I was just trying to wake you up.'

'I was already awake. I was just pretending to be asleep. I dream better that way.'

They took a cab to Stensgården. A boxing practice was still in session. Tea-Bag looked at the boys in the ring with frank fascination. Pelle Törnblom was standing by the ropes. He motioned for them to go to his office, but Tea-Bag didn't move. Her eyes were trained on the exchange of blows. Törnblom blew on a whistle and the boys left the ring.

'Tea-Bag,' Törnblom said. 'That's a great name. Where is it you come from again? I've never really been sure about that.'

Humlin waited anxiously for the answer.

'Nigeria.'

Humlin made a note of this answer.

'I had a couple of boxers here from Nigeria. Just a couple of years ago,' Törnblom said. 'But then one of them disappeared. People around here claimed he had supernatural powers, that his father was some kind of magician. I don't know about that. He sure didn't have any powers that kept him from being knocked out in the ring. The other one met a Finnish girl and last I heard they were living in Helsinki.'

Tea-Bag pointed to a pair of gloves lying on a chair.

'Can I try those?'

Törnblom nodded. He helped her on with the gloves then stood back as she started attacking a punchbag with surprising violence. Her thick jacket was still zipped up to her neck. Sweat started running down her face.

'Not bad. She's quick,' Törnblom whispered to Humlin. 'But I wonder who that punchbag is.'

'What do you mean?'

'I've learned a little bit about human psychology over the years. She's hitting someone. A lot of the guys who come down here hit their dads or uncles or whoever it is that's pissed them off.

Three times a week they come down here and beat someone up. People in the shape of punchbags, that is.'

Tea-Bag stopped abruptly. Törnblom helped her off with the gloves and turned to Humlin.

'The TV crew will be downstairs in the lecture room in about five minutes.'

Humlin wondered briefly if he should bring Tea-Bag with him or not. It seemed like the natural thing to do, but he decided he wanted to do the interview alone. A few moments alone in front of the camera might be just what his rather battered ego needed at this point.

'Wait here,' he said to Tea-Bag. 'I'll be back soon.'

Törnblom frowned.

'She's not coming with you?'

'I think I had better handle this alone.'

'But I thought this was about the girls? Why should you have the starring role?'

'This is not about a starring role. This is about the way I've decided to handle things.'

Tea-Bag sat down on a stool. Humlin turned and walked down the stairs without giving Törnblom a chance to continue the conversation.

*

The TV crew were already there, setting up their equipment. There were three of them: a camera operator, sound engineer and reporter. All three were women. Very young women.

'I take it you are waiting for me?'

'Don't think so. Where are the girls?'

Humlin was thrown off balance. The girl who had spoken

to him had a foreign accent and did not hide her impatience.

'My name is Azar Petterson,' she said. 'I will be doing this interview. But I had taken it for granted that the young women in your seminar would be present.'

'For now I would like to handle this situation with the utmost discretion,' Humlin answered. 'There's a chance that we cannot continue our work in peace if there is too much publicity and unwanted attention.'

Azar looked critically at him.

'What should I ask you?'

Humlin was starting to feel nervous.

'I thought it was your job to come up with the questions.'

Azar shrugged then turned to her crew.

'We'll do a short interview,' she said to the fat young woman holding the camera. 'Then we'll come back another time and shoot the girls.'

Humlin was very uncomfortable by this point. He had never been in a situation where the reporter showed such reluctance towards her task.

'Where do you want me to stand?'

'Right there is fine.'

The red light on the camera started glowing and the boom hung down over his head.

'Stensgården is one of the suburbs outside Gothenburg that has unfairly earned the reputation of a slum, simply because of the high percentage of immigrants that live here. Right now I am standing in Pelle Törnblom's Boxing Club where the author Jesper Hultin has been conducting a writing seminar for immigrant girls. Tell me, why did you decide to do this?'

'It felt important.'

Azar turned to the camera woman.

'We'll cut here.'

Humlin's mouth dropped.

'That's it?'

'We can use it as an intro to the segment with the girls.'

'My name is Humlin, not Hultin.'

'I'll cut that.'

Azar handed him her card.

'Call me a few days before your next meeting. And make sure the girls are going to be there.'

'They'll be here soon.'

'We don't have time to wait around.'

The TV crew packed up and left. Humlin felt humiliated, but did not have time to ponder his hurt feelings. Haiman came in through the door. Humlin's feelings turned to fear. Haiman was coming straight at him, holding a plastic bag in one hand.

'I did not mean to hurt you. I'm sorry.'

'That's all right.'

'If I had been really angry, the blow would have killed you.'

'I believe you.'

Haiman took a stained and worn rugby ball from the bag and held it out to Humlin.

'I hope we can be friends.'

'It's all behind us,' Humlin said breezily. 'I've already forgotten about it.'

Haiman frowned.

'I have not forgotten. I never forget what I do.'

'Of course we both remember what happened. But we just won't think about it any more.'

Haiman looked at him in a confused way. The furrow in his brow grew deeper.

'I don't understand you.'

Humlin broke out in a light sweat.

'I mean the same thing you do. Neither one of us has forgotten what happened but now you give me this wonderful rugby ball and we are friends.'

Haiman smiled.

'That's exactly what I mean. Do you like rugby?'

'It is one of my favourite sports.'

Törnblom appeared in the doorway and said it was time to start. When Humlin walked into the room he saw that Leila's large family was once again in attendance. Leyla, Tanya and Tea-Bag were sitting up in the front waiting for him. He pushed his way through the throng. The chatter died away. Humlin waited until there was complete silence in the room.

'We are now at the point where we can start the course in earnest. Tonight I want you to take twenty minutes to write down the most important thing that happened to you today. You can write in any format you please: a poem, whatever you like. But you only get twenty minutes. Then we'll read what you've written. Don't talk to each other. And please, no chatter from the audience.'

'What about what we wrote last time?' Leyla asked. 'Aren't we going to talk about that?'

The tone of her voice irritated Humlin, but he tried not to show it.

'Of course we'll talk about it. Just not right now.'

Leyla got up and walked over to a corner of the room, asking some of her relatives to move. Tea-Bag stayed in her chair hunched up in her thick coat. Tanya moved as far away from the others as possible. There was complete silence in the room. Humlin looked at Tea-Bag and her bowed head. She seemed completely oblivious of her surroundings. He got to his feet.

'I'll be back when the time is up,' he said, and left.

*

Törnblom had brewed some coffee in his office. Humlin looked at the old boxing posters and thought about how appropriate it was – not that it had ever been his decision – to hold these writing seminars in a place devoted to the art of fighting.

'Things are going well,' Törnblom said and squeezed himself into a chair behind the overflowing desk.

'How can you say that? We've hardly started.'

'Life isn't what you think it is, Humlin.'

Humlin was immediately on guard.

'And what do I think it is?'

'That this is an essentially peaceful and harmonious country.'

'Of course I don't think that.'

'Well, your poetry certainly doesn't betray any knowledge of reality.'

Humlin got up at once at this insult.

'Sit, sit,' Törnblom said. 'You're overreacting again. None of these girls have had an easy time of it. It's still not easy for them.'

Törnblom was right, Humlin thought. He sat down again with the feeling that he should try to get out of this whole thing as fast as he could. Maybe it would even be better to capitulate and write that thriller that Lundin and the oil executives wanted.

A noise at the door made him jump. Haiman was in the doorway.

'I just want to say that the girl called Tea-Bag isn't writing anything. If you like I can have a word with her so she'll do as she's told.'

Humlin could easily imagine Tea-Bag's reaction to such a thing.

'It's probably best to let her be,' he said.

'Then I think we should tell her to leave.'

'We can't force anyone to write against their will.'

'She will have a bad influence on the other two. They're writing. I've walked around and checked them.'

Humlin was glad he wasn't alone with Haiman.

'We don't need a writing police in this seminar.'

'I want order in the classroom.'

'If we leave them in peace I'm sure they'll do just fine.'

Haiman left the room, but more because of Törnblom's look than Humlin's words.

'I don't want him here,' Humlin hissed when Haiman had left. 'I don't want anyone walking around checking up on them.'

'Haiman is a good sort. He just wants to maintain order in there.'

'Is he one of Leila's relatives?'

'No, he's just a person with a strong sense of responsibility.'

*

After exactly twenty minutes Humlin went back into the room. Tea-Bag was still hunched up in her coat just as she had been when he left. Tanya and Leyla got up from their respective corners and returned to the table.

'Let's see what you've written,' Humlin said. 'Who wants to start?'

He turned to Tanya.

'Did you write anything?'

She looked at him angrily.

'Why do you ask that? Why wouldn't I have written anything?'

'You didn't write anything last time, that's all.'

Tanya waved her crumpled paper in front of him.

'Read it,' Humlin said.

Tanya took a breath. Tea-Bag was still enveloped by her voluminous coat and her thoughts. Leyla looked worried. Humlin sensed that she was nervous that Tanya might have written something better than her.

Tanya started reading.

'*The most important thing that happened to me today was that I woke up.*'

Humlin waited but there was nothing else.

'That was it?' he asked carefully.

Tanya turned on him furiously.

'You didn't say it had to be long. Did you? No, you didn't. This is – a poem.'

Humlin backtracked to the best of his ability.

'I was just checking,' he said. 'That was wonderful, Tanya. *The most important thing that happened to me today was that I woke up.* Wonderful. That is so true. And what would have happened if you hadn't woken up?'

'I would have been dead.'

Humlin realised he was not going to be able to get her to develop her insight any further. He turned to Tea-Bag.

'I haven't written anything.'

'Why not?'

'Nothing important happened today.'

'Nothing at all?'

'No.'

'Even when something doesn't feel profoundly important it can sometimes be worth writing down. Don't you think?'

Leyla suddenly jumped in as if to defend Tea-Bag.

'Did anything important happen to *you* today?'

Humlin gave up and was about to ask Leyla to read what she had written when Tea-Bag grabbed Tanya's pad of paper and ripped out a blank page. Then she stood up and spoke, as if reading from the blank page.

*

She, the other one, the one who is not me but who could have been my sister, the one who sells the yellow plastic frogs in the street next to the florist, she has become the only friend I have, she has told me that her name is Laurinda, just like her mother, the old Laurinda. She has a white mark that runs down her cheek like a dried-up riverbed and continues over her shoulder. She swears it is true, not as if she were swearing an oath by God because she no longer believes in such things – how could she when she has lived for so long as a person who is not allowed to exist? She proves it in another way. She has said we live in a time when no one knows any more what another's name really is, no one knows where anyone comes from or where they are going. It is when you get to some place where you don't have to run any more that you can say your real name, and her name is Laurinda.

She has been on the run for nine years and everyone around her has whipped her with their invisible whips so that she won't stay, so that she won't exist, won't be seen, won't stop, but will keep going the whole time as if she were in eternal orbit, an orbit where life slowly crumbles away into death and emptiness. It has gone on for so long that she has started becoming invisible even to herself. She can no longer see her face in the mirror or her reflection in the shop windows. The only thing she sees is a shadow, moving abruptly as if it too were afraid of being caught.

And she has also become invisible on the inside; once where there were memories there is now only a shell as if from the nuts that a monkey has eaten and tossed away. No real memories, just the shell of reminiscence, not even smells are left, everything is gone. She only recalls the music as a noise in the distance, the songs that her mother, the old Laurinda, used to sing for her.

Sometimes she is overcome by a blinding rage, it rushes up in her like a volcano, a volcano that has been sleeping for a thousand years and suddenly awakens with a roar. Then she speaks to her mother: Be quiet! Don't speak. Why can't you let your mouth be closed? Words are not coming out any longer, your insides are coming out. Be quiet!

You don't have to speak any longer about my father's head that was blown off by the grenade. I have that splinter inside me, it is tearing me up inside. I don't want to talk about what happened to my father, it is so terrible, but you force me to with your words. You speak so much I have started hating all the words. I don't know what they mean any more, do they mean anything? If I ask you something you start speaking about something completely different. I get no answers and I don't know what you are talking about, but the worst thing is that even you don't understand all the words coming out of your mouth. It is making me crazy, all the words coming out of your mouth are beginning to stink and if you don't shut up my nails will stop growing. It's true, you talk so much my body is going to stop working.

I know you don't like it when I talk about these things but I need you to know how it is. I can hardly piss any more, even if we're not supposed to talk about that, it is something so natural it has become unnatural, when I was little I was made to understand that it was as shameful as lying. I never dared tell you when I wet my pants even though it was perfectly natural, all children wet their pants. Have you ever been a child? Perhaps you deny that you were once a child too, that it is something your parents lie about. Is that how it is? And that is why you torment me?

The other place we won't even talk about, it hurts all the time and the stuff that comes out is green like sticky seaweed and it's so disgusting it makes me vomit. Gall and shit is what it is. And my periods aren't regular any more; blood gushes out at any time without warning – haven't you wondered why I'm always washing myself? But I don't care any more. Nothing you say is of any importance.

My toenails are growing, but not the nails on my fingers – well, my thumbnails are but not on the other fingers. The nails are curling over and growing crooked. They don't look like nails any more, they look like fish scales. All of me is turning into a lizard – you are turning me into a cave lizard. That's a species that only exists among people like me, people who are chased in and out of trucks and containers and don't know if they're alive or if they're dead and lying at the bottom of the sea. I look in the mirror in the morning and I don't believe what I see there, I try not to but I can't help it and I look in the mirror and I think I see an old hag staring back at me.

When I was little there was a widow who lived in one of those houses that wasn't a house any more, it had collapsed and lay along the path that went up to the mountains – do you remember her? I remember her perfectly, she was so hideously ugly. We were afraid of her but I understand now that she was nice and just old, not ugly, perhaps she had simply lived too long – that is exactly what I look like now when I look in the mirror, like that old widow. She must have been very poor. I don't think she had children and she was probably already dead without really knowing.

The eyes that I see – I'm talking about my eyes now, not the old widow's – are so horrible. They stare back at me with hatred. I don't want those eyes, they're not mine, and my tongue – do you want to see my tongue? – no, you don't, it has a strange furry coating and it feels as if I have an animal in my mouth and that's because you talk too much. Can't you just be quiet, if not for my sake then for someone else's? My father is dead; you can't do anything more to him. I loved my father and I loved you too but I want you to be quiet. I know it's hard for you and you are afraid – if anyone can understand that it's me, I don't even think my father really understood it. If you don't stop talking I'm going to claw out your eyes. Watch out for my thumbnails, I mean it.

You're always lying. We'll be there soon, soon we'll exist again, oh my God, when will that be? Tell me! No, don't say anything, I don't want to know, it doesn't matter anyway since it isn't true what you say. I am a prisoner of my invisibility, not just because I'm on the run but because you are keeping me prisoner, you keep saying we'll be there soon but you have become a prison guard. Do you want to know what I think? Sometimes I think I'll just disappear, that I'm going to let myself freeze to death just so I won't hear your lies any more. I don't mean to hurt you, I'm telling you this because I love you and because you can't manage to formulate a single sensible thought any more. Can you understand that I'm not being mean, can you understand that? You will if you listen to me, not the words but the meaning. Are you listening to me or my words? Can you see that I'm standing here or have I become invisible for you too? And what's the point in that case?

I don't really know what the point is any more, but I have to make a decision now because otherwise nothing will happen. In the middle of all this talking and spitting I've discovered something. Do you know what it is? I'm not sure that I can explain it and even if I could I'm not sure that you would understand it, or would want to understand it since you always insist you know best. But you don't know what's best any more. I don't either but at least I'm trying. It's as if for the first time I feel something that seems like it has to do with freedom – can you understand that? A strange feeling of not being locked up any more and what I have the most trouble understanding is how one can feel the least bit free sitting in a cave and not even existing.

I'm not a child any more. I'm not an adult either, but I understand something now that I didn't before, when I was careful never to offend you, when my whole life centred on this. That was thanks to the tradition you were always talking about, the respect that is really just another word for the noose around my neck since I was born a woman and not a man. I look at the others my age, the girls, I mean, the ones who live in this country, not the boys, don't worry I only look at them in secret since I'm actually quite shy. I'm not going to change that about myself even with a new name. It would make you crazy to see them – the girls, I mean – they don't go hiding behind shawls and respect and traditions and they aren't afraid of fathers who think they can do whatever they like. I see something I haven't seen before and maybe it's not a good thing but I want to find that out for myself. I'm not going to let you answer for me. I'm going to judge for myself.

Up until now you were my hero, Mum. Until now. But not any more. Of course I love you, I do, don't think any different. I'm going to love you as long as I live, I would probably give my life for you if it came to that and I know you would do the same for me but this can't go on any longer. If we're going to make it out of this cave we're going to have to do what I say from now on.

That's how she used to talk to the old Laurinda. It was the volcano that spewed out the glowing remains of feelings and thoughts she could no longer control. And the old Laurinda listened, she turned her face away but she never said anything.

Every day it is as if she falls off a cliff, as if every day she wakes up in a new place in a body she doesn't recognise. Even her heartbeat is unfamiliar, as if someone is tapping a secret code inside her body, a prisoner in there who is sending his message out into the world. That's what her heart sounds like.

Sometimes she senses memories of dreams she doesn't know if she has had or if someone else passed by while she was sleeping and left them beside her, as if she were already dead and lying on the stretcher. She can sometimes remember a truck driving down the side of a cliff while grenades explode all around them. The last image she has of her father is when his head is torn away by the grenade. Only she, her mother, and siblings were left. They arrived in Sweden on a ferry that shook like an animal. They had disposed of their papers by tearing them up into small pieces and flushing them down the toilet because the unwritten rules of refugees insisted on this, that it was harder to get rid of a person without papers than if one still had a name, an identity. This is what it has come to that the ones who don't exist are more true to themselves than those who refuse to give up their identities.

In Sweden they were provided with socks, warm coats and teabags in a chilly youth hostel right next to the cold grey sea that was the border to all that had happened before. It was as if they had torn up all their memories of their earlier life along with their papers. Kind people with frozen smiles had shown them to this place and then left them there. At night they had picked frozen apples and raided bird feeders. They had arrived around Christmas time. The old Laurinda understood that they had finally arrived at their destination and had lain down to die.

After that they had broken up. Her siblings were sent away to be cared for, Laurinda was also supposed to be cared for but she ran away. She walked along a road that went through the brown fields and then someone had stopped and given her a ride and each time this happened her silence was so frightening that the driver stopped and kicked her out. She continued walking. Each step was like a struggle with the earth that was trying to claim her but she didn't stop until she found the black rubbish bag by the side of the road. It must have fallen from a truck. Perhaps someone had simply thrown it there.

The bag was full of yellow plastic frogs, the whole ditch was full of them. At first she thought they were real frogs that had frozen to death and she had tossed them back because she was afraid they might be poisonous. But when the frogs didn't move she picked one up again and that's when she saw the price tag on its underside. She had kept the bag and when she arrived at the next town she poured them out on the pavement and waited. She wasn't sure if she was waiting for the frogs to come back to life or for someone to buy them but she didn't even care.

That was where she was when I came past. When I saw Laurinda crouching over her pile of frozen plastic frogs I knew I had to stop. I asked her if she had seen my monkey but she shook her head and I stayed and then she told me her story. I remember her voice. It was like the voice of the earth, of earth and pain, a hoarse voice that comes singing from a great distance.

I can't remember when this happened any more. It might have been yesterday or a thousand years ago. It doesn't matter. But today when I woke up I remembered what she had told me and the fact that this memory that has been gone so long has now returned is the most important thing that happened to me today.

*

Tea-Bag finished talking and sat down. The blank piece of paper she had been holding she now folded and laid in front of her on the table. Everyone in the room was silent and still. Humlin wondered what they all felt, if they felt that they had been through something earth-shattering, as if Tea-Bag's narrative had painted the room in new colours. It's deeper than that, he thought, but it goes so deep I can't express what it is.

In this atmosphere that was like the silence after an earthquake, Leyla got up. Humlin thought she looked like she had put on even more weight since last time. But nonetheless she seemed to shimmer. She was smiling.

It was as if Tea-Bag's big smile was being passed around the girls like a baton. Now, in the moment that Leyla got to her feet, it was her turn to wear it.

15

The words started coming out of Leyla's mouth first as a gentle trickle and then as an ever-increasing flood. She spoke in a low voice, forcing Humlin to lean forward to catch her words about the unexpected things that had happened to her on this frozen late-winter's day.

*

Oh God, I say, oh God, and I know I shouldn't use his name in vain but I am anyway, I'm going to say 'Oh God', because nothing was the way it should have been when I woke up today: everything was wrong. I remember thinking that it was going to be just another forgettable day. Yet another day that was not going to leave any traces, only sweep through my life like a stray wind. Another day that would make me feel like it was mocking me.

It was far too early in the morning. I hate waking up before I have to but I had been dreaming about apples – I was driven wild by them in the dream – apples that gleamed on the outside but tasted of rotten fish, or perhaps more like the remains of that cat I found once as a child. It was lying on the other side of a fence and someone had cut the paws off and it was covered in maggots. Me and some kids beat it with sticks, although perhaps all we managed to do was hit the fence, or maybe it was each other. I don't know why we were doing it. Perhaps we just needed to hit something since life was so hard.

I can't say for sure what it was that woke me up, if it was the apples or the memory of that cat, but I was furious. It was only six o'clock in the morning and I never wake up at six of my own free will. I suppose that's not actually true, strictly speaking; I often wake up early but then I manage to fall back asleep. That's a habit from when I was very little, probably from around the time that my brother Ahmed was shot. I used to wake up because I was afraid my father wouldn't be there when I got up in the morning. I was always afraid someone would try to kill him too. I thought I could see Ahmed standing in the shadows telling me everything was all right, that I should go back to sleep. Every night was the same, even though I knew Ahmed was dead. I had seen him when they carried him away on the stretcher and his face was so peaceful, as if he were sleeping up there on the stretcher being carried away on the angry men's shoulders. I woke up every night and every night he was there to comfort me and tell me to go back to sleep.

Now I don't see him any more. Perhaps he doesn't feel comfortable here in the Swedish light. But I wake up anyway and sometimes it takes me a long time to fall back to sleep. But this morning I didn't want to wake up, I wanted to sleep. Why should I wake up and go to a school where I don't understand anything anyway? I don't know what it was but I got up because I was so anxious. I put on my clothes and went outside. It can be beautiful in this country at dawn. There are almost no people around and the tall apartment buildings look like frozen pillars carved from huge granite slabs.

It was cold and suddenly I knew I had to visit my grandmother who lives in Nydalen. She and my father, her son-in-law, don't get on so she can't live with us. I don't know why they fight. We gather at every holiday and once every other month she comes over to eat: Ramadan, the end of Ramadan, all of these holidays we celebrate together but otherwise she and my father never want to see each other. I looked in on my parents before I left; sleeping people always make me nervous, they seem so unreachable as if they are already dead.

I can't remember the last time I went out so early in the morning. There were no people anywhere. I walked over to the tram stop and there was a man there called Johansson and he's Swedish, although I think he's originally from Russia. He gets drunk every Friday and he hangs around the tram stop, never going anywhere, just standing there as if he were waiting for someone who never comes and the whole time he mumbles to himself. Me and my sister tried to get really close to him one time to hear what he was saying but all we heard was 'Trouble, trouble, too much trouble.' It is as if he were saying his Friday prayers there. He must be close to a hundred years old, maybe he's already dead and doesn't know it, maybe he has no relatives to bury him.

The tram was almost empty. I sat in the very back. I like it when the cars are empty; it's like riding in a white luxury limousine. It seems to make the trip last longer and you can imagine that you are on your way to anywhere, like Hollywood or New Zealand, which is a place I've dreamed of because it's on the other side of the earth. I've seen it on maps in school and on a computer: Auckland, Wellington, and all the sheep. But I know I'll never get there.

The tram line to Nydalen goes through the city centre. It's like travelling from a country called 'Stensgården' to another called 'City Centre' and then crossing the border into Nydalen. Maybe some day we'll have to show our passports when we get on the tram; whenever I go to the centre on Saturday night it's the same thing. I don't feel welcome, at the very least I don't feel as if I belong.

Sitting on the tram I started wondering what I was doing. My grandmother was probably still sleeping. She can be sulky or happy, you never know until you get there. Somewhere close to the bridge it started to snow. I think snow is beautiful but I wish it was warm like sand. Why can't the snow be related to sand instead of ice? But it is beautiful. Snow was falling over the river and on a boat that was leaving the city. The sun had just come up over the horizon. I had never seen it look like that before. Mostly yellow, but a little red where the rays hit the clouds and then blue behind it.

A few people with familiar faces boarded the tram. I recognised a man – I think he is Greek and has a newspaper stand in the centre – he yawned so widely you could see all the way down into his intestines. He didn't sit down even though there were plenty of empty seats. Then some guys got on who looked like football fans. They were wearing blue and white scarves and acted confused, as though they had been in hibernation and woken up too early. I've never seen such grey faces, grey like the cliffs that Dad and I dive off in the summer. I got such a strong urge just then – it's terrible – but I wanted to stand up and start telling everyone about the slum where I was born. I almost had to jump off the tram to stop myself.

People kept getting on and off, a lot of people got off at the hospital. Most of them were women who probably worked there. And then we started leaving the city again. Because of its name you would think Nydalen – New-valley – lay in a valley, but it doesn't, it's up on a hill. My grandmother has tried to find out how it got its name but even though she's asked everyone she's never found an answer. 'The superintendent is going crazy,' I heard Dad say once to Mum. 'If she doesn't stop asking silly questions they're going to lock her up one day.'

In Nydalen there are nine high-rise apartment buildings on top of a steep hillside. My grandmother says people have killed themselves by jumping off the cliff but she says a lot of things and even though she is my grandmother I can tell you she tells a lot of lies. Maybe that's why Dad has such a hard time with her. She lies to me as well. She'll call out of the blue and say there were four masked men in her apartment – she lives alone except when her cousin who lives up in the north is visiting – and that they have taken everything she owns. But when Mum goes over to see, it turns out there's nothing missing, only some little thing my grandmother can't find, and then when Mum helps her find it there's no longer any talk of the four masked men.

My grandmother tells lies, everyone does, I do it too, not to mention Dad, but my grandmother is better than us in making them sound believable. She doesn't know anything about this country, she just talks about how afraid she used to be of the people who were going to come and kill us in the night. But now she's also grown afraid of the cold and she doesn't dare go outside. She even thinks it's cold in summer sometimes when it's actually sweltering. We have to open her windows when she isn't looking, otherwise she thinks it's going to kill her. She can't speak a word of Swedish and when she got ill one time we had to go in the ambulance with her and she was convinced that the doctors – who she thought looked too young – were going to kill her.

But my grandmother – her name is Nasrin – can also do things no one else can. She can tell how a person is really feeling just from looking at their face. I know, because I can go over to her place and be feeling down but smile and laugh and then she says 'Why are you laughing when you are crying inside?' You can't fool her.

I got off the tram in Nydalen and it had started to snow even harder. The ground was almost totally white. Nana lives on the ground floor in the building that is the furthest away from the edge of the cliff. I walked into the stairwell where someone had scrawled 'Terror' on the wall and again I started wondering what I was doing there. Why wasn't I still at home or on my way to school? But I rang the doorbell and thought maybe she'll be happy to see me. I know she likes me, she pays almost no attention to anyone else when she comes over to our house.

The door opened and at first I thought I had made a mistake. A young man had opened the door. He was about my age and he stared at me as much as I stared at him. I saw at once that he was Swedish, not because he was blond, which he wasn't, but because he had that look in his eyes that only those people born in this country have when they look at people who are not from here. Oh God, I thought, but I kept looking at him and he kept looking at me.

'Who are you?' he asked.

'Who are you?' I replied.

'My name is Torsten and I'm Nasrin's assistant.'

'Nana doesn't have an assistant. You're a burglar.'

He started to protest but I was panicking at the thought that something had happened to Nana. I had never heard that she had any help at home and I was sure I would have since Dad loves to talk about Nana even though he can't stand her. But Nana was sat in a chair watching TV, even though she couldn't understand a single thing the people were saying. She lit up when she saw me.

'I dreamed about you last night,' she said. 'There was a red bird pecking at the pillow next to my ear. The sound forced its way all through my dream and that's how I knew you would come. Every time a bird visits me in my dreams I know you are on your way. When I dream of wriggling fish washed up on the shore it is your father who is coming.'

'I didn't know you had help, Nana.'

Nana looked momentarily confused, as if she too had no idea what the stranger with the duster was doing in her apartment. Then she waved me closer and whispered that it was a secret. She and Mum had agreed to go behind Dad's back on this since he was so stingy. Mum paid for the help, and arranged for Nana's other children to chip in and Dad was on no account to hear of any of it.

I asked her why she hadn't come to me for help with cleaning the apartment and combing her hair but when she said she didn't want me to neglect my studies I felt bad for the first time that I almost never go to school. But of course I didn't say anything about that. I took off my coat and the whole time we were talking the guy called Torsten was dusting Nana's photographs. Nana's apartment almost looks like a photo studio because there are so many photographs on all the walls. There are even old photographs in the bathroom that are so faded you can hardly make out the outlines of people's faces any more.

Technically in our religion we aren't supposed to even own photographs. I don't know why exactly. But Nana wants all these old pictures on her walls, she says the photos ward off evil spirits and the thoughts of those who don't wish her well – the ones who forced us to flee. This way, wherever she is in the apartment, she has loving eyes looking at her and that helps calm her down. Every time I come over Nana leans on my arm and then we walk around together looking at all the pictures. Even if I have been there two days in a row she forgets that she's just showed me the pictures. She tells me who they are and what their names are and says they are family, even though it's not true.

Mum is the one who told me that ever since she came to Sweden Nana has been collecting old pictures that others have thrown out.

She's looked for them around the rubbish bins and in the basement storage area, and every single picture she's found has gone up on the wall. She gives the faces names and makes them cousins or second cousins or even more remote family connections. She has given them dates of birth and decided if they died peacefully in their beds or in terrible accidents. She has given them occupations and let them be poets or singers or remarkable prophets who have wandered in the desert and had visions, or women who have given birth to children with diamonds in their mouths. Even though I know nothing of what she tells me is true I always go around with her and she never changes a single word of her stories. These pictures are Nana's family and sometimes it feels as if it were all quite real.

The whole time we walked around together Torsten was cleaning in the background. I felt him looking at me when my back was turned and I blushed even though he couldn't see my face. The picture Nana always ends with is of a man carrying a rifle. He is laughing and Nana calls him Ajeb, the chieftain who hides out somewhere in the desert and who will one day perform a miracle that will transform our lives. I once tried to press Nana on exactly what this miracle was going to be, but that made her angry and she slapped me. It is the only time she's ever done that. She doesn't want me to ask anything, just listen.

When we were finished with our tour of the photographs and Nana was back in her chair in front of the TV with a blanket over her legs, Torsten came and said he was done for the day and that he was going to be leaving now but that he would be back on Friday. I was disappointed and wanted to say something but I didn't dare. Nana patted him on the cheek and then he left.

'He's a good boy,' Nana said and ran a hand over her hair. 'I never knew before that a man could be so good at combing hair.'

I saw then that Nana's hair had been brushed so it gleamed. She has long hair that reaches all the way down her back. I couldn't understand how Nana who is so afraid of everything in this country could let a boy like Torsten comb her hair. I wanted to ask her more about him, where he came from and how they had found him, but I didn't because I was afraid she would get angry.

Suddenly Nana grabbed my hand and pointed to the screen. There was a programme on about a refugee camp in Africa. A little black girl – so very thin – was walking around in a desert landscape dotted with low bushes. She walked slowly and hesitantly and then she pointed to something on the ground. Suddenly crushed skulls and white pieces of bone appeared on the TV screen. The girl cried and she was speaking a language I couldn't understand but I could follow the subtitles that said her parents had been killed here by soldiers who had been crazed by alcohol and blood lust and she had seen everything and everyone had died except her because her mother fell on top of her when she died.

We sat completely still and Nana was holding my arm so tightly it almost hurt. She forced us to watch that girl who wandered around and cried among all the dead and all at once both Nana and I started crying. Suddenly the girl turned towards the camera or the people operating the camera and it looked as if she were turning towards us, as if she had heard us crying. Then the programme ended simply by cutting to a black screen and then – without even a moment's pause – a programme came on about cultivating tomatoes in a cold climate.

It was quite a shock to find ourselves looking at tomatoes after that girl weeping among her dead. I tried to hear if the sound of her crying reached the studio where they were talking about soil acidity but there was nothing. Nana grabbed the remote control angrily. She pushes all the buttons – since she doesn't know how it works – until the TV shut down. Then we drank some tea without saying anything. It was as if that little girl was in the apartment with us. I thought about her and I thought about Torsten and Nana was thinking about something so far away that she closed her eyes and forgot to touch her tea until it was cold. It was still snowing outside but not as much. Nana finally pushed her teacup away and asked me why I wasn't in school.

'There's no school today.'

'How can that be?'

'It's some kind of holiday – I don't know exactly.'

'All the children in this building left for school as normal.'

It was getting harder and harder to lie, but there was no way out of it now.

'It's a holiday today in Stensgården.'

Nana nodded. I don't know why I returned to the idea of Nydalen and Stensgården being different countries, just like I had been thinking about on the bus when I was still irritated by the fact that I couldn't sleep. But Nana accepted my answer and didn't pressure me with any more questions. I washed the teacups and then I was at a loss as to what I should do next. I couldn't go home because then Mum would nag at me for not being in school. I supposed I could go to school late and say I had had a stomach ache or that Nana had been ill – no one really cares if you go or not. But I didn't want to go there today. I didn't want to stay with Nana either. If I did she would make me play this card game that she has invented, a game I still don't understand all the rules to and that takes several hours.

I stood up and said I was going home. Nana nodded again, got up awkwardly from her chair and stroked my cheek. When she does that her eyes are the most beautiful thing I've ever seen. I get completely relaxed when she touches me, I stop thinking about the cat with its paws chopped off and I feel how the world calms down around me. When I was younger I used to imagine that I would one day see the man I was going to marry at one of these times when she was touching me. But God help me – the only thing I saw this time was Torsten's face.

I flinched as if Nana's hand had burned me – she couldn't know that I had seen Torsten and not one of the beautiful men she used to talk about like one of Mum's cousins who wasn't simply a picture on the wall but a living person who lived somewhere in a country far away or in a refugee camp. We have relatives all over the world, in Australia, the USA, even in the Philippines. It is as if families on the run are shattered by something other than just grenades. The flight and fear tears us apart and those parts land in all kinds of places – we don't even know where. But we always try to find them afterwards.

I remember a time two years ago when we got a letter from Taala, one of Mum's four sisters who had disappeared and who had now traced us and said she lived in a city called Minneapolis in America. Mum started dancing when she got this letter, Dad sat on the sofa and watched her, he looked so young, like a little boy, and he watched her moving through the rooms of our apartment almost as if he were embarrassed to see her happy after so many years of fear and grief and imprisonment. She danced so the walls started crumbling and the windows opened and she stepped out of herself and she became the person she really was and all because Taala wasn't dead. Taala had breathed on her through that letter and memories had risen up from her words and Mum danced as if she were a young girl again.

But when Nana touched my cheek I saw Torsten. He looked just like he had when he opened the front door and saw me. He was holding a duster in one hand and he was wearing a silly red apron with blue hearts and we stared at each other. You can't love someone who wears a red apron with blue hearts. Nana looked at me and wanted to know what I was thinking. I always blush when I get questions I don't want to answer and she noticed of course and asked me sternly if I had been thinking about a boy and who was it? I don't know how I thought of this but the words came of themselves as if they had been stored inside me for so long they needed to get out.

'I was just thinking of Ahmed.'

'And you call that "just"! To be thinking of your dead brother!'

'I don't mean it like that.'

'How do you mean it?'

'It was so unexpected. It was as if he was there in your hand.'

Nana calmed down.

'He is always in my hand,' she said. 'He is in my hand like I am in God's hand.'

Then she walked back to her chair in front of the TV, pushed some buttons on the remote control and started watching. A programme came on with several men seated around a table, discussing something. Sheep, I think. They talked about sheep-shearing. I said goodbye, took my coat and left. When I came out I looked down into the snow and tried to figure out which footprints belonged to Torsten and which were the ones that I had left.

Then I started walking back to the tram stop and it was light now and the snowflakes didn't feel cold for some reason. I wondered what I should do. When I entered the underpass that leads to the tram stop I stopped short. Torsten was standing there. I stared at him. I thought I must be mistaken. But it was him. He was just standing there and even though I couldn't know, I did know. There was only one reason why he would be standing there and that was that he was waiting for me.

*

Leyla stopped reading abruptly. A man had just entered the room and Humlin recognised him. It was Leyla's father.

'I haven't told you any of this,' she hissed. 'I haven't said anything. Nothing about Nana, nothing about the underpass.'

'What happened after that?' Tanya asked.

'I can't tell you now. Don't you get what I'm saying?'

Leyla's father approached the table. He was short and stocky. He looked around at them suspiciously and then turned to Humlin.

'What is going on here?'

'We're conducting a writing seminar.'

'It shouldn't start without me.'

'I'm sorry if there's been some kind of misunderstanding. I start when all the girls are present. I can't be expected to keep track of all their families.'

'I am not simply a relative; I am Leyla's father.'

He turned to his daughter and grabbed her arm roughly.

'Where have you been all day?'

'At school.'

'No, you haven't. They called home and asked why you weren't there. Where have you been?'

'At the hospital.'

'Are you sick?'

'No,' Tea-Bag said, interrupting, 'she felt dizzy and went to hospital. She's had nightmares and difficulty sleeping.'

Leyla nodded. Her father paused, clearly hesitating as to whether or not he should believe this.

'I can't allow Leyla to participate in this course any longer.'

Humlin saw how Leyla tried to swallow her disappointment – or was it anger? He looked at her round face, shiny with sweat, and thought that her plump exterior hid not only a beautiful face but also a strong will.

'What exactly is the problem?' Humlin asked.

'She's not telling me the truth.'

'What is it that isn't true?'

'She hasn't been to the hospital.'

'I have too,' Leyla said softly.

Her father turned and shouted at her, a tirade of smattering sounds of which Humlin understood nothing. Leyla bowed her head submissively, but Humlin thought he could still see the streak of rebellion in her bearing. Törnblom stepped up and looked as if he were preparing for a boxing match.

'I'm sure we can solve this somehow.'

He didn't get any further. Haiman rose to his feet at that moment and approached the table.

'Of course Leyla will continue her work here.'

'You are not her father. I am her father, I decide.'

'Let the girl decide for herself.'

The exchange between Leyla's father and Haiman grew more heated. They used a kind of Swedish Humlin had never heard before. Suddenly Törnblom jumped in.

'We're expecting a TV crew to arrive soon. I would like to suggest that Leyla's father be present for the interview as a representative of the parents. You would be interviewed with Leyla and Jesper. Damn it, we can't have fights over little things like this.'

Haiman gave Törnblom a stern look, and Törnblom in turn gave Humlin the same stern look. Humlin could not recall a previous mention of this supposed return of the TV crew. He assumed it was an attempt by Törnblom to diffuse the situation.

'It is not a little thing when a father believes his daughter has lied to him.'

'But I'm sure she was at the hospital, like she said. Weren't you, Leyla?'

Leyla nodded. Humlin heard Tanya mutter with anger on her behalf.

'I was just going to suggest the same thing,' Humlin said. 'That you as Leyla's father participate in the interview with us.'

Leyla's father looked unsure for a moment.

'And what would I say?'

'That you are proud of your daughter.'

Leyla's father thought about this.

'What exactly am I proud of?'

'That she wants to learn to write, that she wants to be a serious writer.'

He shook his head.

'I don't care what she does. The most important thing is that she doesn't lie to her family.'

Leyla looked pleadingly at her father.

'Dad, I want to be a soap star or a TV personality – if I don't make it as a writer, that is. This might be my only chance.'

'I also want to be interviewed.'

Everyone looked at Haiman who had made the last comment. Humlin was starting to feel tired.

'There isn't time for everyone to be interviewed.'

'I have much to say of great importance for the Swedish people.'

'I don't doubt that, Haiman, but this is hardly the right time and place to air your views.'

'I will not participate if he does,' Leyla's father said.

Humlin looked at the people around him. The main subjects of the conflict were still seated and following the discussion with sombre faces.

'TV programmes like this are often very short,' Humlin started carefully. 'If everyone is to have a say it will take far too long for the slot they have in mind for us.'

'Then we leave and Leyla will not be able to continue her participation here,' Leyla's father said firmly. 'She cannot be left on her own. After a few times here she has started lying to us. She has never done that before.'

Leyla drew a deep breath.

'You're right, Dad. I didn't go to the hospital. I don't know why I said that. I went to the library in the city centre. I started reading and forgot all about time. I was there to study so that I can do better in school. And to read books by good authors so that I will learn to write better.'

Leyla's father regarded her in silence.

'What did you read?' he asked finally.

'I found a book about rugby.'

'There are books about rugby? What am I supposed to think? Is she lying to me again?'

Haiman got up. Humlin was starting to realise that Leyla was craftier than he had expected.

'There are great books about rugby,' Haiman said. 'She is speaking the truth. This initiative to go to the library is something a father should encourage.'

An appreciative murmur was heard from the audience, mainly

people from Leyla's large family who had not said anything until now. Her father now turned to them and threw out a question that raised a heated debate. The voices died down after a while.

'We have decided,' he said. 'I will stay here and be interviewed by the TV people. We accept for now that Leyla continues the course.'

As Leyla's many family members filed out of the room Humlin thought that he had just won his first fight in Törnblom's boxing club. Leyla's relief was palpable. She sank down on her chair and Tanya squeezed her hand. To Humlin's surprise Törnblom grabbed a towel and waved it at Leyla as if she were a boxer waiting between rounds.

*

Naturally the TV crew never turned up. After an hour Törnblom pretended to call them and then declared that there had been a mix-up with the day. Leyla's father looked put out but Humlin hastened to tell him that the delay would simply enable him to prepare his statements more carefully. Then he turned back to his students.

'Write down your stories,' Humlin said. 'Write what you have told us today – everything. A story without an end is not a good piece of work.'

He saw that Leyla understood.

It was snowing when they came back out on the street. Leyla disappeared with her family, Tanya whispered something after them that Humlin didn't hear. Törnblom locked the door and Tea-Bag ran around in circles making patterns in the wet snow. Tanya pulled her cap on.

'Are you still in the Yüksel family's apartment?' Humlin asked.

'No, they're back.'

'Where are you living now?'

Tanya shrugged her shoulders.

'Maybe in this empty apartment on the other side of the square. Maybe somewhere else. I haven't decided yet.'

Humlin had been meaning to talk to her about the little girl in the photograph, but it was as if she knew what he was thinking. Before he could say anything, she put her arm around Tea-Bag and the two of them left. He watched them walk away and wondered what he was really looking at.

Törnblom drove him to the station.

'It's going great,' he said. 'You should feel good about it.'

'No,' Humlin said. 'It's not going well. I have this constant feeling that I'm on the brink of an enormous disaster.'

'Now you're exaggerating again.'

Humlin didn't bother to reply.

*

Törnblom dropped him off at the train station and Humlin walked into the waiting room. Suddenly he stopped in his tracks. The thought of going back to Stockholm that evening was starting to feel like an impossibility. He sat down. Tea-Bag's face flashed through his mind, then Tanya's and, last of all, Leyla's. He wondered if he was ever going to see her move again from the place by the underpass where she and her story had so suddenly been frozen.

He left the station and checked into the nearest hotel. Before he turned out the light and fell asleep he sat with the phone in his hand for a long time. Andrea. But he didn't call her.

*

He left the hotel at a quarter past eleven the next day. For the first time in a long while he felt fully rested. While he was waiting for his train to arrive he made several calls to the various phone numbers belonging to Burén, but to no avail. Before he turned off the phone he listened to the voice messages that had been left for the original owner, a detective inspector by the name of Sture who clearly spent a lot of his time betting on horses. A person with a lisp had called several times and left the message that 'Lokus Harem is a sure bet.' He was just about to turn the phone off when he saw that there was a text message as well. He stared at the words. Then he realised it was for him, not the unknown Officer Sture.

It was a short message, only four words long: *Help. Tanya. Call Leyla.*

At that moment the train pulled into the station. But Humlin did not get on.

16

He called the boxing club. A young boy who could barely speak comprehensible Swedish answered the phone. After a few minutes Törnblom came to the phone.

'It's Jesper. What's Leyla's phone number?'

'How would I know that? Where are you?'

Humlin had already decided to lie. Why, he wasn't quite sure.

'Back in Stockholm. I thought her brother was a student at your club?'

'I never take down any phone numbers. It makes no sense. People come and go all the time.'

'What about her last name?'

'I can't remember. But I'll check if there's anyone else who might know.'

It took Törnblom almost ten minutes to get back to the phone.

'Allaf.'

'Can you spell that?'

'How would I know how it's spelled? Why do you sound so worked up over this?'

'Because I *am* worked up. I have to go now.'

Humlin called information and got a number for the last name 'Allaf'. A woman answered the phone in a low voice, as if she were afraid of it.

'I'm trying to get hold of Leyla,' Humlin said.

He received no answer. A man who spoke in the same hushed tones came on the line.

'I'm looking for Leyla.'

There was no answer. Another man came on the line.

'I'm looking for Leyla.'

'Whom am I speaking with?'

'This is Jesper Humlin. I need to ask Leyla if she has Tanya's number.'

'Who?'

'Her friend, Tanya.'

'Do you mean Irina?'

'I mean the other girl participating in the writing seminar, the non-African one.'

'That is Irina.'

'Perhaps I can speak with Leyla directly?' Humlin asked gingerly.

'She's not at home.'

'Do you know if she has Tanya's – or Irina's – number written down somewhere?'

'I'll see. Please hold.'

The phone was starting to make strange noises. The battery was about to run out. The man came back on the line and gave Humlin a number. Humlin fumbled around for something to write with.

'What is that noise?' the man asked.

'My battery is about to run out. If we are cut off, it's not because I'm being impolite.'

'We are very happy that you have decided to come back.'

Humlin found a pen.

'Would you mind repeating that number?'

Before the man had a chance to run through the number more

than once, the phone died. Humlin wrote down what he thought was the correct number, on his hand. He went up to a pay phone and dialled, only to reach a noisy car repair shop in Skövde. He reordered the last few digits and tried again. This time a young girl barely old enough to have learned how to speak gurgled into the phone. Humlin tried yet another version of the number and this time he recognised the voice. It was Tanya.

'What's happened?'

'Tea-Bag was about to get caught.'

'What do you mean?'

'The police almost got her. They also found some mobile phones in a bag that she had. I don't think the cops liked finding their own phones.'

Humlin tried to think straight.

'Can you tell me what happened from the beginning, and more calmly?'

'We need help. You have to get over here. Where are you?'

'In Gothenburg. What can I do?'

'You're a famous writer, right? So, help us. I can't talk any more.'

'Where's "here"?'

'Just meet me at the boxing club.'

The line went dead.

*

Humlin did as he was told. He took a taxi to the boxing club which was almost deserted. Two young boys were leaning on each other in the ring. One of them had a nosebleed. They stood locked in a wrestling hold, swaying back and forth as if they had found themselves on a sinking vessel at sea. The office was empty.

In the diary that was lying out Humlin could see that Törnblom was sitting in a dentist's chair at that moment.

He walked back out into the training area. The boys in the ring had stopped swaying and the nosebleed had dried up. Humlin recognised the boy with the bloody nose. He was one of Leyla's relatives. He smiled at Humlin, who only now noticed that the boy's eye was swelling shut.

The boys went into the changing room. Humlin pulled on a pair of boxing gloves and started hitting a sand bag. It hurt. He wished he was punching Olof Lundin. When he broke into a sweat, he stopped. The boy with the nosebleed came back out. He was dressed in baggy pants and a long T-shirt, both articles of clothing covered with images of the American flag.

'Someone's coming.'

'Who is it?'

'I don't know. One of them, but you'd better wait outside.'

The boy left, shortly followed by the other one. Humlin walked out onto the street. It was raining. He was reminded of the night Tanya had turned up out of the shadows and he had thought he was about to be mugged. He jumped. Tanya was right behind him. As usual she had managed not to make a sound.

'Where's Tea-Bag?'

She didn't answer. They started walking.

'Where are we going?'

'The city centre.'

'I thought Tea-Bag was here?'

Again there was no answer. They took the tram. A drunk man tried to talk to Tanya, but she swore at him with startling ferocity. It was like seeing her turn into a dangerous predator. The man immediately backed off.

They got off close to Göta square. The rain had stopped. Tanya led the way onto one of the small but impressive streets above the square where large stone villas lay nestled in expansive, well-tended gardens. Tanya stopped by the gate to one of the less-impressive mansions.

'Is this where Tea-Bag is staying?'

Tanya nodded.

'Who lives here?'

'Gothenburg's Chief of Police.'

Humlin flinched.

'It's no big deal. He's gone to a conference, and his family aren't home either. Plus he has no alarm system.'

Tanya opened the gate. The front door was slightly ajar. The curtains were drawn in the large living room on the ground floor. Tea-Bag lay on the floor watching TV with the sound turned low. The programme was a Swedish film from the 1950s. The actor Hasse Ekman was turning on the charm for some actress Humlin couldn't remember the name of. She's watching a film about an extinct species, Humlin thought. A Sweden whose inhabitants no longer exist.

There was a clatter from the kitchen. Tanya was making a meal. Tea-Bag quickly got up and joined her. Humlin heard them laughing. Then he was startled by the sound of the front door opening. But it wasn't the Chief of Police, it was Leyla. She was red in the face and sweating heavily.

'I love him,' she said.

Then she too disappeared out into the kitchen. Humlin wondered if he was ever going to hear the rest of her story. He joined the girls and sat down next to Tanya who was chopping onions, tears streaming down her face.

'How did you know this house was empty?'

'Someone told me, I can't remember who. After everything me and Tea-Bag have been through I think it's only fair that we get to borrow it for a while.'

'Can I help with anything?'

No one answered.

Slowly the table was filled with the contents of both of the large refrigerators. It was one of the most remarkable meals he had ever had, even compared to his mother's late-night feasts. Everything was brought out and mixed; champagne and juice, pickled herring and jam. This isn't happening, Humlin thought. If I were ever to write about this evening, this meal in the absent police chief's house, no one would believe me.

He tried to remain alert for outside noises, checked that the curtains remained drawn and waited for the doors to be thrown open. But nothing happened. He did not participate in the conversation which simply jumped between the three girls. Giggling teenagers have the same language, he thought, regardless of where they come from.

A strip of passport pictures of the three of them was passed back and forth and finally landed in Humlin's hands. He had done the same thing in his youth, pressed himself into a picture booth, pulled the curtain and had his picture taken. Tea-Bag found a pair of scissors and cut out the four snapshots. They walked into the living room. There was a row of family portraits on the bureau. They picked out a photograph of a large group of people gathered in the shade of a big tree.

'What strange clothes,' Tea-Bag said. 'When was this?'

Humlin looked at the picture.

'That's from the late nineteenth century,' he said.

'This is where we belong,' Tea-Bag said, opening up the back of the frame and stuffing one of the passport pictures into a corner.

'What will they think?' Leyla said when Tea-Bag had replaced the back of the frame and put the picture on the bureau. 'They won't understand. They won't appreciate the riddle – the best gift anyone could get.'

Humlin looked at the picture. The three smiling faces were already blending into the old picture of the people who had posed for the camera one hundred years ago.

They returned to the kitchen. Even though it was warm, Tea-Bag had not taken off her coat. She hadn't even unzipped it. Tanya sat down at one corner of the table where her face was in shadow. Leyla picked at a spot that was growing on one of her nostrils. Tea-Bag rocked back and forth on her chair.

'What happened?' Humlin asked, thinking the moment had arrived.

Tea-Bag shook her head and tucked her chin even deeper into her coat.

'She tried to steal a monkey,' Leyla said.

'A monkey?'

'A Chinese monkey. Made of china. It was in an antique store. It broke. It was pretty expensive.'

'How much was it?'

'Eighty thousand.'

'How could it be so much?'

'It's from some ancient dynasty. Three thousand years old or something. It said something about it on the price tag.'

'Good God. What did they do?'

'The owners locked the front door and called the police. But she ran away. But the bag with the mobile phones was left behind.'

'Why did you want to steal a china monkey, Tea-Bag?'

Tea-Bag didn't answer. She got up and turned off the light. It was dark outside now. A narrow strip of light fell into the kitchen from the hall and living room. Humlin sensed that he was about to hear the continuation of the story that had been interrupted so many times before. He would perhaps even hear it to its end.

*

When I'm at a total loss for what to do next I sometimes choose a shop window at random and peer in to see if there's something there behind the glass that can give me a sign as to what I should do next: where I should go, who I should talk to, what I should avoid. Before I came to Lagos I hadn't even seen a shop window before. There were no shops in the village where I was born or in the small settlements out on the plain where roads came together and where the rivers were wide enough to sail on. Anyway, I saw that china monkey in the window display and its eyes looked straight into mine and I felt I had to hold it for a while. If the owners hadn't started tugging at me I would have simply put it down again and walked away. I looked into the monkey's eyes and knew it was very old, several thousand years probably. It was like looking into the eyes of a very old person, like my grandmother's eyes, Alemwa's eyes. It was like being sucked into a waterfall and then being driven straight into her soul. Perhaps it really was Alemwa's eyes in that china monkey – I don't know – but suddenly it was as if I was back in the village where everything had started. I could see my journey, my whole life, completely clearly, like the stars in the African night sky.

Alemwa, I know you are watching over me although you have

been dead for many years. I still remember, though I was so little at the time, how you lay down and closed your eyes for the last time. I can see how we carried your thin body wrapped in woven grasses and buried you at the bottom of the hillside where the path to the river took a sharp turn. My father said you had been a kind person who always took the time to listen to the problems of others and that was why you should be buried next to a path so that you would never lack company. Everyone said I was like you, especially my mother, and I think she was a little afraid of me in the same way she had been afraid of you. I can still feel your breath on my neck. It happens every day and it happened often on my long journey. I know you are close to me when I am in danger and there seems to be nothing but danger in this world.

Perhaps it was your breath that woke me up, Alemwa, that night when the soldiers came to take away my father. I remember how my mother screamed like an animal with its leg caught in a trap trying to gnaw it off. I think that is what she was trying to do; trying to gnaw off her arms, legs, ears, eyes, when they came for my father. They hit him until he was covered in blood but he was still alive when they dragged him away in the night.

I know I became an adult that night, way too fast, as if childhood were a skin that was torn from my body. I still remember the pain of seeing my father dragged away in a bloody heap by those soldiers, of knowing but not understanding. I think that was what made me grow up; the realisation that brutality could be accompanied by laughter. Every night during the following months my mother sat outside the hut waiting for my father to come back, to suddenly reappear on the roof so that she could lure him down with soft words and they could spend the rest of the night tightly curled up together.

Then there was the night when we heard that the laughing soldiers were on their way back. When my mother heard about it she covered her head with a white cloth and shook. I was the only child at home at that time. When she took the cloth from her face I could see she had been crying. Her face looked completely different, it had turned inward and I could not see any life in her eyes. She struck me with the white cloth and screamed at me to go away. She chased me away so that I would live.

From that moment I just ran. I planted the soles of my feet firmly into the ground as my father had taught me but I kept my speed up the whole time. I was so afraid I did not even stop by your grave, Alemwa. I don't think anyone can really understand what it means to have to flee. To leave everything behind, forced to run for your life. The night I left my village it felt as if all my thoughts and memories hung behind me like a bloody umbilical cord that refused to break until I was a long, long way away. I doubt that anyone who has not been forced to flee and has run from people or weapons or dark shadows threatening to kill them can understand what that means. The most desperate fear can never be described or told in words. One can never quite say what it is like to run into the darkness with death and pain and denigration only a step behind.

I remember nothing of my escape, only the incredible fear I felt until I arrived in Lagos and was sucked into a world I had never known existed. I had no money, no food and no idea whom I could turn to. As soon as I saw a soldier I hid and thought my heart was going to jump out of my chest. I tried to talk to you, Alemwa. But it was the only time I was not able to hear your voice. Perhaps you were sick. I tried to feel your breath but there was nothing there. The breath I felt on my neck at last stank of alcohol and smoke.

How long I was in that city I don't know. But at that point I was so deep in my desperation that I had decided to find a man who would give me enough money to continue my journey. I knew the price I would have to pay. It just had to be a man with enough money, whatever 'enough' was. Where was I headed? I had no idea which direction was safest.

During all of the days and nights I starved in Lagos I met other people who were also fleeing. It was as if we gave off a special smell that only other refugees could smell, drawn to each other like blind animals. Everyone had dreams and plans. Some had decided to head to South Africa. Others wanted to get to the harbour cities in Kenya and Tanzania in order to smuggle themselves onto a ship. But there were also those who had already given up. They had managed to reach Lagos but did not think they would ever be able to leave. Everyone was afraid of the military, of the laughing soldiers. Many had terrible stories to tell, some had escaped from prisons with mortal wounds to their bodies and souls.

I tried to listen to these blind animals, to interpret their smells and to answer the question as to where I myself was headed. I asked every new refugee if they had seen or heard anything about my father. But he remained gone. It was as if those soldiers had torn him apart with their laughter. I tried to speak to you, Alemwa, but I could not hear your voice. It was as if all of the eyes in the city, all these belching machines, made it impossible for me to feel your breath. I have never been as alone as I felt those days and nights in Lagos. I was so alone that I sometimes secretly touched people that I passed in the street. Occasionally they shouted out at me since they thought I was a pickpocket.

I ran, the whole time I ran, even when I was sleeping my legs continued to move. I started looking for the man who was going to help me, but it turned out that he was the one who found me. I was at an outdoor restaurant, loitering in the shadows outside the gate where furious guards chased away all beggars and people who disturbed the wealthy as they were getting out of their chauffeur-driven cars. Suddenly I felt that stinking breath. I flinched and turned around, ready to strike if someone was preparing to attack me.

The man who stood there was small, his face was pale. He was white with a thin moustache. He was breathing right in my face. His smile should have warned me since I had learned that laughing people can kill with brutal precision; I had seen smiling people commit acts of violence and betrayal. But perhaps it was because I was so tired that I didn't care about his stiff smile, or perhaps it was because I could not hear your voice warning me. He asked me what my name was and then told me he was from Italy. His name was Cartini or Cavanini, I can't remember any more. He was an engineer and he had been in Lagos for four months and was about to return home. His work was something to do with steam or coal-driven heating plants, I don't even know, he was speaking so fast and his eyes travelled up and down my body, up and down, and I remember thinking that this was the man who was going to help me.

I didn't know at that time where Italy was. I didn't even know where Africa was, that there were continents in the world separated by great oceans. I had heard about Europe and its riches and I had heard about America but no one had told me there were no direct paths leading to these places. Maybe Europe was a city like Lagos, but without the furious guards at the gate, a city where all doors were open, where even someone like me could enter without fear of threats or assault.

He asked me if I wanted to come along, what my price was, if

I was alone. I thought it was strange that these questions came in the wrong order. He asked me for my price before he even knew if I was for sale. Perhaps he thought all black women could be bought, that there was no dignity in a land where almost everyone lived in poverty. But even though he asked the questions in the wrong order I went with him.

He had a car. I thought we were going to a hotel but he drove to a large villa that lay in a fenced-off area with other villas and dogs who barked in identical ways and guards that all looked like each other and bright lights in front of each house that almost burned. We went into the house. He asked me if I wanted to have a bath and if I was hungry and the whole time his eyes travelled up and down my body. I was wearing a blue dress that had torn in one seam. When I sat and ate at the large table in the kitchen he reached over and touched me through the hole in the seam and I remember that I shivered. He asked me for my price. I had not answered him since a person cannot have a price. This must have been what made me hate him.

I already knew what was coming. When I was thirteen my mother told me it was time for me to get used to what men wanted from women and had a rightful claim to and that it was one of her brothers who was going to show me. I didn't like him. He had a wandering eye and wheezed when he breathed. It was a horrendous experience, like being torn apart by someone kicking their way into my body. Afterwards I cried but my mother said that the worst was over now and that it would get better, or at least not any worse.

We went into the pale little man's bedroom which was on the upper floor. A window was open and the night breeze came in. In the distance I could hear drums and people singing. It was dark in the room and I lay down on the bed, pulled my skirt over my head and waited. I heard him moving about the room and it sounded as if he was sighing. Then he climbed on top of me and I listened to the sound of the drums and the song and the sound grew and became stronger. I never felt him inside me although he must have been, I was only aware of the drums and the song that rose and fell and sometimes changed into a scream.

Suddenly he pulled my skirt away from my face. Even though it was dark in the room with only the streetlight coming in from outside I could see that his smile was gone. He was sweaty and panting, beads of perspiration hung from his moustache. His whole face was distorted as if he was in pain. He started screaming at the same time as he grabbed my throat in his hands and tried to strangle me. I knew he wanted to kill me. I struggled with all my strength, but he was stronger. The whole time he kept screaming. He blamed me for everything, for being in his bed, for being black, for smelling strangely of spices he didn't know, for having the skirt over my face, for selling myself, for existing. Finally I managed to kick him so hard that he lost his hold. I rolled down from the bed and tried to find my shoes. When I turned around he had one arm above his head and in his hand he held a large hook, the kind for catching sharks. I looked straight into his eyes, they were like two heavy doors about to slam shut.

Then there was a sound and he paused, the doors in his eyes stayed open. I saw him turn his head towards the window where a thin white curtain was moving in the warm breeze. A little monkey sat in the window. It had brown-green fur and it was scratching itself on the forehead. I don't know where it came from but it saved my life. I lifted a heavy wooden chair from the foot of the bed and smashed it as hard as I could over the pale little man's head. The monkey looked at me in surprise, then continued its scratching. I don't know if I killed him or not. I simply gathered up my shoes and took the man's wallet and watch that were lying on the bedside table. Then I ran. When I came out in the garden I turned. The monkey was still in the window, a shadow against the white curtain.

I crept through the city afraid of being caught by the laughing soldiers or of being robbed by someone who could smell the presence of the wallet and the watch. I hid by an old bridge. It was very dark and I felt rats brush by my legs and I flipped through the wad of notes in the wallet. It was a lot of money. I heard the monkey who had saved my life tell me that I should leave the city at dawn and take a bus going north. I didn't know where I was headed but I knew the monkey would be waiting for me at my destination. When I got on the bus I hid the money and the watch inside my underwear, clasped my hands tightly between my legs and fell asleep.

When I woke up the bus had stopped in the middle of a plain. It was the middle of the day and the sun gave no shadow. The bus had broken down; sweaty men lay under the engine and were trying to fix a leaking oil pan. I got off the bus and started walking. To protect myself from the sun I stuck some palm branches under my headscarf. Sometimes I heard the monkey calling out to me from a tree. I thought about the fact that the one who had saved my life was out there somewhere, watching and waiting. I no longer felt alone as I walked along those dusty roads in the red sand. The monkey was with me, and so were my other invisible companions: my parents and you, Alemwa, you above all.

I kept walking north and became one of the many who wandered along the roads in unruly flocks, running away from their suffering towards a goal that most often was simply a mirage, not even a dream. At last I reached the beach. On the other side of the water lay Europe.

*

Tea-Bag fell silent. She slowly unzipped her jacket and Humlin jumped. He thought he'd seen an animal peek out of her coat, leap down to the floor and run out of the room.

Tea-Bag looked at him and smiled.

He wondered if Tea-Bag's story was over now, or if it was just beginning.

17

The silence took Humlin by surprise.

No one asked Tea-Bag any questions. Had they heard all this before, or was her story a combination of everyone's experiences? Had they even been listening? He didn't know.

Tanya had been at the stove stirring something in a pot the whole time. When Humlin got up to fetch a glass of water he realised to his consternation that the pot was empty and the burner cold. Leyla sat with her watch in her hands, as if she had been timing Tea-Bag's story.

'Why don't you ask her anything?' Humlin finally asked.

'Like what?' Leyla said, continuing to stare at the watch.

'Tea-Bag has just told you a remarkable and gripping story. She certainly doesn't need to attend a writing seminar in order to learn that.'

'I can't write, though,' Tea-Bag said. She had clearly worked up an appetite and was squeezing mayonnaise onto a piece of bread.

A phone rang. Humlin flinched, and even Tea-Bag reacted uneasily. The only one who seemed unaffected was Tanya, who seemed to be able to tell the rings of all mobile phones apart and even to detect if the caller was her enemy or not.

It was Leyla's phone. She looked at the display and then handed it to Tanya.

'It's from home,' she said. 'Can you answer and say we've got our phones mixed up? Tell them you don't know where I am.'

'It'll just cause trouble.'

'Not any more than I'm already in. Go on – just answer it.'

'No, you have to do it.'

'I can't. You don't understand.'

'I do understand. But you still have to answer.'

The phone continued to ring. It lay on the table and was sent back and forth across its surface like a half-dead insect. Humlin saw how afraid Leyla was when she finally grabbed it and answered in her own language. Humlin heard a man. He sounded extremely upset. Leyla initially hunched her shoulders at the sound of this voice but suddenly she straightened her back, shouted back at him and ended the conversation by banging the phone on the table until the battery cover came off. She yelled out something that Humlin didn't understand, got up with clenched fists and then sank down on the chair again and started to cry.

Tanya had resumed stirring her empty pot. Humlin wondered if she were preparing an invisible meal for her daughter who was somewhere far away. Tea-Bag picked up the battery cover from the floor and put the phone back together.

Leyla stopped crying.

'That was my dad.'

Tanya groaned.

'Don't go home. He's not allowed to lock you up. Your brothers are not allowed to hit you.'

'I can't stay here. I can't stay with my grandmother.'

Tanya flicked her tea towel angrily at Leyla's arm.

'But you can't go home. When you told me what happened to your sister I thought you were talking about yourself, right up until the end. It was only then I realised it couldn't be you because you were right there in front of me and your ear wasn't burnt away with acid.'

Humlin drew back in horror.

'What's this – a sister? What ear?'

'I'm not going to tell. At least not with you sitting here.'

Tanya kept flicking the tea towel at Leyla's arm.

'He's our teacher; he's supposed to listen. Perhaps he'll learn something from what you say.'

'I want to hear it,' Tea-Bag said. 'I need to listen to someone else for a while. My head is filled with my own tongues. They fly around in here like misshapen butterflies.'

She rapped her head with her knuckles. Leyla pointed to Humlin.

'Not while he's still here.'

'He can wait out in the hall.'

Tanya gestured for Humlin to leave and so he took his chair and went to sit out in the hall. I'm not supposed to see her in the act of making her confession, he thought. Leyla was quiet for a long time before she started to speak.

*

Once upon a time I had a doll named Nelf. I found it under one of the beds in a room at the refugee camp where people came and went, and where you could hear people scream and cry in their sleep. But there was also an atmosphere of relief there. We had arrived. We were in Sweden. Everything was going to be all right, without anyone actually being able to say what 'all right' was. I thought it was 'good' that I found the doll, and I immediately gave her the name Nelf. I was surprised that no one seemed to understand what it meant. Not even grandmother Nasrin who was still clear-headed those days. But even she didn't pick up that it was the name of a god.

We had just arrived from Iran but I don't remember much about that trip, only that when we were about to land my dad tore up all our documents. My parents' passports, Nasrin's passport – which actually wasn't hers but belonged to Uncle Reza. First we landed in the small Swedish town called Flen where I found the doll and a few months later we moved to Falun where we lived for three years before we came to Gothenburg, to Stensgården.

It was in Falun that my dad decided my sister Fatti was going to marry one of Mehmed's brothers. Mehmed lived in Södertälje and was one of the first to move to Sweden; he came even before the Shah was overthrown and Khomeini had us all under surveillance and was in the process of making the country into something better and which maybe one day it actually will be. But Fatti had eavesdropped on the conversations between Dad and Mehmed – she had been told to stay out of the way – by crouching down outside the door to the living room and when she crept back to bed in the room that we shared I heard her cry.

I got up and crawled into bed with her, which is something we always do when someone is sad or has a nightmare or is just alone. Fatti dredged up the terrible words she had just heard through the closed door, sobbing as she told me. She had heard Mehmed and Dad agree to marry her to Mehmed's brother Faruk. Both of us knew who he was, he had a little shop in Hedemora and everyone took it for granted that Mehmed was supporting him since there were never any customers in there. Faruk often came to visit us at the weekends. Neither Fatti nor I liked him. He was nice, but perhaps it was that he was too nice, so you actually became afraid of him. And now Fatti was going to have to marry him.

She said she would run away, but she didn't know where to. We both knew you can't run away from your father; he would look for you for a thousand years and finally find you. I said this to my sister and that there had to be another way for her to escape a marriage with Faruk. Our mother was not going to be a help; she never did anything without asking Dad first, but maybe Nasrin could stand up to him. The following day was Midsummer's Eve. I remember that Fatti and I walked down to the lake through the birch trees and talked with Nasrin. But Nana just got angry and said that Fatti should be grateful to get someone like Mehmed as a relative. I'll never forget the fact that Nasrin talked about Mehmed the whole time even though Faruk was the man Fatti was supposed to marry. I could see how desperate Fatti was getting. Nasrin had been her last hope. She pleaded with her for help but Nasrin just kept on talking about how wonderful it would be to have such a well-established man as Mehmed in the family.

That night I crawled into Fatti's bed again. She told me she was going to run away but I didn't believe her. Where would she go? Sometimes girls from families like ours run away but I've never heard of anyone who didn't eventually come back. Even the ones who commit suicide are brought back. But when I woke up the next morning the bed was empty. Fatti was gone. At first I thought she was in the bathroom or out on the balcony wrapped in a blanket, but she was gone. I peeked in all the rooms. Dad was snoring, Mum's foot was hanging down on the floor. Fatti's red coat was gone. She had not taken very much with her. The only bag that was missing was her little black backpack. I walked out on the balcony. It was still early. A bird somewhere was chirping, the sun was rising out of the mist, and I wondered where Fatti could have gone. I thought that I should have gone with her because Fatti and

I are really the same person. Fatti is thinner than I am. That's the only difference.

I will always remember when I stood on the balcony in Falun and realised that Fatti had run away, and I remember thinking that everything would be different from then on. They found Fatti in Sala four days later. She had fallen asleep on a park bench, or else she had fainted. The police drove her home and when they had left, Dad hit her so hard that she fell and got a deep gash in her neck. Dad wasn't the only one who hit her, he wasn't the worst, he only hit her that one time. My brother came down from Gothenburg and he didn't even bother taking off his hat before he dislocated her shoulder. Fatti was no longer allowed to go out after that. She was nineteen, she wanted to be a nurse and she had been interested in the sport of orienteering. I don't know why, but she was drawn to the idea of running around in a forest, looking for the most indecipherable clues marked out on maps.

Nothing came of all that. We still shared the same room and whispered to each other at night. I saw her face in the moonlight and it looked like Nasrin's face: dried up, turned inward. The whole time she kept talking about the four days she had been on the run, how she had been afraid but also had the feeling of complete freedom. Something happened during that time that she never told me about. Under her pillow she kept a gleaming metallic nut with bevelled edges. Sometimes when she thought I was sleeping she would get it out and look at it. Someone must have given it to her, but why would anyone give her something like that? What was it she wasn't telling me? I don't know. Of all the riddles I have been given, this is the biggest: the gleaming nut that Fatti kept hidden under her pillow.

It was a time I don't like to think about. Fatti was so afraid of being beaten that she wet herself, even though she was nineteen years old. I remember her saying, 'I'm going to be slaughtered. I'm going to end up in a slaughterhouse.' I didn't understand then what she was talking about. The following year Fatti was married to Faruk and they moved to Hedemora. She still had no children after two years. We had moved to Gothenburg by then and I wanted to visit her but was not allowed to. I couldn't even call her since only Faruk answered the phone. When he wasn't at home he disconnected the line. Then it happened again. Fatti ran away. She ran away in the dead of winter wearing only her nightdress. I don't know what had happened but I think Faruk used to beat her because she didn't have any children. When Faruk dragged her back she refused to sleep in the same room as him. It didn't help that Mum talked to her, and Nasrin. She didn't care about being beaten any more. She had made up her mind. She didn't want to be married to Faruk.

I still don't know if it was Faruk or Mehmed who threw that container of burning acid in her face. A neighbour heard a terrifying scream from the apartment and when she opened her door she saw a man running down the stairs, but we never found out who it was. Both of them denied it, both had alibis. Fatti's whole face was deformed, especially her cheek and one ear. She never goes out any more. She lives in an apartment here in Gothenburg with her curtains drawn. She never talks to anyone; she's just waiting for it all to end. I have called out to her through the letterbox in the door. I've asked her to let me in but she always tells me to go away. The only one who visits her is Mum. Dad never talks about her, nor do Faruk or Mehmed.

Faruk is remarried now. No one was ever punished for destroying Fatti's face. I think about her all the time, my sister in her dark apartment, and I know I never want my life to turn out like hers. She wanted to wait until she found someone she really wanted to share her life with, she wanted to be the one making the decision.

I can't understand my father. He always says that we left our homeland in search of freedom, but when we want to be free that's wrong. I wonder what happened during those four days that Fatti was free. I think freedom – if it actually exists – is always threatened, hunted, always on the run.

I know Fatti met someone during those four days, someone who gave her that gleaming nut with the bevelled edges. Each night before I fall asleep I hope, I pray that Fatti will get to dream about that person who gave her the nut when she was free and terribly afraid. Maybe that's why I want to learn to write; I would want to write about those four days, I would want to write about everything that happened to her then, everything that people walking past her on the street would not have noticed.

If I don't care about Fatti, who else is going to do it? Mum loves her, and Dad probably does too in his way. I know that I have to defend love where it exists and where it doesn't exist and I know it exists even for me since he waited for me in the underpass, and he must have done so because he knew I would go that way to get to the tram stop.

*

There was a loud knock on the door. Humlin flinched on his chair out in the hall, Tea-Bag zipped up her coat as if she were pulling out a gun and only Tanya didn't move. Leyla slowly got to her feet, pushing the hair of her sweaty forehead and walked to the front door. When she came back there was a young man by her side. He looked anxiously around the room.

'This is Torsten,' Leyla said. 'The one from the underpass. The one from my story.'

Nasrin's temporary home assistant, Torsten Emanuel Rudin, had a terrible stammer. Tea-Bag started giggling when she first heard him speak. Leyla was furious with her and Tanya had to come between them in order to stop Leyla from punching Tea-Bag.

'Are you the one who writes c-c-c-c-c-c—'

'No,' Humlin broke in sharply. 'I don't write crime novels.'

'I mean those concise, minimalist poems,' Torsten said.

Leyla stood between them.

'This is my professor,' she said proudly. 'He is going to teach me to be a great writer. He knows all the words there are.'

Then she sat down in Torsten's lap. The chair groaned beneath them. Love takes many forms, Humlin thought. This may be one of the most beautiful I've seen.

'I've run away from home,' Leyla announced.

Torsten was taken by surprise. His exclamation died away in a long stutter.

'I'm frightened,' Leyla said, 'but I've done what I had to do. Now my family will hunt for me as long as I live.'

She looked at Humlin.

'They're going to think it's your doing.'

Humlin immediately felt a sense of panic.

'Why would they think that?'

'They've seen you pat girls on the cheek. They think we send secret messages to each other.'

'I'm shocked by what you have told me about your sister. But that convinces me all the more that you need to speak to your parents about this.'

'About what?'

'About the fact that there's someone in your life,' Humlin said nodding at Torsten.

'They'll kill me and lock me up for ever.'

'They'll hardly kill you first and then lock you up. As far as I have understood what happened, no one in your family had anything to do with what happened to Fatti.'

'She doesn't exist.'

Humlin gasped.

'What do you mean?'

'Of course she exists. What I mean is, it's as if she's never existed. As if she closed all the doors, pulled a scarf over her head and stopped existing. Even though she's still alive.'

'You can be dead even though you're alive, and alive although you're dead.'

It was Torsten who spoke, and he did so without a single stutter. He smiled. Leyla smiled. Everyone smiled. It was a shared triumph.

*

The conversation died away.

Tea-Bag and Tanya washed the dishes while Leyla and Torsten went off together somewhere in the big house. Humlin walked down into the den in the basement. There was a large jumping jack in the shape of a policeman hanging on a wall. Something about it made Humlin feel uneasy. It was eleven o'clock. He hesitated, then dialled Andrea's number. She picked up straight away.

'I hope I didn't wake you up.'

'I had just fallen asleep. Where are you?'

'Gothenburg.'

'Why are you calling?'

'I wanted to talk to you. Isn't that what people do? I thought we were a couple.'

'"I thought we were a couple." Listen to yourself. You sound like someone from an old Swedish movie. I want to end this relationship right now.'

'I can't manage without you, Andrea.'

'You'll manage perfectly well without me. If you don't, that's your problem. When are you coming back?'

'I don't know. Don't you at least want to know what's happened?'

'Is anyone dead?'

'No.'

'Seriously injured?'

'No.'

'Then I don't want to know. Call me when you get back. Good night.'

Andrea hung up. Humlin stared at the jumping jack. That's not a police officer, he thought. It's me.

Humlin walked back up the stairs. The kitchen and living room were empty. He continued to the first floor. Through a half-open door he saw Tea-Bag and Tanya stretched out on a double bed. They were holding hands. Tea-Bag still had her coat on. Tanya's mouth was moving but he couldn't hear what they were saying. The door to the next room was closed. When he pushed his ear up against the door he could hear Torsten's stuttering voice. He walked back downstairs.

This would be the right moment to leave, he thought. The seminar is over, the seminar that never was. But I can't leave yet. I haven't heard the end of Tanya's story. And I don't know if that monkey I sometimes see is real or not.

*

Humlin finally fell asleep in an armchair. He immediately started to dream. Olof Lundin was rowing across a bay with furious speed. Humlin was in a boat with Tea-Bag, fishing. Suddenly police dogs were swimming towards them from all sides. He drew back and woke up when one of the dogs bit him on the shoulder. It was Tanya shaking his arm. Humlin looked at his watch in confusion. A quarter to two. He hadn't been asleep for more than twenty minutes. He saw Tea-Bag behind Tanya.

'She's real,' Tanya said.

'Who?'

'Fatti, Leyla's sister. I know where she lives. Do you want to meet her?'

'According to Leyla, Fatti sits in an apartment with the curtains drawn and a silk scarf over her head – why on earth would she want to meet me?'

'Leyla visits her every day. That's why she's never in school. She's been taking care of her sister.'

'Why didn't she say that?'

'Don't you have any secrets?'

'This isn't about that.'

Tea-Bag broke into the conversation.

'Should we leave?'

'Can't this wait?'

'Do you want to meet Fatti or not?'

*

Tanya called a taxi. They sat in silence during the trip. Leyla's sister lived in a building that was squeezed between a steep hill-side and the ruins of an old brick factory. They got out. Humlin noticed he was shivering with cold.

'How do we get back?'

Tanya showed him some mobile phones that had not been in the bag confiscated by the police.

'But I don't know why you have to ask about that when we only just got here.'

Humlin looked up at the dark building. He started having misgivings about this visit.

'I don't want to meet her,' he said. 'I don't want to see a young woman whose face has been burned away with acid. I don't understand why I'm here.'

'She has a silk scarf over her face,' Tanya said soothingly. 'It's dark inside anyway. Of course you want to meet her – you're curious.'

'It's the middle of the night. She must be sleeping.'

'She sleeps during the day. She's awake at night.'

'She won't open her door.'

'Fatti will think it's Leyla.'

The front door of the building was unlocked. Someone had spilled jam in the lift. Fatti lived on the top floor. Tanya took out her collection of skeleton keys. Tea-Bag gave her a sharp look.

'Shouldn't we knock? Or ring the doorbell?'

'In the middle of the night?'

Tanya started working on the lock. Humlin wondered drily if Leyla also picked the lock when she came over to visit.

The lock gave way. Tanya pushed the door open and put her equipment back in her backpack. Tea-Bag pushed him into the hall. The apartment had a stale smell, like bitter berries. But there was also something sweet in the air. Humlin was reminded of the smell of the exotic meals his mother made in the middle of the night.

'Who is there?'

The voice called out from a room at the end of the hall. Some light from the streetlamp fell in through a crack in the curtains.

'See, she's waiting for you,' Tanya hissed.

Humlin resisted.

'I don't know who she is. I don't want to see her: I don't even know what we're doing here.'

'She has a veil over her head. You're the one she's waiting for.'

'She can't be waiting for me; she doesn't even know who I am.'

'She knows you. We'll be waiting downstairs.'

Before Humlin had time to react, Tea-Bag and Tanya had left the apartment. He was about to go after them when he saw a figure in the doorway at the end of the hall.

'Who is it?'

She had a strong accent, but she still reminded him of Leyla.

'My name is Jesper Humlin. I'm so sorry to disturb you.'

'There is no need to apologise.'

'But it's two o'clock in the morning.'

'I sleep during the day. I've been expecting to hear from you.'

'Excuse me?'

'I said, I've been expecting you.'

Fatti turned on a lamp in a corner of the room. A white cloth had been thrown over the lampshade, and the light that came on was very soft. She gestured for him to approach her. Had he misunderstood? Had she really been expecting him? There was a thick rug in the living room. There was nothing on the walls, a few simple chairs, a table without a tablecloth, some gaping shelves with only a few books and newspapers; no trinkets or ornaments of any kind. Fatti sat down across from him. She was wearing a long black dress and a light-blue silk scarf over her head. Humlin thought he could see the outline of her nose and chin through the thin cloth. The thought of her deformed features made him feel sick.

'Don't be afraid. I won't show you what he did to me.'

'I'm not afraid. Why do you say you've been expecting me?'

'I knew Leyla would tell you about me sooner or later. And I imagine an author likes to see for himself what he cannot quite believe, or what he has never come across before.'

Humlin was starting to feel more and more uncomfortable. He tried to think of something other than the disfigured face beneath the veil.

'I'm right, aren't I? Isn't that what you are trying to teach Leyla: to be curious? If you think she has what it takes to become a writer, that is. Do you think she does?'

'I'm not sure I can answer that question.'

'Why not?'

'It's too early to tell.'

Fatti leaned forward. Humlin flinched.

'Who is going to speak for me? Who is going to tell my story?'

Don't ask me to do it, he thought. I can't bear it.

'Why don't you do it?' he suggested carefully.

'I am no writer. You are.'

It was as if she could see perfectly in spite of the veil.

'Are you afraid I might ask you to do it?' she asked.

He didn't give her an answer, and she didn't press him for one. She leaned back in her chair without saying anything. Humlin had the feeling she was crying behind the scarf. He held his breath and thought that this moment was something unique, something he would never get to experience again.

Suddenly she stretched out her hand and pressed the play

button on a cassette player next to her. The sound that came from the cassette player was not music, just static. Then he realised it was the sound of the ocean, of waves breaking on the shore, or rather, on a distant reef.

'This is my only solace,' Fatti said. 'The sound of the sea.'

'I once wrote a poem about a drift net,' Humlin said hesitantly.

'What is that?'

'It's a particular kind of net used in fishing. I wrote about how I saw one once down in the clear depths. It was a fishing net that had torn away from its anchors and was floating away. The body of a wild duck and a few fish were entangled in it.'

'What was the theme of the poem?'

'I think the image of the drifting net seemed like an image of freedom to me.'

'Freedom is always adrift?'

'Perhaps. I don't know.'

They were quiet. The roar of the ocean washed over them.

'You are afraid,' she said after a while. 'You are afraid that I might ask you to write my story. And you are especially afraid because you couldn't write it without looking at my face.'

'I am not afraid.'

'I won't ask you to, don't worry.'

She paused and he waited but she didn't say anything else. After half an hour of silence he said, very carefully,

'I think I'd best be going now.'

Fatti didn't answer. Humlin got up and left the apartment. As he shut the door behind him it came to him that the sweet smell in the apartment was cinnamon.

*

Tea-Bag and Tanya were waiting for him down on the street. They looked at him attentively. Tea-Bag leaned forward with frank curiosity.

'Did you see her face?'

'No.'

'I've seen it. It looks like someone carved a map into it: islands, crags and waterways.'

'I don't want to hear any more. Please call a taxi. Our priority right now is figuring out what to do with you. Where are you going to hide?'

'I have to hide too,' Tanya said. 'And Leyla. We all need hiding.'

They returned to the Chief of Police's house where Torsten and Leyla were waiting for them.

'How long can we stay here?' Humlin asked.

'Someone may be coming tomorrow morning. We should be gone by then.'

'That gives us a few more hours, until dawn. Who might be coming?'

'A cleaning lady.'

'When does she get here?'

'Not before nine o'clock.'

'Then we'll leave at eight.'

'Where are we going?'

'I don't know.'

Humlin returned to the armchair where he had fallen asleep a few hours before. Tea-Bag and Tanya went upstairs. I have to take care of this, he thought. I don't know exactly what I have got myself into, nor what my responsibilities are. But I'm caught all the same, like having a foot stuck in the railway tracks when the train is thundering down the line.

He tried to sleep but the image of the woman with the light-blue headscarf wouldn't leave him. Tea-Bag and Tanya were also in his dreams, rowing a boat over an ocean the same colour as the silk scarf.

*

He woke up at dawn.

He still didn't have the faintest idea what they were going to do next.

18

A rubbish truck clattered past outside.

Humlin got up out of the armchair where he had been trying – in vain – to get some sleep. He had forced himself to arrive at a decision. He didn't know if it was the right thing to do, but at least there seemed to be no better alternative. He went up to the first floor and looked into the room where Tanya and Tea-Bag were sleeping. Tea-Bag had finally removed her coat, Tanya lay curled up with a pillow over her face. Tea-Bag woke with a start when Humlin entered the room. He saw the flash of fear in her eyes.

'It's me. It's time for us to leave.'

'Where are we going?'

'I'll tell you when we've assembled downstairs.'

He left the room and knocked on the other bedroom door. Torsten called out something unintelligible in a weak stammer.

'Come in,' Leyla's voice shouted.

They lay with the blanket pulled up to their necks. Torsten looked tiny next to Leyla.

'Get up and get dressed,' Humlin said. 'The girls and I have to go.'

'I'm coming along too,' Torsten said.

'Don't you have work to go to?'

Torsten started to stutter his reply.

'He only temps right now,' Leyla answered. 'My grandmother already has someone else helping her.'

It was seven o'clock. Humlin walked down the stairs. He already dreaded the phone call he was about to make; there was nothing his mother hated as much as being woken up early in the morning.

He sat down at a desk with a phone. He heard Tea-Bag and Tanya's voices rising and falling from the upper floor. My family, he thought. All these children Andrea is always pestering me about. He lifted the receiver and dialled the number. His mother picked up after fourteen rings. She sounded as if she were about to die. This is her real voice, Humlin thought bitterly. Not a voice ready to moan for money or a voice ready to commandeer the rest of the world. It is the voice of an old woman who feels the earth calling out to her, trying to claim her.

'Who is it?'

'It's me.'

'What time is it?'

'Seven.'

'Are you trying to kill me?'

'I have to talk to you.'

'I'm always asleep at this time, as you know. I had only just managed to get to sleep, in fact. You'll have to call back tonight.'

'I can't. I only need you to stay awake for a few more minutes so you can hear what I have to say.'

'You never have anything to say.'

'Today I do. I'm calling from Gothenburg.'

'Are you still carrying on with those Indian girls?'

'They're not Indian. There's one from Iran, Russia, Nigeria and also a boy named Torsten who stutters and is from Gothenburg.'

'That sounds like quite a mixed bag. What about the boy – why does he stutter?'

'I don't know. When I was younger I used to stutter whenever I was nervous. Or when I talked with someone else who had a stutter.'

'One can always overcome a stutter. It's only a matter of will-power.'

'Tell that to the people who have suffered from it their whole lives. Anyway, I didn't call you at seven to discuss the issue of stammering.'

'I'm going back to bed.'

'Not before you've heard me out.'

'Good night.'

'If you put that phone down I'm going to cut off all contact with you – I mean it.'

'Well then, what is it that's so important, Jesper?'

'Later on today I'll be coming by your place with them.'

'Why would you do that?'

'They're going to stay with you, I don't know for how long exactly. But it's extremely important that you don't mention this to anyone. Understood?'

'Can I go back to bed now?'

'Sleep well.'

Humlin noticed that his hand was shaking when he put down the phone. But he was convinced his mother had understood the main thing: that she was not to say anything about Humlin making his way to Stockholm with an unorthodox assortment of companions.

*

They arrived in the early afternoon. During the trip he had made them spread out to various parts of the train. When they were just pulling out of the Södertälje station he asked to borrow one of Tanya's phones.

'Whose phone is this?'

'It works fine.'

'That's not what I was asking. Am I still using phones that belong to police officers and prosecutors?'

'This one belongs to one of the train conductors.'

Humlin was taken aback. Then he locked himself in the toilet and called his mother, who picked up immediately.

'I'm waiting for you. When will you get here?'

'We've just passed Södertälje.'

'I thought for a while that I had been dreaming. I take it you are bringing them here because they need a place to hide out?'

'Yes.'

'How many are they? Ten, twelve?'

'Just four.'

'Are you also staying here?'

'No.'

'I'm looking forward to meeting these Indian girls. I'm wearing an Indian shawl your father gave me while we were engaged.'

'They're not Indian, Mother. I told you this morning. Take off that shawl and don't make any strange food. I would also be grateful if you could refrain from moaning on the phone this evening.'

'I've already called the others about it.'

Humlin was horrified.

'What did you say?'

'Naturally I said nothing about you coming over with the girls. I just said I didn't have the energy to work tonight.'

Humlin finished the conversation and then tried to flush the phone down the toilet. It got stuck. He left the toilets and went back to his seat.

Once they got to the Central station he looked for a taxi big enough to hold them all. A police car drove by and Tanya and Tea-Bag waved to it. One of the officers waved back. They think I can guarantee their safety, Humlin thought. They don't understand that I'm unable to give guarantees of any sort.

*

The initial meeting between his mother and the girls did nothing to assuage Humlin's fears. The girls embraced his mother with an outpouring of affection and warmth from the first. He was forced to admit to himself that she could be charming when she wanted. She mixed up their names, insisted that Leyla was Indian, called Tea-Bag 'the beautiful girl from Sumatra' and kept referring to Tanya as 'Elsa'. But it didn't seem to matter. The girls even appeared to change their attitudes to him now that it turned out that he had such a wonderful mother.

There seemed to be a limitless sense of security in her large apartment, as if it were sealed off from the rest of the world by diplomatic immunity. She had made up all available beds and after only a few minutes they had all been shown to their spot. Tea-Bag and Tanya were still sharing a room, Leyla had her own and Torsten was camped out on a folding camp bed in the hallway.

'I simply can't let an unmarried couple share a room.'

'That's very old-fashioned of you, Mother.'

'I am old-fashioned.'

'What about the Mature Women's Hotline?'

His mother didn't reply. She had already turned her back to him.

*

A little later Humlin left to go shopping. He took Tanya along to help him carry the groceries. He had asked Torsten first but Leyla had looked so unhappy about this that he changed his mind. On the way to the shop Tanya suddenly stopped outside a bar.

'I'm thirsty.'

She opened the door and walked in. Humlin followed her, just in time to see her order a beer.

'I'll get you one too, if you like,' she said. 'But you're paying. I have phones, not cash.'

'Isn't it a little early in the day for a beer?'

Tanya muttered something under her breath, then sat down at a table. Humlin joined her with a cup of coffee. He saw how tense she was – her eyes travelled nervously around the room.

'Do you want to be left alone for a while?' he asked.

Again she didn't answer. Humlin waited and she emptied her glass of beer. Then she got up and walked out to the toilets. One of her phones was lying on the table and it started to ring. That's her, he thought. She's doing what she did in the Yüksels' apartment. She calls when she has something important to say. He answered the phone.

'Associate Judge Hansson at the Administrative Court of Appeals wishes to speak to Prosecutor Westin. May I put him through?'

'He's in a meeting,' Humlin said and hung up.

The phone rang again. Humlin fumbled with the phone to

see if there was caller ID, but didn't find anything. He gave up and answered the phone.

'I think we were interrupted. I was trying to get through to Prosecutor Westin?'

'He's still busy.'

Humlin was starting to sweat. The doors to the toilets remained closed. After a while he got up and walked over to them. He listened for sounds from the women's toilets but heard nothing. He knocked, but there was no reply. Then he opened the door. There was no one there. He tried to open the window at the far end but the latches were rusty and stuck. She didn't leave by this way, he thought. Then he went into the men's toilets.

Tanya was sitting on the floor next to the urinals. She was holding a paper towel up to her face. At first Humlin thought she had had an accident and was trying to stem a nosebleed but then he realised she was sniffing something concealed in the paper towel. He grabbed it out of her hands. It looked like a messy bar of soap but then he saw it was a bar of scented cleaning solution that must have come from a urinal. He had heard about this from somewhere, that the urine released ammonia from these bars, which could then be inhaled. But it was still hard for him to believe his eyes: Tanya's glassy gaze, the paper towel with the sticky blue bar. He tried to pull her up off the ground but she hit him in the face and screamed something at him in Russian.

A man came in and Humlin ordered him to use the women's toilets. The man quickly left.

Humlin kept fighting Tanya for the scented bar. They crawled around on the floor. She scratched him in the face with her nails, which made him furious. He grabbed her around the waist and forced her up against the wall. Both of them were covered in urine. He screamed at her to calm down but when she kept resisting and tried to fish yet another scented block out of the urinal he slapped her. Her nose started to bleed and she became absolutely still.

Humlin heard someone's steps outside the door and forced her quickly into one of the cubicles. A man came in who coughed and urinated for a long time. Humlin sat down on the toilet with Tanya on his lap. She was breathing heavily and her eyes were closed. He wondered if she was about to pass out. After the man had left, Humlin shook her.

'What's going on?' he asked. 'Why are you doing this to yourself?'

Tanya shook her head.

'Let me sleep.'

'We can't stay here,' he said. 'We have to go pick up some food. The others are waiting for us.'

'Only for a little while. I haven't sat on anyone's lap since I was a little girl and my aunt held me like this on her knee.'

'We're sitting on a toilet,' Humlin said.

Suddenly she got up and leaned against the wall.

'I'm going to puke.'

Humlin got up and left the cubicle. He heard her throw up, then everything was quiet. He opened the door and handed her a wet paper towel. She wiped her face and followed him out. As they were leaving the toilets they met a man who was pulling down his zip. He looked at Tanya with interest and then winked conspiratorially at Humlin, who came very close to punching him.

They walked out of the bar. Tanya pointed to a small cemetery on the other side of the street.

'Can't we go there?'

'We have to buy some food.'

'Ten minutes. That's all.'

Humlin pushed open the rusty gate to the cemetery. An old woman sat propped up against a gravestone that was pushed half on its side. Its inscription was no longer legible. The woman's clothes were tattered and several plastic bags and packets of newspapers wrapped up in twine lay strewn about her. Tanya stopped and looked at her.

'Do you think she needs a phone?' she asked.

'I doubt she has anyone to call. But I suppose she could always sell it.'

Tanya took out one of her phones and laid it next to the sleeping woman's cheek. They continued walking through the empty graveyard. Tanya sat down on a bench. Humlin joined her.

'Maybe I should call the bag lady,' she said. 'The phone I gave her plays a lovely, old-fashioned lullaby when the phone rings. It's a heavenly way to wake up.'

'I'd let her sleep. What kind of life does she wake up to anyway?'

Tanya whimpered, as if she had been struck by a whip.

'Don't say that,' she said. 'What kind of life do I wake up to, for that matter? Do you want me to wish I were dead? I have wanted that, I've stood on the bridge and almost thrown myself off, I've put needles in my arm without knowing or caring what was in the syringe. But deep down inside I've still always wanted to wake up again. Do you think I did what I did back there because I wanted to die? You're wrong. I just wanted to get away for a little while, just to have a moment's peace. No words, no voices, nothing. I remember when I was growing up that there was a little black pond in the forest nestled in between the high trees. I always went there when I was upset. The water was absolutely still and shiny like a mirror and I used to think that that was what I wanted inside. Peace, nothing else. I still crave that sense of peace.'

Tanya stopped talking and looked around for something in her backpack. Humlin counted the phones that she laid out on the bench: seven. At last she found what she was looking for, which was a crumpled pack of cigarettes. He hadn't seen her smoke before. She inhaled the smoke as if it were oxygen. But just as suddenly she dropped the cigarette into the gravel and killed it with her heel.

*

What I don't understand and what I will keep asking myself all my life and won't even stop when I die is the question of how it could be possible for me to feel any joy after all the hell that I have been through. Or hasn't it even been that bad? Yesterday, when Tea-Bag and I were lying on the police chief's bed, she told me that I haven't had it any worse than anyone else. Then she fell asleep. Is she right? I don't know. But I don't understand how I'm supposed to be able to laugh after all the humiliation I've been through. And I'm someone who thinks it's necessary for people to be able to feel an uncomplicated, simple joy in their lives since we are going to be dead for such a long time. Death is not what is frightening to me, not the fact that the flame goes out, but this fact that we are going to be dead so very long.

I still think about that time four years ago when we stood out by the main road, four girls in skirts that were much too short. We were the East, nothing more. We knew how Westerners saw us, as those poor Easterners, those wretches. And there we were in our short skirts in the middle of winter, still mired in the poverty and misery that was our life in the vodka-stinking hole that was all that was left after the Communist collapse. Four girls: fourteen, sixteen, seventeen and nineteen. I was the oldest and we were laughing as we stood out there in the cold, wild with joy – can you understand that? We were so close to being free! When that old rusty car came down the road it could just as well have been Jesus or Buddha or Muhammad come down from the clouds. It was the car that was going to carry us to freedom, no matter that it stunk of mould and unwashed feet.

Why do people leave? Why do they pull up their roots and go? I suppose some people are chased away and forced to flee. Maybe it's war or hunger or fear – it's always fear. But sometimes you choose to leave because it's the clever thing to do. A teenage girl might very well ask the same question as a holy patriarch: where can I find a life for myself, a life far away from everything here that I despise?

There was an abandoned barn in a field behind Mischa's cabin, Mischa who was old, crazy and a little dangerous. We used to hang out there, Inez, Tatyana, Natalia and I. We had all known each other so long we couldn't even remember how we first met. We staged trials in that barn. Inez had stolen some rope from one of the barges that went up and down the river. She was crazy; she had jumped into the cold water with a knife between her teeth and cut off a few lengths of rope that she tied to her legs and swam back to shore with. We made a few nooses – Natalia had a brother who had been in the KGB so he knew what a real hangman's noose looked like. Then we proceeded to hang our enemies. We put straw and stones in the bags, pronounced the sentence and hanged them from one of the beams in the roof, one by one. We hanged our teachers and our parents; Tatyana's dad was particularly mean and used to beat her once a week. I don't think we ever thought too closely about what we were doing. There was just life and death, punishment and mercy. But we didn't show anyone mercy; they didn't deserve it.

There we were, four avenging angels in the little village outside Smolensk. We had given ourselves a name, the 'Slumrats'. That's how we saw ourselves. Creatures of the underworld without value, hunted, filled with self-loathing. But we didn't just conduct trials in that barn, we prayed to gods of our own choosing. Inez had stolen a book from her step-father, a book filled with pictures of big cities in North America and Western Europe. Inez used to steal all the time; she was the one who taught me how, not my dad. When I told you that I was lying. My dad was a worm who couldn't even have broken a bike lock. But Inez was never afraid. She would break into churches and steal the elaborate frames they use for icons. We would tear pictures out of our books and slip them into these old icon frames, hang them up and then pray to them. We prayed that we would one day get to see these cities. Then – so that no one would find the pictures – we buried them in one corner of the barn underneath the rotting floorboards.

I'm still not sure who gave the Slumrats their order to flee. Maybe it was me; it should have been me since I was the oldest. We were always dreaming of better places because we only saw hopelessness around us. Political borders may have fallen, but the only difference for us was the fact that now we could see what was on the other side. The rich life was out there, waiting for us. But how were we going to get there? How to cross the invisible border that still existed?

We hated the feeling of being trapped, we kept executing our enemies and we started taking any kind of drug we could lay our hands on. None of us went to school, none of us worked. Inez taught me how it was done, she let me watch her when she picked people's pockets or broke into houses. But we never kept the money for long. We bought drugs and clothes and then we had to start all over again. I don't think I was clear-headed for a single day during that time, I was always high on something.

I don't know who first heard of the Woolglove. I think it was Inez, but I'm not sure. There was a rumour that he could get girls well-paid jobs in the West. They had to be good-looking, independent, ready for anything. He was staying at a hotel in the city and he was only going to be in town for two days. We made up our minds on the spot. We put on our best clothes, made ourselves up, slipped glue tubes into our pockets and jumped on the bus. On the way, we took out the glue and sniffed it. Tatyana had to throw up before we went into the hotel. The man who opened the door – I still remember it was room 345 – was actually wearing white wool gloves. Later he said something about having eczema on his hands and treating them with a special cream. That was why he had to wear those gloves. He promised to get us jobs in a restaurant in Tallinn. We would be waitresses and get good pay, not to mention tips. He told us what girls usually made per day and he made it sound like we would earn all this money for about two hours of work. It was a restaurant that only catered to foreigners, he said. He also told us we would be sharing a big apartment together.

We drank in every word. He was wearing those strange wool gloves, but his suit was expensive and he smiled the whole time. He told us his name was Peter Ludorf, and he threw in a German word now and again to impress us. He wrote down our names on a small notepad. Then another man suddenly turned up. I don't think I've ever heard anyone move so quietly. It still gives me the shivers to think about it. He took pictures of us and then left. And that was it.

A few weeks later we stood on the side of the road in our short skirts in the middle of winter, waiting for Peter Ludorf's car to come and get us. But some unshaven men who smelled of vodka were driving the car. We stopped at various houses on the way and new men of the same sort took over the driving. We got almost nothing to eat, just a little water and enough time to jump out and pee in the snow.

Peter Ludorf had arranged new identities and passports for us. At first that had freaked us out, that our old identities had been taken away. Tatyana said it was like someone slowly scraping away our old faces. But we trusted Peter Ludorf. He smiled, he gave us clothes and talked to us like grown-ups. What else could we do? We had already put our lives in his hands. He was the one who had come to take us away from our old lives, to give us a chance at freedom – a raft with which we could paddle away from the vodka marsh where slumrats like us had no future.

We arrived in the middle of the night. The truck pulled into a dark yard where there were growling dogs pulling at their leads. I remember that Tatyana grabbed my arm and whispered, 'It's not right. Something isn't right.' We got out of the truck. It was cold and damp and there were foreign smells all around. Somewhere in the darkness among the growling dogs we heard voices speaking in a language we couldn't understand. One man smiled and chuckled and I realised he was making comments about us standing there in our short skirts.

We were led into a room where the walls were clad in a red plush fabric. There were large gilt mirrors on the walls and Peter Ludorf sat there on a sofa with his white gloves on, smiling at us. He looked us over, then got up from the couch. At that moment it was as if a light had been turned off in his face. His eyes changed colour and even his voice seemed different. He stood right in front of me and told us that we would be staying in some rooms on the first floor. We were to service all the men who were sent up. We had to give him our passports.

To show us that he was serious, that he wasn't making idle threats, he instructed us to walk over to the table right next to the sofa. There was a wooden box on the table, about twenty centimetres high and about as wide. He kept on talking the whole time, telling us that other girls had made the same trip that we had just done but that they had not understood that he meant business. He opened the box and took out two glass jars. In one jar was a pair of lips, preserved in some kind of ether. None of us knew what we were looking at. The other jar contained a finger with a ring still on it. The nail was painted red. It was only when we saw that that we realised the first jar had held a pair of lips.

The whole time Peter Ludorf kept talking. He told us the lips belonged to a girl called Virginia. She had tried to escape by stabbing one of her clients – an elite member of the French trade delegation – in the chest with a screwdriver. Peter Ludorf sounded almost wistful when he told us that he had cut her lips off himself in order to show all of us what happened to girls who misunderstood their situation and thought that rebellion and escape attempts would be tolerated. The girl who lost her finger – Peter Ludorf had used the kind of tool that blacksmiths use to extract old stitches out of horses' hooves when they reshoe them – was called Nadia and she had been seventeen. She had also tried to escape, this time by climbing out of a window and stealing a car that she rammed straight into the wall of the house across the street.

Peter Ludorf put the jars back and closed the lid to the box. I don't think his words had really sunk in yet. We were all too cold and hungry to focus on anything except food. We were taken to the kitchen where an emaciated woman was stirring a pot. She chain-smoked and she had no teeth left, even though she couldn't have been older than thirty. There was no real restaurant there, just a bar they used as a cover. We were in a real live brothel. Peter Ludorf had betrayed us in the same way that he had betrayed many others before us. He had known exactly what to say to lure a group of slumrats like us.

None of us knew what kind of life was waiting for us. We ate some of the bad-tasting soup that the emaciated woman put in front of us, and then we were locked into our rooms. I could hear Tatyana crying through the wall. I think we were all crying, but you could only hear Tatyana. That night I remember thinking: what am I going to wake up to? Why don't I try to fall asleep and stay somewhere deep inside myself where I never need to wake up again? At the same time I felt a growing rage inside. Was I really going to let someone like Peter Ludorf win?

The rest of the night I just waited for dawn to come. I had no other thought than escape. We were not going to allow ourselves to be humiliated in this brothel. None of us were virgins exactly, but no one would ever have thought of selling herself either. I know Tea-Bag had to do it; she had no other choice. But I wanted us to break out, not turn into a couple of chopped-off body parts in a wooden box in a room where the walls were the same colour as blood. But when I heard a noise at the door the next morning I was paralysed.

I don't need to tell you about what we had to go through. For half a year I stood at that door each morning prepared to attack whoever came through the door. But I never did. I didn't have the guts. It took me six months for that, six months of unending, unimaginable hell.

One night a deep rage that I hadn't even known was in me, came over me and I unscrewed two of the legs of the bed. They were made of steel. I tied them together with the help of a pillowcase and then I had my weapon. The next morning I finally struck back.

I had never seen the man who came into the room that day. I hit him as hard as I could so that blood spurted from his head. He died immediately. Then I grabbed the keys from him and unlocked the door next to mine. It was like opening the door to a chamber of horror. Tatyana just sat curled up on the floor staring at me. I screamed at her to get up, that we were leaving, but she didn't move. I pulled at her, but nothing helped. I opened the door to Inez's room but it was empty. I finally realised that she had hidden behind the bed. I tried to pull her out, I pleaded with her, but she was so frightened she didn't dare crawl out. I opened the door to Natalia's room and she was the only one who was willing to come with me.

The two of us tried to get the others to come along. We screamed at them and pulled their arms but with no success. Then we had to get going: we heard voices in the stairwell. We jumped out of the window and onto the roof of a garage. I ran and thought Natalia was right behind me. It was only when I had no more energy to run that I realised she wasn't there. Maybe she had hurt herself when she landed on the roof. I don't know.

I can normally keep the pain at a distance, controlling it like you control an unruly horse with the reins. But sometimes it doesn't work. Then I sniff scent blocks in men's urinals and wish that Peter Ludorf were dead and all my friends set free. I don't know anything about what happened to them after I left. In my dreams I see us standing there on that road outside Smolensk, waiting in our short skirts, waiting for a car to bring us to freedom but that will actually plunge us into endless darkness. A darkness I am still waiting to find my way out of.

*

Tanya stopped.

I should ask about Irina, Humlin thought. But now is hardly the time.

Tanya took a phone out of her pocket and dialled a number. Humlin thought he heard a lullaby start playing nearby, in a place he couldn't see from where he was sitting, but where he imagined the bag lady was still sleeping with her head resting against the old gravestone.

A gravestone where the inscription had long since crumbled away.

19

After the interlude in the cemetery, Humlin and Tanya went shopping and carried home bags full of groceries. His mother was preparing a meal in the kitchen. Humlin sat down in the living room and listened to the sound of laughter and clattering pots. He knew he needed to think of what to do next. The girls couldn't stay here for ever. I have to draft the next chapter, he thought, as if what was happening was only part of a novel and not something real. The phone rang and his mother answered. Humlin listened anxiously but her voice sounded quite normal, no moaning. She came over and handed him the receiver.

'How can it be for me? No one knows I'm here.'

'I made sure to tell the people who needed to know.'

'But I specifically asked you not to mention this to a soul.'

'I haven't said anything about the girls and that boy. But we never said anything about keeping your whereabouts secret.'

'Who is it?' Humlin asked.

'Your wife.'

'I don't have a wife. Is it Andrea?'

'Who else would it be?'

Andrea was clearly irritated.

'Why haven't you called me?'

'I thought I made it clear that certain difficulties had presented themselves, difficulties that needed my immediate attention.'

'That still doesn't mean you can't pick up the phone once in a while.'

'I can't talk right now. I don't have the energy.'

'Get back in touch when you regain it, then. But don't be too sure I'll be waiting around for you.'

'What does that mean?'

'Exactly what you think it does. Olof Lundin called, by the way. He had something important to discuss with you.'

'What was it?'

'He didn't tell me. You can call him at the office. Oh, and someone called Anders Burén called. He said he had a great idea he wanted to run by you.'

'He always does. Last time he wanted to make me into the equivalent of a tourist hotel in the mountains. I don't want to talk to him.'

'And I don't want to be your secretary.'

Andrea hung up. I'm the one who makes her sound whiny, Humlin thought despondently. She wasn't like that when we met. As usual the fault lies with me.

He dialled Lundin's number.

'Why don't you ever call?'

Lundin was out of breath and Humlin imagined he must have just jumped off the rowing machine.

'I've been in Gothenburg dealing with some things.'

'You mean those fat girls? How many times do I have to tell you, you don't have time for that right now. We're getting ready to publish the first chapter of *The Ninth Horseman* in next month's issue of our in-house magazine.'

'What book is that?'

'The book you are in the process of writing. I was forced to come up with a title. It's not half bad, is it?'

Humlin turned cold.

'I've already told you I'm not writing a crime novel and you can shove that title up your arse.'

'I don't much care for your language. Unfortunately it's too late to change the title at this stage.'

Humlin lost his composure and started to scream. Tea-Bag came into the room at that moment, carrying a tray with plates and silverware. She stopped when she caught sight of him, looking at him with curiosity. In some way her presence gave him more courage and strength than he would ordinarily have been able to muster.

'I'm not going to write your damned crime novel. How could you have come up with such an idiotic title? How have you even had the nerve to write the blurb of a book that doesn't exist? That will never get written? I'm leaving your company.'

'You say that, but you don't mean it.'

'I have never been so outraged in my entire life.'

'But we both agreed on this. You mean to say you're going back on your word?'

'*We* didn't agree on anything. *You* agreed to it all by yourself. I'm not writing a book about nine or any other number of horsemen.'

'I don't understand you, Humlin. For the first time in your life you have the opportunity to write something that will sell in big numbers. What more is there to think about?'

Humlin looked at Tea-Bag who was busy setting the table.

'I'm going to write a book about immigrants.'

'Good God, I think he's serious.'

Humlin came very close to telling Lundin the whole truth, that he was currently hiding three young foreign women and a stuttering Swedish youth in his mother's apartment, that two of the girls were illegal aliens and that the third had just experienced the miracle of love. But he restrained himself this time. Lundin would never understand.

'I don't have anything more to say to you, Lundin.'

'Of course you do. I don't know why you insist on getting yourself worked up like this. Call me tomorrow.'

The conversation ended. Humlin carefully replaced the receiver, as if he was afraid of bringing the conversation back to life again.

*

It was a sumptuous dinner. It was also the first time in years that Humlin had actually felt hungry as he sat down to dine at his mother's table. He noticed the respect with which the girls treated her. It was as if nothing from the past or the present could touch them while they sat there in the sanctuary of the apartment. Humlin should have invited Andrea. If she had been able to experience this for herself she would perhaps have been able to understand why these girls had become so important to him. That was also true for Viktor Leander, his doctor, Burén; everyone in his inner circle. But there was another important person missing from this gathering.

Humlin got up and called Törnblom from the phone in his mother's study. Amanda answered.

'I'm cleaning up the office. Otherwise it gets to be such a mess that no one can work in here.'

'I don't think I've ever told you what a great man you're married to.'

'There are millions of men in the world, but a real Man is rare. Pelle is a Man.'

Humlin tried to understand the difference while he waited for her to get Törnblom. When he came on, Humlin told him about the hasty get-away from Gothenburg and all that it had entailed. Törnblom chuckled.

'The Chief of Police? Really?'

'That's what Tanya said. I don't think she's the kind to lie.'

'She lies constantly, but not about these sorts of things. What are you going to do now?'

'It's not a question of what I'm going to do now. I've learned one thing about these girls and that's that they take care of themselves. They're far from helpless victims. They win every boxing match they're forced into.'

'I told you it would all turn out for the best, didn't I?'

'Nothing has turned out the way I expected it to. I thought I was teaching them to write. But the longest story I've received is just a few scribbled lines.'

'Whoever said something had to be written down on paper to be a story? The most important thing is that they are telling their stories at all. Keep me posted. I have to go now – a couple of guys look like they're getting into a fight.'

Törnblom hung up. Humlin stayed at the desk for a while, listening to the excited chatter from the dining room. He suddenly realised he would not be able to join them until he had made a decision. Was he going to give in to Lundin and write a bestselling crime novel after all, and improve his now disastrous financial situation? Was there an alternative? What did he want to do? In relation to Tea-Bag, Tanya and Leyla he suddenly felt like a pick-pocket. Their stories were finding their way into his hands just like Tanya collected those phones.

He got up and walked over to the window. He was reminded

of how he had seen Tea-Bag turn the corner with something that looked like a little monkey on her back. Tea-Bag, who had come to Sweden after meeting a Swedish man in a refugee camp in Spain, a man who had shown an interest in her life's story. This is how it has to be, he thought. He saw it clearly now. Hiding out was wrong. Tea-Bag and Tanya didn't have to keep hiding – that was part of the problem. Instead they would attract the media with the only weapon they had: that they were illegal aliens; that they had much to tell about a life that few Swedes knew anything about.

He didn't need to think it through any longer. His mind was made up. He took out the phone book and started making calls. Soon he had spoken to reporters from all the major newspapers. They were in business.

*

He stayed at the desk so long his mother finally came out to see what had happened to him. She had drunk a lot of wine and was clearly enjoying herself.

'Why are you sitting here?'

'I need to think.'

'Well, no one back there misses you very much.'

That made him furious.

'Everyone misses me. Not you. But everyone else. If the only reason you came out here was to tell me that, you can leave. I want to be left alone.'

'Someone's in a bad mood, I can tell.'

'I'm just being honest with you, for once.'

'So are you planning to stay here and sulk?'

'I'm not sulking, I'm thinking. I've made an important decision. Go on, go back to them. I'll be out shortly.'

His mother looked anxious and started whispering.

'You haven't told any of the girls out there what I do in order to try to secure your inheritance, have you?'

'Not a word.'

The front doorbell rang.

'Who could that be?'

Humlin got up.

'I think I have an idea.'

'Jesper, I don't like you inviting people over without talking to me about it first.'

'I haven't invited anyone over, Mother. But Tea-Bag, Tanya and Leyla are about to meet some people who are much more able to help them than we can.'

Humlin went to open the door. The reporters had started arriving. One of them set off a flash in his mother's face.

'Reporters, Jesper? Why did you let them in?'

'It's the best thing we can do.'

'What about the diplomatic immunity I was supposed to offer them? I thought the girls were refugees?'

'You've had too much wine, Mother. You don't understand what's happening.'

'I know enough not to let reporters into my home.'

Despite her resistance Humlin ushered the reporters into the dining room. Before he had a chance to say anything and explain the situation, Leyla got up and started screaming.

'I can't be in the papers! If my parents see this they'll kill me!'

'Calm down, I'll explain. Just listen.'

But no one listened. Tea-Bag pummelled him with her fists.

'Why are they here? Why did you let them in?'

'I'll explain.'

Tea-Bag kept punching him.

'Why are they taking pictures of us? Every policeman who's been trying to deport us will see those pictures. What do you think will happen to Leyla who hasn't told her parents yet about Torsten? Why are you doing this to us?'

'Because it's the only way. People have to know about this, about everything you've told me.'

Tea-Bag wasn't listening, she just kept hitting him. In sheer desperation he finally slapped her. A camera flash went off. Tea-Bag's eyes were full of tears.

'I think this is the right thing to do,' Humlin said.

But Tea-Bag cried. Tanya threw a plate of spaghetti at one of the reporters, then pulled Tea-Bag with her out into the hallway. Humlin followed them and closed the door behind him.

'You can't just disappear. I'm doing this for you. Where are you going? How will I get hold of you?'

'You won't!' Tea-Bag screamed. 'The seminar is over. We've learned everything we needed to learn.'

Tanya swore at him in Russian, perhaps it was closer to a curse. Then they were gone. He heard their footsteps in the stairwell and then the front door downstairs slammed. Leyla and Torsten came out into the hallway. Leyla was crying.

'Where are the reporters?'

'They're talking to your mother. We're leaving.'

'Where will you go? There are no trains to Gothenburg at this time of night.'

Leyla grabbed him by the arms and shook him. But she didn't say anything.

Humlin felt paralysed. It's not my fault, he thought. They're the ones who have misunderstood the situation. For once in my life I thought I was doing the right thing.

He sat down on a chair. One of the reporters came out into the hallway and smiled at him.

'"Jesper Humlin: the poet whose eyes were opened."'

'What are you talking about?'

'You've never displayed much of a social conscience in your poetry until now.'

'That's not true.'

'Of course it's true. But don't worry. I won't write about this. It's a good enough story on its own: "Illegal immigrants on the run. A poet and his old mother try to help them find their way."'

The reporter tilted an imaginary hat and left. The others also left shortly afterwards. Humlin got up. Shards of china and spaghetti lay scattered on the dining-room rug. His mother stood in the doorway and looked at him. He spread his arms wide.

'I know what you're thinking. You don't have to say it. But I meant well.'

She didn't answer. He bent down and started picking at the smashed porcelain pieces among the spaghetti.

*

It was two o'clock in the morning by the time they were finished cleaning and washing up. They sat down in the living room and had a glass of wine each. Neither of them spoke. Humlin got up to leave and his mother followed him out. He was about to open the door when she grabbed his arm.

'Will they be all right?'

'I don't know.'

He opened the door, but she didn't let go.

'What kind of animal was it she had, you know, that girl Tea-Bag?'

'She doesn't have any animals.'

'That's strange. I'm quite sure I saw something peeking out from behind her back.'

'What did it look like?'

'A big squirrel.'

Humlin reached out and stroked his mother's cheek.

'It's just your imagination,' he said. 'That's all.'

Humlin walked home through the city. From time to time he stopped and turned around, but there was no one to be seen in the shadows.

*

Two days later he went back to the church in the Valley of the Dogs. Tea-Bag had not been seen there. On his way home in the taxi he changed his mind and asked the driver to take him to the Central station. Then he went to the spot where he had arranged to meet Tea-Bag before. But she didn't turn up, nor did Tanya. The next day he went back to the train station, this time at the precise hour that he had been supposed to meet Tea-Bag on the day they travelled to Gothenburg together and she had jumped off in Hallsberg. But again no one came.

That evening he was to have had dinner with Viktor Leander, but he called and made the excuse that he was coming down with a cold. He could tell that Leander didn't believe him, but he didn't care.

The following day he was back at the Central station, at the same time, the same place. Suddenly he spotted Tanya. She was watching him through the window of the florists. He felt as if her gaze had drawn him to her, rather than that he had found her of his own accord. Tea-Bag came around the corner shortly thereafter. She went and stood next to Tanya. Humlin started walking over to them. When he was so close that he could see their faces clearly he noted that even Tea-Bag looked pale. Her thick coat was zipped up to her neck as usual.

'I'm alone,' he told them. 'There's no one with me. It was wrong of me to call those reporters. All I can say is that I thought I was doing the right thing. But I was wrong.'

They sat down on a bench together.

'What happens now?'

Tanya shrugged. Tea-Bag pushed her chin down into her coat.

'Where are you staying? At the church?'

Tanya shrugged again. She was looking around the whole time. She was the one keeping an eye out, not Tea-Bag. Humlin suddenly started worrying that he was losing his hold on them. Tanya and Tea-Bag were just going to disappear if he didn't do something to make them stay, not that he knew exactly why he wanted to hold onto them.

'When should we have the next seminar?'

Tea-Bag sat up straight.

'That's over now,' she said. 'I came to this country to tell my story and now I've done that. No one listened.'

'That's not true.'

'Who listened?'

Her smile was gone. She looked at him as if from far away. Humlin thought about what she had told him about the river that flowed down the mountain, the river with its cool, clear water. She seemed to be looking at him as if from the very cliffs where that river had its source.

'*I* listened to you.'

'You didn't hear my voice. You only heard your own. You didn't see me. You saw a person who was born through your own words.'

'That's not true.'

Tea-Bag shrugged.

'True or not, what does it even really matter?'

'What's going to happen now?'

'We travel around. You see us disappear into the crowd and then we're gone. Nothing else. Stockholm is as good a city for invisible people as any other. I don't exist, just as Tanya doesn't exist. We are shadows that have to keep to the edge of the light. From time to time we put a hand or a foot or even a bit of our face into the sun, but then we quickly pull back again. We're trying to achieve the right to exist in this country. How we will win this right, I don't know. But as long as we keep ourselves hidden, as long as we're nothing but shadows and you only see a hand or a foot, we are slowly getting there. One day we can perhaps emerge fully into the light and not have to keep to the edges. But Leyla is already there. She has found the way out of this shadow-world.'

They're slipping out of my hands, he thought again.

He tried to keep them with his questions.

'What about the photograph of that child, Tanya? Is that your daughter?'

She looked at him with surprise.

'I don't have a daughter.'

'Then it must be you, am I right? But that can't be. The picture was taken only a few years ago.'

'It's not my daughter. It isn't me either.'

'Then who is the girl in the picture?'

'Irina.'

‘Who is that?’

‘Natalia’s daughter. I got the picture after we had arrived in Estonia. She had four pictures of her daughter – she had left her with her grandmother back in Smolensk. She gave each of us a picture. Late one night, when the last of the arseholes had left our beds, she gave us each a picture to keep, like an icon. We had to survive for the sake of the child, and make our way back to Smolensk. We all shared the responsibility for Natalia’s daughter. One day I will return and take on responsibility for Irina. That is, if Natalia or one of the others hasn’t done so already. But I don’t think they have.’

Humlin thought about what she had said for a long time. Then he turned to Tea-Bag.

‘I’m thinking about the first time we met. That evening when there was a fight in the audience. Do you remember what you asked me then? Why I didn’t write about people like you. I’m going to do that now, you know.’

Tea-Bag shook her head.

‘You won’t. You’ll forget us as soon as we’re gone.’

‘So little faith? That hurts.’

Tea-Bag looked him deep in the eyes and said:

‘I don’t hurt anyone. Now you will hear the end of my story.’

*

Do you remember how I stood there on the beach, south of Gibraltar? It felt as if it were the holy city of refugees, a palace built from wet sand from which an invisible bridge led to paradise. Many who came there saw that there was water between them and their goal and they despaired. I remember the excitement and fear I felt as if we were waiting for the boat that was to carry us across. Every grain of sand was a watchful soldier. But I also remember a strangely joyous atmosphere; people were humming melodies under their breath and moving in slow, measured victory dances. It was as if we had already arrived. The bridge lay before us and the very last part of our trip was a single jump into a weightless vacuum.

I don't know what made me survive when the boat was smashed against the rocks and desperate people down in the hold were clawing and tearing their way out. But I know that the bridge we all thought we saw as we stood on the beach in the northernmost part of Africa, that continent we were fleeing and already mourning, that bridge will one day be built. It will be built, if only because the mountains of corpses pressed together on the bottom of the ocean will one day rise above the sea like a new country and a bridge of skulls and bones will form the bridge that no one, no guards, dogs, drunk sailors, or smugglers will be able to topple. Only then will this cruel insanity come to a stop, these anxious flocks of people who are driven on in desperation only to end up living their lives in the underworld, becoming the cavemen of modern times.

I survived, I was not consumed by the sea and the betrayal, cowardice and greed. I met a man who held a palm frond in his hand and said that there were people in this land who wanted to hear my story and who would let me stay. But I have never met these people. I have given everyone my smile but what do I get in return? I thought he would be here to greet me, but no one greeted me. And perhaps I will be obliterated. But I think I am stronger than the grey light that wants to render me invisible. I continue to exist even though I am not allowed to exist, I am seen although I live in the shadow-world.

*

Tea-Bag stretched out her arms. She smiled. But then her smile died away, and the two of them were suddenly in a hurry to leave.

Humlin watched them scurry out past the exit doors. He stood up and stretched so that he could keep them in view for as long as possible. Then they were gone, lost in the landscape of illegal existence. He sat back down on the bench and looked around. He asked himself how many of the people he saw did not really exist, how many were living on borrowed time with borrowed identities? After a while he got up and threw a last look up at the roof.

Next to the pigeons on the rafters he thought he saw a little brown-green monkey.

Maybe, Humlin thought, maybe it has a mobile phone in its hand. And maybe it is dreaming about that cool, clear river with its source far away in Tea-Bag's mountains.

Afterword

This is a novel. But Tea-Bag is real. Just like Tanya and Leyla. What their actual names are doesn't matter. What matters is their story.

Many people have helped me along the way. Many impressions, feelings and unfinished stories have been woven into these pages.

Many people have taken up the cause. To all of them I owe my thanks.

Henning Mankell, September 2001